FORBIDDEN

USA TODAY BESTSELLING AUTHOR

TIA LOUISE

"It is impossible to manufacture or imitate love."
—*Horace Slughorn*

CHAPTER 1

Dirk

"**I** HAVE A BAD FEELING ABOUT THIS." MY OLDER BROTHER WATCHES me, hands on his hips.

Standing in front of the half-renovated warehouse I call home, all my belongings fitting neatly in a large duffel bag, I've never felt so unmoored.

"Who are you, Han Solo?" I drop the bag in the back of my Jeep beside a smaller case.

"Sure, if that's the analogy where you're leaving the field in the middle of a battle."

"That would make *me* Han Solo." I exhale a bitter laugh, turning to face him and pulling a ball cap over my messy hair. "There's no battle, Hutch. It's been four years. The case is closed. Hell, even Hugh says it's over."

"You know we can't trust what Hugh says," he growls, refusing to let it go.

Hutch is an intimidating guy—a former Marine with too

many muscles and the attitude to match. We're three years apart in age, but he's always had my back.

It was easy to say yes to joining his private investigation firm eight years ago. He's the muscle, and Oskar Lourde, or Scar as we call him, is Hutch's former military guide, scary as hell and an expert tracker. I'm the tech guy, tracking messages across the dark web, hacking into street cams and security networks to follow suspects throughout the city, often throughout the night. My hours are insane, but I've never been a nine-to-five guy.

All that changed after our last case.

"I won't argue with you, but he paid his bill. We have no reason to keep pursuing it, whatever *it* would be now."

Hugh van Hamilton is our richest client, and he has a bad habit of withholding vital information from the team he's supposed to trust, a.k.a., us. When he hired us to protect his nieces, we discovered their safety was only the tip of the iceberg.

We spent the next year tracking down blackmailers, exposing a money laundering ring, dodging a Russian oligarch, and escaping a murder charge that almost sent Scar away for life (in a Russian prison, no less).

I won't lie—it was fun. The challenge, the excitement, the cat-and-mouse game… we don't get a lot of that in our tiny town, and now that it's done, I've emerged from my tech-cave to discover I'm the only one waking up alone every morning.

"We have plenty of reasons to keep going." Hutch shakes his head. "Their network is still in place. It's only a matter of time before a new leader emerges, and it'll probably be the guy who murdered Simon Petrovich."

"Simon was the head. We cut off the head, and the body died."

"We didn't cut off the head, and whoever did cut it off is going to come back."

That makes me laugh, and I football-charge him with my shoulder. "This isn't a horror film. They're not coming back."

He easily blocks me, pulling me in for a brief hug. "Watch yourself. I don't want to have to kick your ass again."

"Like you ever kicked my ass."

"Only because it would've broken Mom's heart. You were her favorite son."

"Whatever." If that's true, it's because I acted like a son.

Hutch was born to play the dad role, unlike our real dad, who checked out when we were only kids. Our mom leaned on my brother for everything, all the way until she died.

Shaking away that dark memory, I grip his shoulder. "I haven't seen any rumors of a resurgence on any of the chat boards. It's time to let it go. You're married, Scar has a baby on the way… "

My voice trails off as I consider our broody Viking of a partner settled with a wife and baby. Hana's pregnancy was the final straw that made me realize I had to make a change.

"It's time for me to get on with my life." Stepping back, I straighten my jacket, ready to get on the road.

"When we started the firm, we said we'd be partners til the end."

"I'm still your partner." I push back on the guilt his words trigger, icy tendrils creeping across my chest. "But I've been talking about doing this for years. You thought it was a good idea at one point."

"When you wanted to teach one class at the community college in town. Now you're moving to Miranda Bay and actually joining the faculty at Thornton." He glances at my belongings crammed in the back of my vehicle, sounding for all it's worth like a parent saying goodbye to his only child. "This is completely different."

"I'm an hour down the road. I can keep up with anything that pops up, and if I need to come back, it's an easy drive."

"So stay in Hamiltown and commute the days you teach. You could keep your office hours here instead of breaking up the team."

"I'm a faculty member. I don't want to half-ass it. I want to be active in the department. This is the right choice for me, Hutch. I've spent too many nights chasing bad guys. It's time for me to develop human habits, before I wake up at sixty and realize I'm alone."

"Ah, fuck that. You're nowhere near sixty."

"Maybe not, but the last four years went by faster than I like."

My brother runs a hand over his dark scruff. He's quiet, which means he's thinking. Hutch is stubborn, but he's not inflexible.

Finally, he relents. "Just don't get too comfortable around all those kids running around in wool blazers with their scarves flying over their shoulders."

"It's not Hogwarts," I chuckle, gesturing to the warehouse looming behind us. "Anyway, I've still got to finish this dump. You think I'd let all my hard work go to waste?"

I bought the abandoned garment factory on the edge of town when I graduated from Columbia, and I've been slowly renovating it, turning it into an open-floor-plan loft ever since. So far, I've got the upper level completely livable. That just leaves the rest.

Hutch squints up at the massive structure. "You should hire a contractor to finish it while you're gone. We have the money."

"Where's the fun in that?" It's slow going, but I enjoy working with my hands. It's a nice balance to being in front of a screen.

"How long is this teaching thing going to last?"

I slide my backpack off my shoulder as we climb into my Jeep. I'll drive him back to our office in town before I hit the road. "I'm an adjunct professor, so for now it's only a semester-to-semester gig. If they don't like me, it could be a one and done."

"They'll like you."

We drive for a few minutes in silence, and it bothers me that he could be angry at my decision. "I need to do this, Hutch."

He blinks over at me, and the tension in his jaw relaxes. "I know."

A few more minutes of silence, and we're entering town. I parallel park on Main Street in front of our glass door, which reads *Winston and Lourde* in gold lettering. "You take care of yourself and Blake. Let me know when you've got a baby on the way."

"Not sure Blake's ready for motherhood." A sly grin curls his lips, and my eyes narrow.

"I'm not sure if that look means you're wanting to change her mind or you're still enjoying being on your honeymoon."

"Nothing wrong with an extended honeymoon." He holds the door open for me. "And if we have any accidents, that's okay, too."

A pang of something like jealousy twists in my stomach. It's ridiculous, and I dismiss it. I'm happy for my brother, and I'm equally happy returning to campus life, hitting the books, learning what's new and breaking in the world of academia.

"Hey, handsome." A sweet voice greets me as I enter our office building.

"Hana." I catch her in a side hug, her hand resting on the baby belly lifting the front of her black, knee-length dress.

It's short with spaghetti straps, and her pale-blonde spiral curls are gathered up on her head in a messy way, leaving tendrils falling around her cheeks. She's really cute pregnant, and Scar is beaming like I've never seen—he almost looks approachable.

"Professor Winston." Her small nose wrinkles. "I thought you were already on the road. I'm glad I get to tell you goodbye."

"I'm heading out now. Hutch needed a ride to town, and I'm on my way."

Scar walks up to where we're standing. His long hair is

pulled back in the usual samurai bun, and his inked arms extend from his short-sleeved black tee. He slips one around his wife, covering her rounded belly with a large hand.

His torso and arms were severely burned in a fire when he and Hutch were serving together overseas. Elaborate tattoos now cover those scars, and combined with his piercings and wolf eyes, he's an intimidating presence. Hana isn't fazed.

She covers his large hand with her small one, exhaling a light laugh. "Can you believe how fat I am? Just look at me!"

Joy beams in her eyes, but I push back. "You're not fat, you're pregnant."

"But just look how chubby my cheeks are!"

If I didn't know Hana better, I'd think she was shaming herself, but she's not. Hana has struggled with addiction and disordered eating all stemming from the abuse she suffered as a child. She's actually happy.

Scar's eyes smolder with love, and he speaks in a soft growl. "You're beautiful."

She beams up at him, and the heat between them tightens the skin on the back of my neck. I'm not jealous of them…

Okay, fuck it. Maybe I'm a little jealous—of all of them. I'm glad these two wounded souls have found each other. Hell, even Blake and Hutch are pretty incredible together.

Blake is Hana's older sister, and she's fiercely protective of her family, much like my brother. She and Hutch are iron sharpening iron, two powerful forces making each other stronger.

It's all great and happily ever after, the fairytale ending they all deserve, and I'm fucking completely out of the loop. Heat is in my throat, and I force a smile. This is why I need to get out of here, why I need a break.

"Professor." Scar shakes his head with a chuckle. "I don't know how you're going to handle all those teenagers."

"It's a three-hundred-level course, so they'll be a little older."

"Just don't do anything stupid. I won't be there to bail you out."

"Got it. No punching the students." I glance around our small office at the computer system I installed, the server and firewall, all the tech I maintain. "Think you can handle all this while I'm gone? I am taking the brains with me."

"Last I checked, your brains were in your briefs."

"That does it—" I lunge at him, and he grabs my arms, taking a step back.

For a minute, we push against each other like two rams locking horns over the high ground.

"Good lord, don't break the office." Blake scolds as she enters through the glass door.

"He couldn't leave without a fight." Hutch puts his hands on our shoulders, parting us.

We're both red-faced, breathing hard, and grinning, and I scoop my cap off the floor, putting it back on my head.

"You've been working out." Scar nods at me.

"More like you're getting soft in your old age, Pops."

He makes a move like he might come at me again, but Hutch steps between us, giving Hana a hug. "Hey, sis, you look good."

"Is this what I have to look forward to with boys?" Hana returns his hug, arching an eyebrow at us. "Remind me not to buy anything breakable."

"I'm pretty sure everything in our house was glued together." I laugh, taking my laptop off my desk and slipping it into my backpack. "I've got to hit the road. Let me know if anything comes up. I'll be busy, but not too busy to work remotely."

Scar's lips tighten, and he nods, a hint of a smile telling me he knows why I'm doing this, even if I won't say it out loud.

My brother's send-off is more ominous. "Stay close to your phone. My gut says this is the calm before the storm."

Another tight smile, and I head out, climbing into my Jeep and slamming the door. It's not the first time I've said goodbye to Hamiltown, South Carolina, but it's the first time I've felt like I'm starting something new outside it. It's an unusual feeling, a mixture of excitement and dread, like anything could happen.

Turning the wheel, my mind drifts to what's coming. I'm starting a new road, forging a new path. After a tense, stressful, dangerous few years, I'm ready to see if I can make a life for myself.

My brother's anticipating a storm, but I'm looking for a silver lining in those clouds.

CHAPTER 2

Reanna

"LET ME OUT!" PANIC SEIZES MY CHEST, AND I'M COVERED IN A cold sweat.

I'm on my feet, squatting in the middle of my bed, fighting invisible enemies. Sunlight shines through the open blinds and pain blasts through my temples. I drop my head in my hands shivering as shadows of the nightmare filter through my mind. Large hands drag me away. I fight against them, trying to get to him, trying to stop the bleeding as my insides collapse, as my dad lies dead on the ground.

Vodka usually stops the memories, but here I am, burning eyes, a Sousa march pounding in my skull, and my heart beating out of my chest. I need water. I need coffee.

Sitting back, my elbow collides with a shirtless, male body stretched out at my side, and like a record scratch, I recoil to see who the fuck is in my bed.

When I recognize his face, my teeth grind. "Get out!"

Planting my foot on Rick's side, I push hard, sending him

falling to the floor with a loud groan taking all the blankets with him.

"What the fuck?" His voice is muffled from inside the roll of sheets, but I don't care.

"What the fuck is right!" I shade my eyes. "There's not enough alcohol in Manhattan for me to sleep with you. Why are you in my bed?"

"I got in late and needed a place to crash."

Glancing down at my body, I'm relieved my black tank top, underwear, and shorts are securely in place. I was pretty drunk last night, but I see no signs I was coerced into making an extremely bad decision with this jacked up, wannabe gangster.

"You can crash in your car. How the hell did you get a key to my apartment anyway?"

"Natasha has keys to all our shit, girl." He sits up, lifting a gold ring with a single key dangling on it from the nightstand. "You just gotta know where to look."

My eyes narrow. Natasha Petrovna has appointed herself leader of our small band of outlaws since her uncle Simon was killed four years ago. Still, I don't like her having keys to my place without my knowledge.

I snatch the ring from his hand. "You do not have permission to sleep in my bed. *Ever*."

He snorts a laugh as he pushes off the floor, sauntering to the kitchen in only his boxer briefs. "You'll feel better after some coffee."

Staggering to the bathroom, I grimace at the mascara smeared under my eyes. I didn't wash my face before I went to bed, so I turn on the water, drowning out the noise of Rick digging in my cabinets.

He thinks he can do whatever he wants now that only four of us are left. I never believed I'd miss the days when Greg or Trip were around to keep his ass in line.

After Simon's brother Victor was killed and Greg was killed and Trip disappeared and finally Simon was killed (*I know, Jesus*

Christ), Natasha took over their criminal enterprise. The problem is we're the only ones left in the city, and the big guys in Europe won't even acknowledge her existence. Misogynist pigs.

Rick sticks around, I'm sure, because he's looking for a way to make bank out of what's left, perhaps to insert himself into any abandoned deals.

Marco, Simon's driver, had nowhere to go, and me? What's my excuse? Good question.

I was pulled into this shitshow crime-world before I was old enough to say no. I went from being the only daughter of a loving father I adored on the beautiful shores of the Black Sea to an orphan, living with my "uncle" Simon and my "cousin" Natasha.

My father's death always felt like an inside job, but I've never been able to prove it.

Closing my eyes to wash away the cleanser, I can still see Natasha's nine-year-old face scowling when I arrived, curling her nose like I was an ant invading her picnic. I'm still that ant, threatening what she's hungered for since she was old enough to know what it meant—control of this corrupt empire.

At first, I played it safe, following her like a minion, but now I'm twenty-two, and everyone's dead. And I want answers.

I want to know who killed my dad, and then I want to make him pay.

When I return, patting a towel against my face, Rick gazes at me from the kitchen in a way I don't like.

"Say, girl, you really filled out these last few years. I remember when you were a runty little kid, but now," he smacks his lips, smiling to reveal a gold tooth as his eyes glide lustily from my tank down to my sleep shorts. "You lookin good."

I'm legitimately revolted. Rick Ivanov is a slippery con man who dabbles in porn and would blackmail his own mother if it would make a buck—and probably has.

Turning away from him, I go to my armoire. "I couldn't be less interested in your opinion."

I know how I look. With ice-blue eyes and deep, chest-nut-brown hair, I've attracted unwanted attention since I was young, a dangerous thing in this world. So I bleached my hair and wore brown contact lenses.

Done. *Invisible.*

"All those years you acted like you were nothing." He crosses his arms, leaning against the counter. "Why would you do that?"

So losers like you would stay the fuck away, I muse.

"I have my reasons." I take out a hoodie and sweats, quickly covering my body in baggy fabric. "We're supposed to be meeting Natasha at the firing range at…" *Shit.* "In ten minutes."

"Just chill, baby girl. I got my car out front. I'll drive us." He scoops a pair of jeans off the floor and jerks them over his lean hips. A metal chain dangles from the pocket to the belt loop, and he quickly pulls on a white tank and a plaid overshirt-jacket.

I run a brush through my long hair, whipping it into a ponytail.

"How did you manage to park your car out front?" My loft apartment is in the part of Hell's Kitchen that never has street parking available.

"Get on the parking payola, and they'll save a spot for you." He pours us each a go-cup of coffee. "Let's hit it."

No telling what he's told the guys running the lot across the street. They probably think we're sleeping together, which makes me ill.

Grabbing my black bag from under my bed, I slip my socked feet into my Adidas slides and follow him out the door, down the stairs, coffee in hand. He slaps the hand of the guy at the booth, slipping him some amount of cash, and they give him the keys to his late-model Subaru. It's sporty enough and completely impractical for this town.

"We should've hailed a cab." I settle into the passenger's seat, surveying the traffic. "It'll take longer than ten minutes to get to Chelsea, and there's definitely no parking there."

"Just drink your coffee and leave it to me." He lays on the horn at a cab taking too long in the intersection, and I sip my drink.

I'll give Rick credit. He makes good coffee.

We're moving slower than I can walk, and he glances at me. "You were pretty shit-faced last night. Why you drinking so much? I heard they put your name on a bottle of vodka at Gibson's."

"So sphincters can ask why." It's a childish response, and he blows air through his lips, shaking his head as he looks out the window.

Gibson's is the underground cigar bar in the Financial District that serves as the unofficial headquarters of the "RDIF Investment group," which serves as the legitimate front for our organization. I grew up in it, but Rick came on the scene about five years ago.

"Why are you still hanging around anyway? You're like one of those vultures picking at the carcass."

"I remember when you were sweeter."

"I was never sweet."

He remembers me as a scared teen doing my best to blend into the scenery, but I've spent four years training my body and learning how to navigate the dark web. I'm building a file, so when I find what I'm looking for, there will be consequences.

Another abrupt stop, and I'm ready to get out and walk. Between my throbbing head and his driving, I'm nauseated. Setting the coffee in a cup holder, I roll down the window to let the cool breeze blow around us. Fall is creeping in on little cat feet, and I'm ready to bundle up in wool and textures.

"Don't barf in my car," he snaps.

"I'm not going to throw up."

I *would* like to know why Natasha is summoning us on a Saturday morning at this hour. It had better be something important.

We finally reach the stately old building, and Rick pulls

up to the curb. "Go in and tell her I'm parking. That way she won't go off on her 'no respect' rant."

I check the traffic before hopping out and circling the front of his car. The entrance to the antique store is two stately brass doors with *Dezer Building* printed in gold lettering on the transom. The exterior looks like it could've been a bank in a previous century, but inside it's just a run of the mill Army surplus store.

Assorted camping gear is arranged in the front. Old military coats hang on mannequins, and plaques with assorted sizes and types of bullets adorn the walls. The shelves are crowded with taxidermied animals, and a sign taped to the glass reads, *Making good people helpless won't make bad people harmless.*

Everything is covered in a layer of dust, and it smells like old paper. I nod to the old guy at the register before following a narrow hall to a flight of stairs leading underground where an old parking garage has been converted into a firing range with stalls for individual practice.

Metal clips are attached to mechanical wiring along the ceiling, transporting the black and white paper targets of male torsos back and forth.

Natasha has a pair of black headphones around her neck. Her hair is dyed red these days and styled in a French twist. She's wearing tan slacks and a black turtleneck, and she's not smiling. "What took you so long?"

I glance at the digital clock overhead. "Give me a break, Nat. We're five minutes late."

"Where's Rick?"

"Parking his car. What's this all about?"

Cocking her hip to the side, she crosses her arms. "I'm curious, Rain. Show me how useful you are to me after binge drinking all night."

I don't even hesitate. I unzip my duffel and take out the only possession I have from my father, a pearl-handled, 9mm Ruger.

Simon gave it to me on my sixteenth birthday, and when he told me my father would've wanted me to have it, I knew he was a liar.

My father would've never wanted me to need a gun.

After they took my older brother, he took us off the grid. We lived on the coast for easy escape, and he didn't like using electricity or having any kind of "locating services" like the Internet or phones.

We had a root cellar and a garden, goats and chickens, and everything we owned, we either made or harvested. We stayed hidden for a long time, but they found us. I'll never forget the day they came.

I was so young, it's mostly shadow memories… until I fall asleep. Then my body remembers what my mind tries to forget.

Lifting the handgun, I squint one eye, exhaling slowly as I gently pull the trigger… *Pop-pop-pop-pop-pop!* My arms don't move as I do what I've spent four years mastering, along with Krav Maga and tracking.

Stepping back, I flip the switch to return the target to us. The five bullets I shot are clustered in a tight circle around the heart on the black and white paper torso.

"How useful is that?"

Natasha's arms are still crossed, her flat expression crackling with annoyance. It's always been that way with her, from the first day I appeared in Simon's house, begrudging acceptance.

"You've grown up a lot since Simon died." Approval is not in her tone. "He always said your true colors would emerge, but I didn't believe him."

She doesn't have to tell me she didn't. She made it abundantly clear. What's not so clear is the meaning of my true colors, but I'll leave her in the dark for now. As it is, I'm still trapped in this cage.

Holstering my gun, I return to my original question, "What are we doing here?"

Rick trots down the stairs, the chain on his jeans jangling. Nat lifts her chin, indicating for him to join us. Once we're all together, she motions for us to take a seat. I gladly comply, and she paces a tight line, speaking quietly, urgently.

"It's difficult to take the lead in this world, assuming the mantle with no guidance or support." She looks around as if someone might be listening. "The old guard thinks they'll steal what's left and remove me without any accountability, but I'm one step ahead of them."

She inhales deeply, straightening her back. She wants us to ask how she's ahead, but those days are over for me. If she has something to say, she can say it.

So she continues. "Victor kept a ledger of every member of the RDIF's dealings. How much they collected and paid, to whom, and most importantly, how deeply they were involved. Five years ago, Andre Bertonelli stole it. It was a pointless act, because the information only makes sense if you're in our organization."

"Okay." I sit straighter, growing more interested.

A book like she's describing could help me find what I'm looking for.

"I have to get it back," she continues. "That book will give me all the information I need, the receipts to force everyone back to the table."

"Do you know where it is?" I ask.

"From what I've been able to learn, Hugh van Hamilton gave it to Hutch Winston's younger brother Dirk. He's their computer geek, so it's either still with him or it's somewhere at Hugh van Hamilton's estate in South Carolina."

Blinking fast, I know where she means. "In Hamiltown…"

She nods, and I remember Greg and Trip going there to search for something stolen. Mystery solved—although, I take it they never found the ledger.

"Do you have a plan?"

"The Winstons and the van Hamiltons all know me, and they know Rick."

My brows furrow. "They know me as well. We partied with Hana and Blake all the time, and Hutch and Scar were with us at the Belmont Gala and in Gibson's."

"Yes." She takes a few steps nodding, her arms still crossed. "But you've never met Dirk, and he doesn't know you."

"I've been photographed with them, I have social media. I'm sure he knows what I look like."

"Not necessarily. You always changed your hair color, your eyes, and a photograph is very different from meeting someone in person."

I'm not convinced this will work. "But if Blake and Hana are there, they'll know me."

"*Professor* Dirk Winston has taken a faculty position at Thornton College in Miranda Bay, about an hour west of Hamiltown. He's teaching a course there this fall, and he's living on campus." She walks directly to where I'm sitting and stops. "You'll enroll in that class as Reanna Lorak, get to know him, and get me that book."

Rick blows air through his lips, laughing like it's the funniest thing he's ever heard. I'm still as a statue, considering what she's saying.

It's a risky plan that could blow up in my face, but I'm intrigued by the prospect of getting my hands on such an important item and being eight hundred miles away when I do.

I could finally learn what happened to my father's estate after he died, and I could follow the money to his killer.

Natasha scans me briefly. "Rick, can you hack into the college enrollment system and create her student account?"

"Can do, boss." He sits forward, ready to get started.

"Don't make her stand out too much. We don't want to raise questions. Classes start next week, so find her a room in one of the dorms. "

"I'll take care of it. No worries." He heads up the stairs,

and I'm on my feet now as well, sorting out my plan to bag this new professor.

"It's his first semester, so he won't know any of the students, new or old."

I need to have regular, private access to him that won't raise eyebrows or come across as stalkerish. "Would it be possible for me to be his teaching assistant?"

"That might raise questions about your identity. You'll have to work it out while you're there, have a problem in the class, meet with him after hours for *special help*." Her eyebrow arches.

"I'm not sleeping with him just to get a book."

"It's a very important book." Natasha returns the headphones to a hook on the wall. "I can tell you have ambitions. Get me that ledger, and I'll make you my second in command."

"I'll get the ledger." I scoop up my bag and head for the exit.

I don't say she can shove the number two job, or Rick can keep it for all I care. When I do get that book, I'll be calling the shots. What happens next will be up to me.

CHAPTER 3

Dirk

"**W**ELCOME, PROFESSOR WINSTON!" DR. BOWERMAN GREETS me with a broad smile, gripping my elbow and passing me a crystal tumbler of brown liquor.

He's a stocky man in his late sixties, head of the psychology department, and the guy who hired me. He looks exactly how you'd imagine a faculty head to look—corduroy slacks, wool sweater, tweed blazer. His gray hair is brushed back from his face, and a scant, salt-and-pepper beard covers his jaw. An unlit pipe is tucked in the breast pocket of his coat, and I admire his old-school, friendly nature.

"Thank you, sir." I take the glass.

"We're so glad you could make our little gathering."

Classes begin tomorrow, and I've been invited to a meet-and-greet for new faculty, which, as far as I can tell, is only me.

"Dr. Chase wanted me to apologize on her behalf," he continues. "She has a sick child at home and couldn't stay."

"I completely understand." I sip the drink, a nice, smoky bourbon.

The faculty lounge is as elegant as the rest of campus, with dark mahogany wainscoting, highly polished oak tables and leather chairs. Brass floor and table lamps provide soft yellow lighting, and the built-in bookshelves are filled with hardcover editions of every psychology text you could possibly desire.

The scent of ancient pipe smoke and aging knowledge lingers in the fabric of this cozy space, which by day serves as a communal study and after hours as a place to have a drink and relax.

"I trust you had no problems getting settled into your housing?" he asks.

"Yes, thank you. It's much better than I expected."

My furnished, one-bedroom faculty cottage is similarly decorated as the rest of campus—beige limestone on the exterior, dark wood, built-in bookshelves, and leather furnishings on the interior.

"And what exactly were you expecting?" A superior-sounding male strolls up to where we're standing.

He's dressed similarly to Dr. Bowerman in brown pants and a brown tweed blazer over a beige sweater. His light-brown hair is neatly trimmed, and his beard is also starting to gray.

A scotch is in one hand, and he extends the other to me. "Landon O'Toole, clinical psych."

"Nice to meet you." I feel too casual in my jeans and blue crewneck sweater, and now I'm thinking I should probably get my hair trimmed. "My only experience with campus housing was the men's dorm at Columbia, and they were not concerned about our comfort."

Dr. Bowerman chuckles. "I've often considered having the boy's dormitory completely stripped and fumigated between semesters. I might do it yet."

"Not a bad idea," I quip.

"Welcome, Professor Winston." A smiling, younger

woman in a calf-length tweed skirt and long-sleeved brown turtleneck strides into the room. Her long, dark hair is smooth with bangs, and she gives off a very Allison in *Umbrella Academy* vibe. "I'm Sharon Stead, Ph.D. candidate and graduate assistant, a.k.a., department slave."

"Call me Dirk." I shake her hand.

"Now, Sharon, it's not as bad as that. You have a stipend and housing." Dr. Bowerman hands her a drink.

"It's the very least you could do." She gives the old guy a wink.

Sharon is fresh-faced, and her turtleneck shows off nice curves, which I notice O'Toole studying a bit too long. *Interesting.*

"I think you're the first faculty member we've ever had with real-world experience." Then she cups her hand beside her mouth as if sharing a secret. "Definitely the most handsome."

Dr. Bowerman blusters something between a cough and a chuckle. "Now don't make the man uncomfortable."

"I can take a joke." I deflect quickly, hoping to put him at ease. "Being a professor is new to me, so I'm just as impressed by all of you."

"Mm-hm." Sharon arches an eyebrow, and it's clear she likes to stir up the mothballs in this ancient establishment.

I like it, and I'm ready to join in the fun, but O'Toole cuts us off.

"As long as we keep such jokes inside these four walls. Remember what happened to Effington last year—the reason we had an opening in the first place."

I look at Dr. Bowerman, and he pats my back. "Your predecessor forgot the invisible line between professors and students, and we had to let him go."

"He was screwing our wealthiest donor's daughter," O'Toole expands loudly. "A parent busted him in the faculty bathroom with his head between her legs."

"Whoa." My eyebrows rise, and I sip more bourbon.

"Our college operates through a strict endowment," he continues. "If we lose it, we all lose."

Frowning, I glance from him to Dr. Bowerman. "What does that mean?"

"Don't shit where you eat." O'Toole's tone is flat.

"That's enough, Landon." Dr. Bowerman waves a hand, brushing him aside. "We're all professionals here. We know how to behave, and as for teaching, Dirk, you'll get the hang of it in no time. If you need anything, just reach out. Sharon divides her time between the three full-time faculty, and she knows where all the bodies are buried."

Sharon smiles up at me, and I realize she's more Naomi than Alison. Her attention to me clearly irritates the Tool, and it makes me want to mess with him, although not in front of Dr. Bowerman.

I'll have to tell Scar he was wrong—he predicted the students were going to be the assholes, not my coworkers.

"Thank you. I'm ready to get started."

"I'll take care of him. Don't worry, Dr. B." Sharon slips her hand into the crook of my arm. "I'm looking forward to your class. I can't wait to get a glimpse inside the criminal mind and understand how it works."

I pat her hand, and for fun, I turn on a little extra charm. "I warn you, it's pretty basic stuff. If I had all the answers, there'd be no unsolved cases, and then I'd be out of a job."

The clap of a tumbler on wood draws our attention. "We'd better get going. Classes start early." O'Toole starts for the door, and the old man follows slowly.

I see a maintenance worker waiting outside the door and decide he has a point. We'd better wrap it up and let everyone go home.

"Thank you again for the warm welcome." My tone is only slightly sarcastic. Only one member was less than welcoming.

Sharon follows me into the hall. "Sorry it's such a small group. Dr. Bowerman, Landon, and Pamela, er, Dr. Chase, are the only full-time faculty besides you. The part-timers typically don't hang around for these after-hours things."

"I'm sure they have a lot going on."

She hands me a card. "Here's all my contact info if you need anything. Feel free to call… whenever."

A little wink, and she turns, walking slowly away from me, up the hall. I'm pretty sure she adds an extra ass-shake with each step. Studying her card, I turn back with a grin…

Right into O'Toole.

"The invisible line between faculty and students is real." His pompous voice annoys me. "Any hint of impropriety is grounds for immediate dismissal. Our good, Christian alumni won't tolerate it."

I tuck Sharon's card in my back pocket, leveling my gaze on this asshole. I might not be as tall as Hutch and Scar, but at six feet, I can hold my own. "Thanks for the tip, Landon. I've been taking care of my shit a long time."

He holds up both hands. "Just trying to help. Workplace politics can be tricky, especially when wealthy donors are involved."

"I got this."

He huffs a smile and falls back. "Like I said, just trying to help."

I watch as he quickly strides away in the direction Sharon went. I follow them out at a slower pace. It's not what I expected on my first night, but I'm a fast learner, and I don't put up with bullshit.

A cool breeze lightens the air as I walk back to my small cottage. Laughter and music echo from the large fraternity houses lining a long, grassy rectangle, and I slow my pace, taking in the sounds of college life. Thornton is a small campus. The entire place covers about ten blocks, which makes it feel close-knit and welcoming.

I stroll past a group of kids in the quad beside a giant statue of a dog. The distinct aroma of pot drifts through the air, but I'm not here to play narc. Continuing on, I pass couples lying on blankets looking up at the stars. A few guys are throwing a football.

A sharp whistle cuts through the noise, and I glance over to see a group of girls sitting in a circle on the grass watching me. When our eyes catch, they collapse inward, giggling, and I exhale a laugh, shaking my head as I continue walking.

It's night, but with all the lights and the back to school festivities happening, it's not dark. I pass the open doors of a frat house and see kids crowded around a keg with red cups. Streamers and balloons dangle from the rafters, and a guy has his arm around a girl, his face buried in her neck.

My stomach tightens, and I remember the feel of soft skin against my cheek, under my lips. It's been a long time since I was in a relationship, and a phantom heaviness presses on my chest. It would be nice to have the secure satisfaction of someone to go home with, to sleep with, but I made choices that precluded such a thing years ago.

I walked away from it in New York, and I don't regret my decision. I don't like being alone, but perhaps things will change.

Turning away, I continue in the direction of my house when my phone buzzes in my pocket.

Taking it out I see a text from Hana on the screen. *Hey, big brother. We're all dying to know how it's going. Has anyone given you an apple yet?*

It's such a silly question and so Hana. I pause to tap out a quick reply. *No apples—did get a giant tin of gourmet popcorn from faculty housing.*

Gray dots precede her answer, which makes me smile. *Popcorn is the new apple.*

Like orange is the new black?

Orange will never replace black. She inserts an eye-roll emoji. *We miss you, but I hope you have a blast.*

Heart emojis line the end of her sentence, and I add a thumbs up to indicate my approval.

I know my brother is annoyed by my choice to come here. Blake is supportive, while gently trying to woo him around to my side. Scar has a one-track mind these days, and it's focused on Hana and the baby.

I don't know what I'm hoping to get out of this experience. Maybe it's only a break from the routine. Maybe it's the start of a new life. One thing is certain, the definition of insanity is doing the same thing over and over and expecting different results.

I'm not insane, and I'm ready for something new.

Later, after I've had a sandwich and a shower and changed into shorts and a tee, I navigate over to a streaming service to find a Harry Potter film. It's dark, the colors and music are calming, and it's my go-to when I'm too keyed up to drift off on my own.

Harry, the Weasleys, and the Diggorys all put their hands on an old shoe, and I'm asleep before they even make it to the Quidditch World Cup.

CHAPTER 4

Reanna

"**H**AVE YOU FOUND JESUS?" AN EARNEST YOUNG WOMAN WITH braids and a crocheted poncho holds a pamphlet directly in my path.

I'm pushing a canvas bin containing my suitcase, all my toiletries, and everything I expect to need for a semester on campus across the quadrangle in the direction of the girls' dorm, where Rick placed me.

"I didn't know he was lost," I quip, and her eyes narrow as she turns away with a scoff. I call after her, "Jesus would've laughed at that."

I continue rolling, pushing the bin to Amanda Egret dorm. It's an ancient building with soaring ceilings and dark-marble floors. I'm pretty sure it's a hundred years old, especially when I board the rickety elevator taking me to the tenth floor.

No breakdowns, and I actually have a brass key in my hand to unlock the door as I wheel the squeaky bin down the black-marble hall. I'm in Room 1013, but when I arrive at what

I'm pretty sure is the place, I'm startled to find the door wide open.

"Sorry, is this Room 1013?" I hesitate, pretty sure it is.

"Are you Reanna?" A petite girl with platinum-blonde hair turns from hanging posters on the wall to approach me with her hand outstretched. "I'm Ali!"

She says it like *Ah-lee*, the boxer, and I shake her hand carefully, still frozen in the doorway. "I'm Reanna, and I… I wasn't supposed to have a roommate."

Now that I'm saying it, it seems pretty wasteful when you consider the size of this room. It only has two beds, but it could easily fit four. A bathroom is between this room and another, technically making it a suite.

"Reanna! That's such a pretty name." She puts a hand on her chest. "And I know, it's a last-minute switch for me, too. Surprise!" She does a little cheery, jazz-hands movement.

I don't like surprises. "What happened?"

"Not sure exactly." Turning away, she goes back to hanging a poster of a young male singer-turned-actor on the wall. "It seems my assigned roommate found somebody she liked better… And she has the connections and the money to get me bumped to your room. Sorry I'm the turd in your punchbowl."

My shoulders drop, and I push the large bin into the room to start unloading. I'm ready to call Natasha and let Rick have it. A roommate is going to make my job infinitely more complicated, and it was already a gamble.

Still, dressed in jeans and a fuzzy pink sweater, Ali is a beam of sunshine in the clouds darkening my mood. "I'm from Savannah, so not too far from home. Where are you from?"

She finishes taping the last poster and turns, dropping on her bed and facing me expectantly. This is exactly why I don't need a roommate. A semester is a long time to keep details straight, and I've never been a great liar.

So I draw on my childhood experience. "Odesa."

I lift my suitcase out along with a plastic kit holding my

toiletries. Placing both on the desk, I return to the bin to dig out sheets, so I can get my bed made and start stacking stuff on it.

"As in Texas?" Her brow is furrowed, and she sits on her perfectly made Hello Kitty comforter.

"As in the Ukraine. I'm a transfer student."

"Oh!" she gasps, cupping both hands over her mouth. "I'm so sorry! Were you like in the fighting?"

Her blue eyes are so big, and now I don't have the heart to tell her I lived there ages ago, when I was a child. "No, not where we were. My family sent me here just in case, for safety."

"That's so scary." Her voice is a soft whisper, and I'm sorry I went there.

"It's really okay. I promise. We're all good. Really."

"Okay." She nods, lowering her hands. "I guess you won't have any family visits, then?"

That almost makes me laugh. "No, but I'm good with that. You?"

She shrugs. "My mom has a store near the art school in Savannah. She sells a lot of their stuff in it, so during the semesters, she's pretty busy."

"That's cool." I nod, continuing to unpack my few belongings. "Is she an artist?"

"She does some things, but mostly she works with the students now."

Carrying my clothes to the narrow closet, I sort them out on hangers. "You didn't want to go to art school?"

"I'm no artist." She laughs. "Much to my mother's dismay!"

"I'm sure that's not true."

"I'm not so sure." She shakes her head. "But I try to meet her halfway by being mystical."

My brow furrows, and I take the small bucket of toiletries out of my case. "You're a witch?"

"No, I'm majoring in psychoanalysis. I'm all about digging into your psyche and finding out where you're broken."

Great. I'm glad my back is turned. "Got any favorite theories?"

"Well, it's pretty dated, but I love studying dear old Siggy." I cut her a confused look, and she clarifies. "Freud. Sigmund."

"Ah." I lift my chin, and the last of my shit is unpacked. I push the bin to the door, glancing from her sparkly pink, Sanrio surprise explosion to my relatively bland, beige side, and I state the obvious. "My half looks pretty sparse."

"It's just the beginning of the year." She jumps up, holding her arms wide. "You have plenty of time to express yourself!"

"I guess." Expressing myself is one way to put what I'll be doing.

"Check this out." She takes a sheet from her desk, holding it to me. "Back to school frat party tonight. Let's go!"

I quickly scan the paper, not the least bit interested. "It says it's happening right now. I'm not even dressed for a party."

Not to mention, frat parties are on my *Not* to Do list.

"You're dressed like a college kid. Just put on some lipstick, and let's get out of here."

Hesitating briefly, I weigh the alternatives. I do need to get to know the campus better. "You're on. Let's go."

"Huskies, Huskies, Huskies for the win!" A group of very drunk frat boys hang over the railing at the top of the stairs chanting what I assume is the school's fight song.

I lean into Ali's ear. "We're the Huskies?"

"I mean, they're pretty cool dogs, you have to admit." She leans away, quickly scooping up two red Solo cups full of beer. "To fall semester and the best roommates ever!"

Everyone in this giant house is periodically either shrieking greetings to friends or boyfriends or shouting at the top of their lungs about how great it is to be back…

"I don't remember being this enthusiastic when I was in college," I say, forgetting my earlier lie.

Luckily, Ali doesn't notice. "Probably because you were in a war zone. I imagine that would overshadow just about everything."

I don't bother correcting her, noticing two guys heading in our direction.

"Hello, beautiful ladies, I'm Ryan and this is Evan, and on behalf of Delta Rho, welcome back to Thornton."

"Well, aren't you the sweetest?" Ali's nose wrinkles, and she grins up at Ryan, whose curly brown hair is shoved behind his ears.

He's tall like a football player, dressed in a long-sleeved maroon Henley and jeans, and he sways a little closer to my roommate. "I am, yes. I am very sweet."

I snort into my cup, and he smiles at me, revealing an impressively straight set of white teeth.

"You have really nice teeth," I note over the music.

"Thanks, it's a long story, and you are?"

Frowning at his odd response, I motion between the two of us. "I'm Reanna, and this is Ali."

"Roommates?" Evan speaks, and his player tone puts me on guard.

"Yeah," I nod. "I'm guessing you're not as sweet."

Dropping his chin, he exhales a laugh. "I can be when I try."

"At least you're honest," Ali shouts over the noise.

"Not always," Ryan yells back, scooping four shot glasses of clear liquor off a passing tray.

The guy with the tray shakes his head, heading back to the bar, and my eyebrows rise.

"Don't worry! The pledges are here to serve." Ryan hands each of us a glass. "This beautiful new friendship calls for shots."

We shoot what turns out to be straight vodka, and I'm the

only one who doesn't squint and yell, or shriek as in Ali's case. It's pretty cheap shit, but it'll do the job.

More shots follow, and as the night wears on, our small group tightens. Looking around, I notice the other groups leaning close enough to talk, drinking, holding up shot glasses and laughing. Excited energy hums in the air, and everyone's smiling and ready to start the semester. It almost makes me forget why I'm here.

Almost.

I'm not here to make friends. I'm here to get to know a certain professor better and then take back what he stole—or what the old man hired Andre the rat to steal.

"I think I'd better head back to the dorm." Ali sways, leaning heavily on my arm. "I'm never going to make it to class this way."

Ryan and Evan follow behind us. "See you two later?" Ryan asks.

I hesitate, but Ali nods enthusiastically "For sure. We'll look for you on campus."

It's small enough, I don't think they'll be hard to find. Evan starts to say something, but I put my arm around Ali's waist, speaking with finality. "Have a great night."

With that, we head for the door, and start the short walk back to our dorm. Ali wobbles all over the place, pointing out the dog statue at the top of the quad, the lights on the library bell tower, the welcome back banners on all the frat houses. They were all there before, but she's an amateur drunk. I'm not even feeling much of a buzz.

When we finally get to the room, she goes straight and falls face-first on her bed. She's breathing heavily as I walk to the bathroom to wash my face and get ready for sleep.

A text is waiting on my phone when I return. Of course it's Natasha. **Have you made contact?**

Shaking my head, I quickly tap back. **First class is tomorrow. I'll see him then.**

Gray dots, and her reply annoys me. **We don't have time to waste.**

I'm tapping my reply before I even finish hers. **Then you shouldn't have given me a roommate.**

My phone goes silent, and I plug it in before falling back on my bed. It's been a while since I went to bed somewhat sober, and I'm not sure what to expect. Lying in the darkness, I think about how I'm going to do this. I'm not even sure what Dirk Winston looks like exactly. Hutch is a sexy giant with dark hair and muscles. I can't picture a data-nerd, college professor looking like him.

He's probably the exact opposite, glasses, skinny. Short. I expect it'll be easy to get close to someone like that—he probably never gets any female attention in the shadow of a brother like Hutch. Not to mention Scar, with his tattooed, Viking-biker-thing going on.

My eyes grow heavy, and I feel pretty confident about my ability to manipulate Professor Winston. Then on a whisper, sleep takes me…

Gray clouds hang low overhead, and I'm sitting on a flat rock on the shores of a solid-black sea so big it could be the ocean. A cool wind pushes my pigtails behind my shoulders, and I'm carefully taking my favorite toy apart, arranging the pieces in a line.

It's a simple Russian nesting doll, a matryoshka. *She's nowhere near as ornate as the ones in the shops, but I love her so much. I open each cone, delighted as the dolls inside get smaller and smaller, until the tenth piece is so very tiny, the size of a grain of rice, with the same painted face and shawl on her head as the biggest one.*

A strong gust of wind, and my heart plunges as I almost drop her. With trembling fingers, I put her back in her mother's belly and carefully restore the other nine pieces. I've just screwed the top on the biggest one when I hear the sound of raised voices coming from the direction of our house.

Scooping up my doll, I run over the uneven, rocky shore. I've

*stayed out longer than I should've, and it's time for supper. A drop
of cold rain hits my cheek, and my eyes are fixed on the ground, so I
don't fall. It's not until I reach the dark gray sand that I look up, all
the way across the grassy field to where my father should be.*

*It's when I see them standing there. Three men I don't know, fac-
ing down my papa. Our eyes meet, and he holds out a hand. "Stay
back, Ahren… Stay ba—"*

*A staccato pop!, and he falls to his knees. He's a tall man, so his
head still reaches their chest.*

*His eyes are still on mine, and my legs cramp as I try to run
faster. Ahren means angel, his pet name for me. Another pop, and he
falls flat on his face, his limbs limp at his sides. I drop to the ground
as if I've been shot, my voice a shrill wail. My face is in the sand, my
fingers curling in the soft silt. Strong hands grasp my arms, dragging me away.*

*My doll… I clutch her in my palm. She's all I have left of him.
Struggling, I try to fight them off, to push them away, but I'm too little. I have no power. Papa…*

"Reanna, it's okay… Shh, it's okay."

With a yelp, I realize I'm in my bed on all fours, searching
like a child, throwing my blankets aside, a thin sheen of sweat
coating my body.

Ali is at my bedside shushing me, and my forehead drops
to my hands. I struggle to catch my breath, fighting against the
hot tears threatening my eyes.

"It's all gone," I whisper.

"You were having a bad dream."

I sit on my heels, struggling for calm. "I'm sorry, I…"

I don't know what to say.

"Were you dreaming about the war?" Her voice is calm,
mascara-smudged eyes round with empathy.

Pressing my lips together, I decide to lean into her narrative, even if it's false. "Maybe? I don't really remember."

I remember.

She sits carefully on my bed. "You know my major is psychotherapy, but my focus is on dreams and dream therapy."

I'm not talking to her about this one, so I try to play off what just happened. "You can major in dream interpretation?"

Pushing off the bed, I go to where I set out my clothes for today. I intentionally chose something memorable, and I need to focus on my future, not the past.

"It's more talking about the stressors behind your dreams." She stands and takes a floral dress out of her closet. "It's based on Freudian dream theory. Dreams are expressions of repressed and unconscious wishes. Your dream is the fulfillment of that wish."

"Cool." I go to the bathroom to brush my teeth and apply some light makeup.

Ali is right behind me. "If you ever want to talk, I'm not licensed yet, but I'm a good listener."

"I don't want to talk about it." Grabbing the brush, I smooth it through my hair, giving my outfit and face a quick inspection.

Low-cut jeans, short, tight top, red lips and a hint of mascara on my blue eyes. This should get his attention.

"You look really pretty." Ali frowns at herself in the mirror. "I look like I got run over by a truck. Remind me not to do shots again."

"I'll try." If I remember college correctly, it won't matter.

Heading back into the room, I grab my books, and she pulls on a pair of ankle boots.

"Coffee? Hot chocolate?" She stands, and I nod, thinking. "Coffee."

Waiting in line at the coffee cart in the quad, Ali surveys her schedule. "I can't believe we don't have a single class together."

"I'm not a psych major."

"But you're taking criminal psychology with Professor Winston."

Nodding, I quickly place my order for coffee: two creams,

no sugar. Ali orders hot chocolate. We swipe our student cards, and head for the psychology department.

"So you're a criminal justice major." My roommate scrunches her nose. "Sounds like an oxymoron. Do criminals deserve justice?"

"Everyone deserves justice." I recognize that male voice from last night.

Evan slides up beside us, and Ali gives him a bright smile. "Hey! I knew we'd see you guys around again."

"The campus is not that big," I quietly note, stopping at the door of my class.

"No way—are you headed in here?" He motions to the door, and my stomach sinks.

Forcing a smile, I blink up at him. "Sure am. You?"

"Yes…" He does a little fist pump. "Homework buddy."

Great. Another complication.

A loud male voice from inside draws my notice.

"They're starting." I grab the door to the small auditorium, and hold it open. "After you."

Evan heads inside, and I take a beat. Ali waves, heading down the hall, and I wait a few seconds longer. I want to have his full attention when I enter.

The male voice comes closer, and the door pushes open a bit while I'm holding it. "Are you coming in?"

Lifting my chin, my eyes lock with intense, green-hazel and my chest squeezes. Dirk Winston is not skinny. He's not a computer geek. He's not even short.

I'm five-eight, which is tall for a girl, so he's got to be six foot. His brown hair is slightly wavy and attractively messy, and he smells like clean citrus and fresh soap. I can tell he's muscular by the way his slim button-down shirt stretches over his chest and shoulders.

Full lips part over straight-white teeth, and he gives me an all-American-hero smile. "We're starting now, Miss…?"

Blinking away quickly, I try to catch my breath. Professor

Dirk Winston is lose your panties, fall to your knees, thank (not-lost) Jesus, fucking hot as sin.

My dream from this morning, my papa's murder, echoes in my memory, and I'm ashamed. I don't fall for marks. I'm a soldier, and this job is the chance of my life, to find answers, to avenge my father.

"Sorry..." I clear my throat, finding my focus. "Lorak. Reanna Lorak."

"If you'll take your seat, Miss Lorak." He turns, and his ass is perfectly tight in those jeans.

I almost exhale a delighted sigh, but a hissing sound snaps me out of my lust-filled gaze. Evan tilts his head towards the empty seat beside him, and I remember how to walk.

Professor Panty-dropper continues his course introduction as I quickly take my seat and get my shit together. I'm better than this. So what if he's even hotter than his older brother?

An image of Natasha's scowling face flashes across my brain, melting my lust into anger. Nothing has changed about this job, and in an hour, I'll make the first move.

CHAPTER 5

Dirk

FIRST CLASS IN THE CAN. I'M STANDING AT THE FRONT OF THE SMALL auditorium, disconnecting my laptop from the podium and making a note of where I stopped. I added a few bonus readings to the homework assignment, so I need to update my syllabus on the campus intranet.

Campus life is a little different from when I was at Columbia, with everything online now. Dr. Broadman told me since it's my first year, I should expect to update my lesson plans, assignments, and readings regularly, based on our actual progress. He called it "first-year problems."

Sharon sat in on the class, helping with attendance, and I'm pleased to have a good-sized group of students. I wasn't sure what to expect, but they were very engaged. Of course, they're paying money to be here, so they're attentive, asking questions, and taking notes.

So far, being back on campus, being a professor is scratching that itch, that need for something more.

Only one hiccup in the beginning, the girl Reanna Lorak charging in late and then staring up at me a little too long and with a little too much interest. It caught me off-guard.

Long, dark hair, stunning blue eyes… Something was strangely familiar about her, her eyes, her face. I couldn't place it. I could swear it was as if we'd met before, and for a second, it nearly threw off the whole rhythm of the class, which was potentially embarrassing.

Of course, being the professional I am, I shook off the phantom feeling and got down to business. I couldn't possibly know that young woman.

Heading for the door, I notice the guy she sat with hanging around Sharon's seat in the risers.

"So you're the class enforcer?" He's clearly flirting.

Sharon smiles in a dismissive way. "I'll be grading your quizzes and taking attendance. That's as much as I do."

"Pretty powerful." His hands are in his pockets, and he's a decent-looking fellow if a bit smarmy—not that it matters. Sharon can do what she wants.

"Sorry to interrupt." I pause beside them. "Just heading back to my office. Sharon, thanks for your help today."

She's on her feet at once, sliding her notebook and laptop into the messenger bag at her feet. "I'll walk with you."

In the hall, the sea of students has thinned to a trickle as the next hour of classes begins. Glancing back, I notice the guy heading out the door of the building.

"Looks like you picked up an admirer," I tease.

"One for me, twenty-five for you," she teases right back, but I dismiss her comment with a wave.

"That's a non-starter, but you and that guy are both students. You could pursue it."

"No way." Her lip curls. "He's bad news."

"Is that so?" I exhale a laugh. "What is your definition of *bad news*, Miss Stead?"

She shakes her head. "He's a fuckboy. Women are notches on his bedpost, and his dates *always* do the walk of shame."

"Hm," I nod, knowing the type. "But you're a strong young woman. No judgment here if you want to blow off a little steam."

"No thanks. I don't expect commitment, but I do expect courtesy."

"Smart girl."

"Woman." She corrects me, bumping my arm with her elbow. "Anyway, I've got to get to Landon's class. See you tomorrow."

"See ya, and hey, let me know if you have any problems with that guy." I don't like fuckboys either, and it's possible my experience with Hana has made me a bit overprotective.

"You're sweet, and I will." She gives me a wink before hurrying away.

Taking out my key, I unlock the door to my office. I plan to hop online, make those syllabus updates, then head out to lunch.

I've just sat down when a soft tapping starts on my door. "Professor Winston?"

It's a low female voice, smoky with the faintest hint of an accent, and even though I've only heard it once, I recognize it immediately.

"Come in." My stomach tightens as Reanna Lorak steps into the small space I share with my computer. Alone.

Her blue eyes are so intense, and she's tall with that magnetic quality models have. She's still in those jeans and that top, tiny spaghetti straps, no bra, nipples pointed. She's fit like an athlete, and I blink a few times, tearing my eyes away from her midriff.

Jesus, fuck that. I'm not ogling her body, what the hell? I'm the professor.

She's the student.

The end.

"Miss Lorak, is it?" I take a beat, picking up my glasses and clearing my mind as I slide them over my eyes.

I have no problems with boundaries. I'm just out of practice.

Her full, pink lips part in a smile revealing straight, white teeth. "You remembered my name."

Of course, I did. "Did you need something?"

She's holding a laptop, and her long hair is pulled over one shoulder. It's shiny and straight with a slight wave near the bottom.

"I'm sorry…" She blinks long lashes onto her cheeks. "I'm a transfer student, so I wanted to meet all my professors."

I give her a controlled smile. "In that case, welcome. It's nice to meet you."

Her forehead relaxes, and she exhales a laugh. "The truth is I'm a little worried about your class. I'm not from this country, and our laws are so different. I need to do well."

"Where are you from?"

"Odesa. I lived with my father in a small house near the Black Sea… until he died."

Her voice trails off, and empathy filters through my chest, lowering my guard. "I'm sorry."

"It was a while ago, but it changed my life." Her nose wrinkles, and she points to my face. "You wear glasses, but not in class?"

"Yes, actually." I take them off, studying them in my hands. "I'm right on the border of not being able to see without them, so I can still get away with forgetting."

"They look nice on you." She blinks slowly.

Tension radiates across my shoulders like a warning. This conversation is becoming problematic. She speaks and carries herself in a way that feels more mature than a typical college student.

"How old are you, Miss Lorak?"

Her blue eyes sparkle up at me through dark lashes. "I'm twenty-two, but I thought it was rude to ask a woman her age."

"Yes, sorry." Clearing my throat, I adopt a detached, scholarly tone. "You were worried about the difference in our laws. The good news is we don't go into law or anything like that. My course is about psychology. The focus will be on understanding how the criminal mind works."

With a gentle nod, she steps closer. "Is it possible to understand such things?"

She's directly in front of me, the heat from her skin vibrating in proximity to mine, and I can't help thinking, if this were a different time or place, I'd suggest we go somewhere and have a drink, get to know each other better.

As it is, I'm her teacher. I'm in a position of trust, and I have no intention of abusing that trust. Taking a step away, I return to my leather chair, putting the enormous mahogany desk between us.

"If you're so worried, it's not too late to drop the course and take something more in your comfort zone." The suggestion sticks in my throat, but I'm doing the right thing, giving her good advice.

More "first-year problems"—developing an immunity to attractive co-eds.

Her blue eyes blink up at me again, and her voice lowers. "What do you know about my comfort zone, Professor Winston?"

It feels like a taunt, and I shift in my seat. In the field with Hutch and Scar, I'm lethal. I'm not afraid to face down anyone or tell them where to go. Now, with this unarmed girl sitting across from me, a heavy mahogany desk as a shield, I'm second-guessing every word.

"You're right. I should've said 'something that would help you adjust more comfortably.'"

"I'm pretty comfortable with you." She tilts her head to the side. "The truth is, since my father died, it's been hard to feel

comfortable with anyone. I've had to make a way for myself
alone in the world. It's why I need to do well in my classes."

There it is—an obvious bid for me to give her a good grade
because she's a pretty girl alone in the world.

I'm not annoyed. College students do it all the time, and
considering her background, she does have my sympathy. It's
possible her situation *is* more compelling than the average trust-
fund kid here on Mom and Pop's dime, but the prejudice of
such a consideration annoys me. Many students have suffered
trauma, and giving her special treatment is wrong.

"If you apply yourself, complete the assignments and the
readings on time, you should have no problem doing well in
my class." My tone is firm, all business.

"I've offended you." Her eyes drop to her lap. "I only
wanted to let you know my situation. I didn't mean to seem
like I was asking for... *anything*."

"I'm not offended." I remain firm. "If you choose to stay
in my class, you'll have to do the work. I'll give you the name
of a tutor if you fall behind—"

"I'd rather study with you." Her eyes meet mine again,
and it's time to end this meeting.

Rising from my chair, I hold out my hand for the door.
"I'm sorry, but tutoring isn't something I do."

"But you're the one grading my assignments. I'd rather
know your opinion than a surrogate's."

"I have regular office hours, and I'll be glad to look over any
assignment before it's due—like I would for any other student."

It's a clear line of demarcation.

"I see." She stands, placing her fingers lightly on my wrist.
"Thank you for seeing me... Professor Winston."

Her full lips say my name as if asking for a kiss, and the
heat circulating in my blood rushes straight to my dick. I do not
imagine ordering her to get on her knees and open her mouth.

"Have a nice day, Miss Lorak." I place my hand on her

shoulder and gently, but forcefully move her into the hall, closing the door solidly.

Anger burns in my throat at my primitive response to this girl. I'm always in control, and that hasn't changed. Then, my eyes land on the laptop she left on the edge of my desk.

Shit, I shoved her out the door, and now I have her computer. Last thing I need is her coming back for it.

Scooping it up, I quickly jerk the door open, stepping out so fast, I nearly collide with her and Evan the Fuckboy talking in the hall.

I stop short, holding out the tablet for her. "You left this."

She smiles up at me like I just saved her life. "Thank you." Her voice is breathless. "You've helped me so much."

Evan smirks at me like we're on the same team, and I want to punch him in the face, which is completely unprofessional. Reanna's fingers brush mine lightly as she takes the laptop from me, and I pull my hand away.

"You're welcome. Next time, please note my office hours." I return to my office, shutting the door firmly on that nonsense.

I'm not a player, and I'm not interested in that student.

I need a drink.

"How will you finish your thesis if you're assisting three professors all the time?" I take a sip of draft beer, leaning on the bar at The Husky Den.

"Somehow I manage." Sharon sips from her pint glass.

The Den is a popular collegiate watering hole within walking distance of campus. It's all-wood and brass and filled with mostly graduate students, a few professors, and some upperclassmen, whom I assume are over twenty-one.

It didn't occur to me that any of my students might be adults. I'd anticipated a bunch of immature teenagers, zero interest, zero temptation. I didn't not anticipate Reanna Lorak.

Following our meeting in my office, I updated my online class information then headed out in search of a drink, bumping into Sharon on the way here.

"Here's to the start of fall semester." She holds up her glass, and I clink it.

It's a good pilsner, slightly bitter but light, and classic rock filters over the low roar of the crowd. I'm pretty sure it's "Creep" by Radiohead.

"Something's on your mind." Sharon studies my face. "And I don't think it's your concern about my workload, which predates you anyway."

Exhaling a grin, I place my glass on the polished bar. "I forgot what it's like to work with professional thinkers."

"You're in college now, Professor Winston."

I like it. I like the nature of strong minds challenging me to dig deeper.

"Okay, I've been thinking about our conversation from earlier. Has that type of thing happened at Thornton before?"

She looks away, into the crowd. "I really shouldn't have said that about Evan. He's probably just a regular guy, and I labeled him without giving him a chance to defend himself. It's the definition of prejudicial behavior."

Possibly. At the same time, I've met opportunists like him before.

"Not the Evan thing. I'm talking about the thing with Effington and the student. Is that something that happens a lot?"

She takes another sip of beer and shrugs. "If it does, nobody talks about it. However, speaking as a Ph.D. candidate in psychoanalysis, it seems inevitable it would happen a lot."

"How so?"

"College women tend to be attracted to highly educated men, and professors are often men who've never been particularly attractive to women, present company excluded, of course."

"Of course," I laugh, taking another sip of beer.

"Suddenly, at a time when many men struggle with mid-life issues, they're being inundated with interest from young, nubile women." She hesitates then grins. "Then, of course, some girls simply have daddy issues, and who better to scratch that itch than a bossy, intelligent professor."

"Ahh…" The pieces click into place. "That makes sense."

Especially if a student, say, lost her father tragically at a young age. *Daddy issues*.

"Which part?"

"All of it, really. You're very observant, Miss Stead."

"Not that it matters. I'm sure you have plenty of admirers on and off campus." She leans closer. "Answer the burning question on all our female minds… Does the very handsome Professor Winston have a significant other?"

"No." I polish off my beer.

Her lips quirk in a frown. "Why not?"

"Lots of reasons. I've never seen a long-term relationship that worked." My dad was the worst fucking role model. "And perhaps I made bad choices when I was younger."

"What's *your* definition of 'bad choices,' Professor?"

She's imitating my question from earlier, and I huff a laugh. "I'll tell you something I've never told anyone. Ready?"

"Definitely." She sets her glass down and squares her shoulders. "Hit me."

"I had a serious girlfriend in college, then after graduation, she wanted to settle down and get married. I didn't." Sharon does a fake gasp, placing her palm on her chest, and I continue. "I still think I was right. We were too young. I wanted to do things, and being married would've held me down. So we broke up. Now she's married with a couple kids, and I've never gotten that close again."

Silence falls between us. She studies me with her dark brows furrowed, and I wait to hear her fresh, psychoanalytical, Ph.D.-candidate opinion.

Finally, she suggests a reason. "So that's it? You're done?"

Fishing cash out of my pocket, I drop a ten on the bar. "I think I missed my chance."

"Bullshit. If *Sex and the City* taught us anything, it's there's no such thing as one soul mate. You gave up."

"I didn't give up." Patting her shoulder, I'm ready to go. "I like my job. I don't like drama. Relationships always turn into drama."

"You're a grinch." Sharon is smug, taking out her card to settle her bill. "A little piece of coal where your heart should be."

"I'm not a grinch. I'm telling you what I've seen and experienced."

Although, my brother seems to have broken that rule—or he's the exception that proves it.

"You're much too handsome and virile to be a confirmed old bachelor. I'm betting this time next year, you'll be settled down, married, and covered in babies. It's why you came back to college—for a second chance."

"Five dollars says you're wrong."

"Done." She holds out her hand, and I shake it.

"Goodnight, Sharon." I grin, heading out into the night, ready to get back to my solo, faculty housing and get some rest.

CHAPTER 6

Reanna

I WANT TO FUCK PROFESSOR DIRK WINSTON.

The realization hit me hard when I left his office after my initial contact. I've never wanted to sleep with a target, but this purported "computer geek" professor is fucking hot.

Sleeping with him is not part of my "get close" master plan. I could get what I want from him without spreading my legs…

But it does make the job more fun.

When I was in his office, it took all my focus not to place my hand over his, to press my soft body against his hard one. I turned on all the charm, pouting my lips, allowing my hair to fall seductively over my shoulder, and he shut me down. *Damn.*

I kind of hoped he'd be easy, but honestly, feeling his anger, his strength when he hit the brakes and turned into Mr. Strictly Business, made him even hotter. He's a good man with good character, and so fucking hot with those glasses and broad shoulders and large hands.

The muscle in his square jaw tightened, and I wanted him

to catch me by the face and tell me I was being a brat. I wanted him to shove my thin top up and squeeze my bare breasts, lick my hardened nipples, and pull them with his teeth. I wanted him to spank me and then bend me over his desk and fuck me hard from behind.

Heat races to my core, and alone in my dorm room, I lie back on the bed, closing my eyes as I slip my hand past my underwear and play out my fantasy...

It starts with him sitting in that leather chair, burning with anger. I walk around his mahogany desk, leaning forward so he can see I've forgotten my panties (*oops*). I bend a little farther and my pussy is right in his face.

I imagine the muscle in his square jaw flexing, his hazel eyes darkening as he struggles with his animal needs versus our human rules. He's right on the edge. The muscles in his arms bulge as he grips his chair tighter. He only needs a little nudge...

"Please," I moan, feeling my wetness leaking onto my thighs. "I want you so much it hurts, professor."

He breaks.

Strong hands grip me by the waist, and he fumbles, sliding his cock up and down between my legs until he locates my entrance. With a firm thrust, he's inside, and we both moan so loudly, it's audible in the hall. It doesn't stop us.

Curses fall from his lips as he punishes me. I'm jeopardizing his career. I'm a student, barely twenty-two, but he's lost all control. He pounds into me feverishly, and my voice is a wailing cry, somewhere between begging and bliss. His cock is so hard, and he's so desperate.

My hand circles faster, massaging my clit as orgasm tingles in my legs. I imagine a drop of sweat tracing down his cheek from how hard he's working. Strong fingers thread in my hair, and he jerks my head back as he drives deeper. He's taking out his frustration on me, hating himself for wanting me. Hating himself for how much he wants to do it again.

"Fuck, yes," I gasp as my orgasm shudders through my core, shaking my thighs and bending my waist. "Oh, fuck…"

I'm so sensitive, my eyes squeeze shut as I ride it out, as a smile curls my lips.

God, that felt so good, even if it was just a fantasy. Turning onto my side, I wonder what it will be like when it happens for real. His hard body against mine, surrounding me with his scent, his salty sweat on my tongue.

He's so fucking lickable.

I've got to find the crack in his walls.

"One aspect of criminal psychology that has fallen out of favor is profiling." The lights in the auditorium are dim, and Dirk stands in front of the screen sliding his hand down each bullet point as he discusses it.

He's become simply Dirk in my mind, although it's hotter to imagine calling him Professor Winston when we're alone, when he spanks my bare ass for being a bad girl. Pressing my lips together, I fight a smile at the thought.

Two weeks have passed, and I'm doing my best to take it slow. Maybe today I can try a different approach. My outfit is more conservative, a blue dress with a cardigan. It's pretty and sweet, not too much to put him on guard.

Subtlety and patience are the most important parts of my job.

My eyes travel over his body as he stands in front of the screen, pointing to the traits of a good FBI Profiler. When he lifts his arms, his muscles move under that thin, button-down shirt stretched over his broad shoulders.

It's really hot how smart he is, and today he's wearing his glasses. I imagine him sliding them off when he sees something he likes… perhaps something he might like to kiss?

"A good profiler can ascertain the level of planning that went into the crime…"

He uses the word *ascertain* perfectly in a sentence.

"…the degree of control used by the offender, if there was an escalation of emotion at the scene…"

I wonder how *controlled* he is when he's fucking. Does he coolly give orders, those intense eyes distant and unreadable? Or do his emotions *escalate*?

If I dropped to my knees in front of him, pulling his hard cock between my lips and giving it a firm suck, would he groan with pleasure or pull my hair and hiss words of approval?

Shifting in my seat, I cross my legs, and his eyes move to mine. Our gaze holds for only a moment, but it's long enough to flood my stomach with heat.

His brow lowers as if he's annoyed, but he doesn't miss a beat, continuing his lecture. His control makes me thirsty, and I wonder if he could read from my pouty lips, I was dreaming of blowing his mind.

"Above all, a good profiler must resist racial stereotypes." No sign he felt anything. "This skill can be useful, but it can also be highly destructive…"

He slides his glasses higher, and I'm barely listening as he gives our reading assignment for the night. Next class we have a writing project due, and I'm so ready to pay him another visit.

The first time laid the groundwork and helped him see me as a sympathetic character. I love that he pushed back when I got too close. I love that he isn't a sleaze, ready to take advantage of a young girl's apparent willingness to please him.

Every man is flattered by a woman who obviously wants him, but Dirk is different. It makes me wonder if there could be something more between us. He's "the enemy," but only because Natasha is giving the orders.

Shit, where the fuck did that come from? I'm not looking for something more.

I have to stay focused if I'm going to complete this mission and find that book. Once I have the truth about my father, I'm leaving these people far behind. I want a new life, something better than what I've had so far. He has his life, and I have my plans. He's a mark, and when I'm finished, I'll walk away.

"As always, if you need to see me, no appointment is necessary during office hours." Still, the low vibration of his voice *is* a tempting sound. "Have a great weekend."

Class ends, and I gather my books. He'll take his time finishing up, and I need to take my time getting to him. Strolling into the quad to wait, I sit on a bench under a tree watching a couple of guys throwing a frisbee.

"Hey, you got a break between classes?" Ryan drops to sit beside me on the bench, smiling brightly.

"Yeah…" I wrap my cardigan tightly around my body as I study his perfect smile, remembering his odd response when I complimented him on it that first night. "You?"

"Done for the day." He leans back proudly, and I glance at the clock.

It's after lunch on a Thursday, and I have a 90-minute class starting at three, not that it matters. I'm only here for one reason.

"Clever guy," I tease, and he gives me another megawatt grin. I can't resist anymore. "So what's the long story?"

"What?" His brow furrows, and he shoves a lock of curly brown hair behind his ear.

"On Welcome Back night, I complimented you on your smile, and you said it was a long story. What's the long story?"

"Oh." His chin drops, and he studies the laces on his shoe.

His knee is bent, and I scoot around, bumping his shoulder with mine. "It's okay, you can tell me. What was it? Car wreck? Teeth never came in like that kid on *Stranger Things*?"

"The kid on *Stranger Things* has cleidocranial dysplasia. It's not that his teeth never came in, more like they take much longer to develop."

"Okay, okay." Holding up my hands, I nod. "Clearly, you're destined to be a dentist. What's your long story?"

His face flushes, and a prickly heat rises in my neck. I wasn't trying to embarrass him. He said it was a long story, like he might tell it sometime. Instead, he seems on the verge of tears, which is very uncomfortable.

I'm ready to shut it down, tell him not to worry about it, when he speaks. "My baby teeth didn't fall out at the right time, and my mouth was too small for all my permanent teeth coming in and the ones still there…"

He hesitates, and I'm confused. He's describing a recipe for disaster, but his smile is perfect.

"Was that bad?"

"When I was thirteen, my teeth were shoved together and became severely crooked. Some went sideways, my front teeth protruded… My parents couldn't afford to have all the dental work done. At school, I became a joke."

A pit is in my stomach. "Kids made fun of you?" He nods, and anger simmers hot in my chest. "But it wasn't your fault."

"It wasn't just kids. The basketball coach called me 'picket fence.'" He hesitates a beat before huffing a bitter laugh. I think I see a glimmer on his bottom lids.

He blinks it away, and my fist tightens. "What was that coach's name?"

I can find him, and I'll make that asshole pay…

"It doesn't matter. I got older, made some money, and fixed my teeth." An edge enters his voice. "Nobody will make me feel ashamed like that again."

"If you'll tell me his name, I'll make sure he never makes anyone feel ashamed ever again." I'm ready to find that motherfucker and beat his head into the ground.

Being a kid is hard enough, but there's a special place in hell for adults who bully children, especially kind ones like Ryan.

"What are you, some kind of hit girl?" Ryan laughs, and I catch my breath, sitting a little straighter.

Easing off the revenge, I wrap an arm around his shoulder, pulling him into a side hug, and giving him a few extra squeezes.

"Wouldn't that be cool?" I deflect. "If I were a hit girl, I'd find that coach and find a way to humiliate him in front of everyone."

"Reanna's secretly a softy," he teases.

Standing, it's time for me to get back on the job. "Don't tell anyone. It'd ruin my street cred."

"I won't." He pats my arm, and I turn, heading back inside the psychology building.

Hurrying down the hall, I let too much time pass, and it's very possible he's not there anymore. I fly around the corner, my shoes squeaking on the linoleum floors, and I hear his low voice mixed with another. It's followed by the soft sounds of laughter, and the skin on my neck prickles.

Creeping closer, I hesitate outside the door listening.

"It's what we call 'back to school voice.'" A woman is talking to him, but I can tell from her tone, she's not a student.

Unexpected jealousy flares to life in my chest.

"How do I get rid of it?" Dirk's low voice is slightly hoarse.

"Don't talk more than you have to outside class. Eventually, your vocal cords will strengthen and adjust. You're not used to speaking so much, and being in the auditorium makes you project more than normal." A crinkling of plastic, and she speaks again. "Here."

"Peppermint?" Dirk is skeptical.

"Hot tea with lemon and honey is also good."

"How about a jolly rancher? I like the green ones."

"What are you, twelve?"

Mental note. Knocking softly on the door, I wait as he walks over to open it. My brow tightens with fear. I'm unsure how he'll react to my being here after last time.

I'm relieved when a smile relaxes his features. "Miss Lorak, I wasn't expecting to see you. Can I help you with something?"

"I'm so sorry to interrupt." When I speak to him, it's soft and low, touched with an accent I learned to hide years ago. "I can come back another time."

"No, this is a good time. Sharon is my graduate assistant. I'm sure you've seen her in class."

"Hi, there." The young woman smiles.

Her hair is long and dark, straight with bangs. She's wearing a shirt that hits above her knees, and her tight sweater that shows off her round breasts. When her eyes move to him, I can tell she wants him, and I instantly hate her.

"Do you need help with the assignment?" he asks me.

"Yes." Snapping out of my annoyance, I tilt my head towards his office. "Could we... speak privately? It's a little embarrassing."

"Of course." He backs up, heading to the door like such a good teacher.

I pass Sharon the slut, and I don't even look at her. My eyes are fixed on the muscles in his ass, flexing when he walks. So hot. As before, he puts the large desk between us, sitting in his leather chair.

My fantasy from last time flashes through my mind, and my neck heats. The place between my thighs flutters, and I almost sigh audibly. How much longer will I have to wait?

As it is, two weeks isn't enough. I have to know him better, although we do see each other twice a week in class...

"What's on your mind?" He leans forward, taking off his glasses and massaging the bridge of his nose before setting them on the desk.

My tongue slips out to wet my bottom lip. "It's about the writing assignment."

"It's not due until Thursday."

"Last time we spoke, you offered to read over my assignments and give suggestions. Would you still do that for me?"

"You've finished it?" His dark brow rises, and I can't tell... *Is he proud of me?*

Warmth blooms in my stomach that he might be, and I blink down to my bag where my laptop is stored. "I'm worried my English is not very good."

The slightest grin curls his full, kissable lips. "Good news—it's not an English class. I'm not grading you on grammar, but on how well you demonstrate your understanding of the reading assignment."

Taking out my laptop, I pull up the assignment. "Would you still look over it for me?"

His shoulders fall, and he holds out a hand. His shirt sleeves are rolled, and the muscle in his forearm flexes as he takes the device.

I scoot my chair around to the side of his desk, leaning forward so the V-neck of my top falls open. If he glances up, he should be able to see most of my bare breasts, my taut nipples beneath the fabric.

Instead his eyes are focused on the screen as he quietly reads, and I glance around his small office, thinking about some way to get his attention.

"She's very beautiful." My voice is quiet, and his eyes flicker from the screen, first to my breasts, then quickly to my eyes.

"Who is?" He frowns, lifting his glasses and putting them on again.

Slow down, Reanna.

"Sharon, your assistant." I straighten, wrapping my cardigan tighter around my body. "Is she your girlfriend?"

Placing my laptop on his desk, his eyes level on mine. "Sharon is not my girlfriend, and it's not your business. I can review your work, or you can visit the writing lab in the library."

I'm torn between happiness at the news and despair at his fortitude. "You're right. It's not my business."

"Now about your paper." Glasses off again, he slides the device in my direction. "I think your worries are unfounded. You have a good grasp of the language as well as the concepts."

I allow myself to smile, pushing my hair behind my ear. "Thank you so much. This means so much to me."

"You're welcome. Now, if that's all, I've got work to do."

I chew my lip, trying to think of another way in. "You must think I'm foolish to be so relieved, but... Have you ever lost someone, Professor Winston?"

His lips part, and he doesn't answer immediately. He seems to be choosing his words. "My mother died when I was very young."

"Oh, I'm so sorry." Without thinking I place my hand on top of his. He pauses, and I quickly take my hand away. "I'm sorry. I shouldn't have done that."

"It's okay. I'm not offended." But he stands, gesturing as if it's time for me to go.

I close the laptop and slide it into my bag, speaking slowly. "I forget sometimes. In my country we're more open to touch. I miss it... the feeling of connection."

"Touch therapy is an emerging area of clinical research." He's waiting as I gather my things, still remaining aloof.

Standing slowly, I attempt to slide the strap of my bag onto my shoulder. It slips, and he catches it quickly, lifting it onto my shoulder for me. His touch is warm, and I lift my chin, wanting him to show me any confirmation he feels this energy simmering between us.

"I miss my father's hugs." My voice is quiet as I speak from my heart. "I scroll on my phone, chat with friends, get advice, but what I miss most is that one simple thing I'll never have again."

As I say the words, I ache at how true they are.

His eyes hold mine. Clean citrus touches my nose, and he's not pushing me away or throwing up walls now. He's looking into my soul.

"Honestly, I miss my mother's hugs." His voice is gentle, as if something shifted.

"You must be lonely… like me." The words hang in the air, and we're so close.

Swaying, I hold my breath, dying for him to move, to pull me into his arms and hug me so tightly, something we both want and miss. I know it would be amazing.

Loud voices erupt in the hall, and the spell breaks.

He takes a step back, going to the door and opening it. "I'll see you in class, Miss Lorak."

Sharon is gone, and I drop my chin, acknowledging defeat as I softly pass him. "Goodbye, professor."

He closes the door, and I pull my cardigan even tighter around my body. It's ridiculous for me to want to cry, but I do.

CHAPTER 7

Dirk

FIRE IS IN MY VEINS, AND I MOVE FAST, SWITCHING THE LOCK ON the door.

Going to the small bathroom behind the bookcase in my office, I slam the door, quickly lowering my jeans to relieve the pressure.

I scoop up the tube of hand cream beside the soap dish on the small sink. A little lube, and I grasp my hard cock, bracing my other hand on the wall and closing my eyes.

Her taut nipples are at my lips, and I pull them into my mouth, biting and tugging at her breasts as I slide my hands down her back and over her round ass.

In my mind, I stand in front of her, rising to my full height. Her head is at my shoulders, and her eyes flash with defiance. She knows exactly what she's doing, licking her full lips, studying my crotch.

I place my hands on her shoulders. "Get on your knees." It's a hoarse order, fueled by weeks of denial.

She blinks up at me, blue eyes round as she obeys. Her face is at my cock, and her eyes are on mine as she lowers her jaw, extending her tongue flat and placing it at the base of my shaft, dragging it to my tip.

"Fuck," I groan as orgasm flares hotter in my pelvis.

I've pretended to be immune to her, and every day that passes, every day she sits in my class watching me, undressing me with her eyes, I'm in a perpetual state of frustrated desire.

This isn't happening.

Only it is.

She wraps her lips around my tip, pulling my cock farther into her mouth, and sucking. My hand moves faster, and I grow angrier, rage fueled by need.

"You want to fuck me for an *A*?" I growl, threading my fingers in her hair and hitting the back of her throat with my dick.

She blinks fast attempting to nod as she holds her breasts, lifting them and pinching her nipples as I fuck her face.

"Then you'd better give me your best effort."

I'm not safe, and she knows it. She's playing with fire, and if she's not careful, I'm going to use her the way she's begging me to. Her head bobs faster, her hands wrapping around my hips, moving to my ass.

"Fuck…" I growl as heat turns to fire in my lower stomach, and my orgasm shakes me to the core. "Fuck, Reanna…"

It's a ragged groan, and I lean my head against my arm as jets pulse from my cock into the open toilet. My knees are weak as I tug slower, coaxing the last drops of come from my body. God, it's been too long since I've gotten laid.

Grinding my jaw, I reach forward to quickly flush the evidence away and reach for a towel to clean my hands. *What the hell, Dirk?*

Stepping to the sink, I turn on the hot water and grab the soap. I wash my hands roughly, scrubbing my skin as if I actually touched her body. Her young body, her perky nipples, her dewy skin…

She's a fucking child.

She's twenty-two, my rebellious brain argues.

"She's a fucking student," I say out loud to shut it down.

Great. Now I'm talking to myself.

I need to get out of here. Snatching my bag off the desk, I storm out into the hall and into the quad, glancing at the lowering sun. It takes less than ten minutes to get from my office to my faculty house.

I drop my bag on the table and head straight to my bedroom where I strip out of my clothes and quickly pull on shorts and a tee. I have an hour until sunset, and I slip AirPods in my ear and set off at a rapid clip.

Running is the only way to kill this tension, so I run until I don't feel it anymore.

The sun is down, and I'm slick with sweat when I get back to my apartment. Halfway through my run, I stripped off my tee. It's fall, but it's still a little warm, and I had already soaked through the thin cotton. Now I toss it near the plastic laundry bin.

Crossing my empty kitchen to the fridge, I grab a bottle of water, rip off the top, and drink it all in one long gulp. My hand is braced on the door, and I lift my head, looking around the empty room.

You must be lonely… like me. Her voice echoes in my ears.

With another growl, I slam the refrigerator door and head for the shower.

Showered and changed, I flick on the TV, looking for anything to distract my mind. After going through three different streaming services and not finding anything, I pick up my phone.

I can't call Hutch. I don't want to hear him say I told you so.

Blake is always easy to talk to, but she'll feel obliged to tell Hutch, and that gets me back to where I started.

Glancing at the clock, I see it's ten, so I decide to start with a text. *How's it going, little mama? Any movement on the baby front?*

Checking in on my pregnant sister-in-law is not out of the ordinary. It doesn't signal I'm stressed or dealing with a hot-assin student who I really, really want to fuck.

Luckily, my phone buzzes with a quick response. *Hey, handsome! Baby's just growing. We miss your face around here. What's new at school?*

The fist in my chest relaxes. Why do I believe if anyone would understand what I'm going through right now, it would be Hana?

Because it's true.

Still, I'm not about to burden her with my irresponsible shit. *Feel like talking?*

A few seconds pass, and my phone vibrates in my hand, indicating a call. I press the green button and Hana's sweet, slightly high, breathy voice is in my ear.

"Hey, what's up with you?" A light laugh is in her tone, and I almost forget how fucked-up I was feeling when I sent her a lifeline.

"Just needed to hear a familiar voice."

"Oh, no! Are you homesick? We're only an hour away if you want to drive back for the weekend. We'd all be so glad to see you."

"Now why didn't I think of that before?" I sound like I'm joking, but I'm actually pretty serious.

I could drive back to Hamiltown, spend some time away, see if that helps me get my head straight.

"You just need to be reminded how much you're loved around here."

A half-smile curls my lips. Hana's been through so much, and yet she's so ready to give love. I guess that's how it works. Those who suffer the most know how important reassurance is.

"Maybe I'll drive home this weekend. I would like to see how much you've grown."

"I'm getting bigger, but not so big I have to sleep sitting up. Yet."

A low voice in the background draws my attention. "Is that Scar?"

"The man himself. Want to say hi?" A scuffing sound is in my ear, and I'm pretty sure she passed the phone.

The next sound is the low voice of my partner. "How's it going, bro? Punched any kids yet?"

"Not even close," I laugh, and he exhales a chuckle.

"Glad to see you're controlling that temper. You know, self-control is a sign of maturity."

"Then I'm the most mature person you know." He has no idea. "Although there is this one professor who's annoying as fuck."

"Bro, you're supposed to make friends with the professors. They're your coworkers."

"So far my only friends are the dean and my graduate assistant. Oh, and this one student who I'm pretty sure wants to get in my pants."

That gets me a loud laugh. "Only one? Or is she the only one who interests you?"

Shaking my head, I can't believe he called me on it. "Maybe I'm not cut out for this line of work."

"Listen." Scar's voice turns serious. "You can't help who you're attracted to. What you can do is figure out if it's simple lust or something more. I'm speaking from experience. Don't shit where you eat... unless you're sure it's the real deal."

My eyes squeeze, but I hear him. I know Scar wrestled with his feelings for Hana for six months before he ever even kissed her.

"Thanks, man. I knew you'd understand."

"I'm here if you need me."

Hana's voice calls in the background. "We love you, Dirk!"

Warmth calms the storm brewing in my chest. "I love you guys."

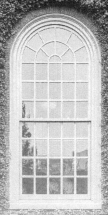

CHAPTER 8

Reanna

"**Y**OU STOLE IT!" HOT TEARS BLIND MY VISION, BUT I CONTINUE searching, ripping the cushions off the couch and throwing the pillows aside. "*Give it back!*"

"I don't have it." Her impudent nose is in the air like it always is.

"You always wanted it. You took it, now give it back."

She stands with her arms crossed watching me like I'm an annoying pest. The more agitated I get, the happier she grows until a cruel smile curls her lips, and she cuts her eyes to the fire.

"It's gone."

I scream so hard my chest quakes. My little doll, my tiniest matryoshka, the one thing I treasured, that I brought from my father's house. I held it in my hand as I fell asleep every night… Now it's burning in the fire.

Pain cuts through my chest, and I fall to my knees in front of the flames. I would shove my hand in and save her if I could. I'm crying, ragged breaths shuddering from my throat.

Strong hands, grown-up hands, grip my shoulders to stop me from screaming. They shake me, but they'll never make it right.

She destroyed it, like she destroys everything.

Now I have nothing left of him.

Nothing.

"It's all gone. I have nothing…" I'm sobbing, repeating the words over and over as the dream fades.

"It's okay, Re-re, I'm here."

A gentle hand strokes the side of my head, and I sit up fast, kicking my feet and scrambling against the wall beside my bed. Blinking fast, I look all around, disoriented.

"Where…" I almost ask where I am before I realize I'm in my dorm room at Thornton, not my uncle's lavish living room with the Persian rugs and velvet armchairs and Tiffany lamps and all the hate.

"Oh my God." Dropping my face in my hand, I feel the dampness on my cheek, and I quickly wipe the tears off my face. "I'm okay. I'm sorry."

Ali presses her lips together, and I know she wants to say something. I tilt my head and give her a look that says *Don't.*

"I'm here if you need to talk."

"Thanks." Climbing out of the bed, I go straight to our small bathroom and turn on the hot water.

When it's finally warm, I scoop handfuls onto my face, trying to calm my jangling insides. I'm stronger than this. I survived Natasha's cruelty already. She doesn't have power over me now.

Only it's not true. I'm here on her orders. She's still calling the shots.

But it's for my purposes. I have my own agenda, and she can't stop me.

More water, I hold my hands against my face trying to calm myself. *Get it together.*

A soft tapping on the door and it slowly opens. Ali hands

me a towel, and I take it, silently patting my face dry. Our eyes meet briefly in the mirror, and hers are full of concern.

"As a psychology major, I know you know it's unhealthy to hold things like this inside." I don't answer, and she continues. "I wouldn't betray your trust. I'd like to think we're friends."

I put the towel on the rack and exhale a sigh. How could Ali possibly understand my life? "I'm a criminal justice major, and we've only known each other a month."

"Isn't that what college is all about? Making new friends?"

But I'm not really a college student. I don't belong here. Friends will only cause problems, which is why I wasn't even supposed to have a roommate.

Going to my closet, I study my wardrobe. We almost hugged last time I was in his office. I can't remember the last time I felt so desperate for a hug. The chemistry crackled around us like static electricity, and when it broke, so did I.

Chewing my lip, I grab a pair of jeans and a tight sweater Miss Graduate Assistant would envy. When I turn, Ali's dressed in a long-sleeved jersey and jeans, but her eyes are downcast, and a dejected expression is on her face.

Thanks again, Rick. Now I feel like shit.

I decide to be as straight with her as I can. Gentling my tone, I walk over and put my hand on her shoulder. "The truth is, Ali, I wasn't supposed to have a roommate this semester."

Her lips tighten, and she nods. "I know."

"It's my last semester, so, you know…" I shrug. "I'm not going to be here much longer."

Honestly, I have no idea if I'll even be back after I've gotten that book.

An unexpected sense of loss filters through my chest. Between Ali and Ryan, I've had moments where I felt like a regular college student, no worries, living in the moment, having fun, making friends. If only it were true, but a normal life, friends—these things have never been mine.

"Thank you for telling me." She lifts her chin, giving me an almost-smile. "I'd assumed we'd be together all year."

"Yeah, so, I guess it makes me feel like," I look around the sparsely decorated room, "I've got one foot out the door."

Ali smiles for real at that, placing her hand on top of mine on her shoulder. "You've been through so much, it's classic self-preservation. But even if it's only for a few months, we can still be friends. You don't have to be alone, Re-re."

She's so positive and upbeat, I can't find it in me to rain on her parade—or ask her to stop calling me Re-re, *jeez*. "You're going to make a really great therapist."

"Dream expert!"

"Right! Dream expert." I shake my head and give her arm a nudge. "How about we get some coffee and head to class? And tonight, we can meet up at the Den for a *friendly* beer."

Looping her arm through mine, she nods. "You're on, friend!"

We enter the psychology building twenty minutes later, coffees in hand, and students filter past us quickly running to their classes before the ten-minute cutoff.

Ali glances up at the entrance to Dirk's class. "It's so unfair you get to spend two mornings a week with Professor Panty-dropper, and I'm stuck with Professor... Poindexter."

I snort a laugh then yelp, holding a hand in front of my face. "You almost made me send coffee through my nose!"

She snorts, and we lean closer laughing. It feels so good, so real. My disturbing dream from last night and exhaustion are stored neatly away in their little boxes in my mind, the way they have to be for me to survive.

"It's true, though!" she cries.

"It's not too late for you to change your schedule. I think we have one more week to drop or add classes."

"Maybe next semester," she sighs, glancing past me as I pull the door open. "Mmm... That man is too hot to be real."

"Gotta go," I whisper, giving her a wave. "See you at the Den at five."

She waves, then I turn to see Dirk in the front of the class, glasses in place. Today he's wearing a brown blazer over a white tee with those jeans. His dark hair is slightly damp on the ends as if he came straight from the shower, and he's reading something on his phone. The muscle in his square jaw moves, and he simply exudes sexy.

I want to get close and sniff his clean scent, but Evan makes a noise to get my attention. Lifting my chin, I smile, climbing the risers to sit beside him in the middle of the small auditorium.

"Was that Ali with you?" he asks.

"Yeah," I whisper, but our conversation is cut off when Dirk begins to speak.

"Sharon is returning your graded assignments." The annoying grad student is making her way up and down the aisles handing out papers. "Overall, it was a good effort for a first writing assignment."

Dirk's eyes meet mine, and heat blooms in my stomach. I lift my stylus to my lips, parting them slowly, and his brow furrows.

He turns to the other side of the room. "I made notes I hope will be helpful going forward. As always, you're welcome to stop by my office during office hours if you have questions."

I hear a few groans behind me, but when my printout is placed on my desk, a bright red *A* is on the first page. Unexpected pride surges in my chest, and I bite my lip against the huge smile trying to split my cheeks.

Glancing up, our eyes meet again as if drawn by an invisible force, and he gives me the slightest hint of a smile. Another wave of happiness floods through me. It's completely unwarranted and honestly ridiculous for me to feel so happy about a grade.

It doesn't matter how I do in this class. It's all fake. It would actually be better if I did poorly so I would need more assistance from Professor Winston. As it is, I'm giddy over an *A*.

I've got to get my head straight.

"Today, we'll discuss the effect of psychosocial factors on brain function, so I hope you finished the reading on the Bobo doll experiment…" He continues speaking, but my mind drifts to after class.

· Thanks to my brilliant performance, I don't need help. Turning my stylus in my hand, I filter through the possibilities as Dirk continues his lecture.

"Exposure has a significant impact on outcomes. Bandura found that children who witnessed violent or aggressive behavior tended to pursue these types of behaviors as adults compared to those who were not exposed to the aggressive model…"

Class continues, but I'm miles away.

Afterwards, Evan waits beside my desk as I slowly collect my belongings and put them in my bag. "We haven't hung out since Welcome Back night."

I wish he'd go away.

Pausing, I straighten in my chair. "Ali and I are going to the Den tonight. You could meet us there at five."

"I definitely will." He slides a hand into his pocket, his lips twitching with a smile. "You're going to be late for your next class if you don't hurry up."

I swallow the growl rumbling in my throat and do not tell him it's none of his business. None of my classes matter.

Standing, I slide the strap securely over my shoulder, and I do not miss his eyes checking out my breasts. It's the effect I want, but not from him.

"Actually, I have to meet with Professor Winston before my next class."

"Don't tell me you're in trouble." We slowly walk down the risers.

"What makes you think I'd be in trouble?"

"Because you clearly don't need help. You made an *A* on that assignment when everyone around us got *B*s or worse."

More pride surges in my chest. Maybe my good grade isn't so bad after all. "I'm just touching base. It's good to know your professors."

He stops short. "Oh, no, don't tell me you're one of those."

My brow lowers, and I turn to face him. "One of whats?"

"You're a brown noser."

"Asshole," I laugh. "I am not."

We're outside the door, and he loops his arm around my waist. "You're not going to visit the young, single-male professor to thank him for your grade, flirt a little, maybe shake that ass…"

"You're gross." I twist out of his embrace. "That is not what I'm doing."

It's exactly what I'm doing.

"Go out with me." Evan catches my hand, pulling me to a stop.

Pausing a beat, I give him a tight smile before sliding my hand out of his. "I think we should just be friends."

"Ugh…" He grasps his chest. "Stab me in the heart next time."

I can't help it. I exhale a laugh. "You and Ryan meet up with Ali and me tonight at the Den. It'll be fun."

"I'll do my best, but you're a hard one to get over, Reanna."

He doesn't even know me. Shaking my head, I do a little wave. "See you there."

Hesitating outside Dirk's office, I wait until the last of the students have disappeared into their classrooms before tapping lightly then opening the door. I'm happy to see Sharon is not here today, and I slip in quickly, closing the door behind me and quietly turning the lock.

"Hey, is someone there?" He steps to the door of his back office, and another almost-sigh catches in my throat.

His coat is gone, and the tee he's wearing shows off

muscled arms and rounded biceps. It hangs over his chest in a way that suggests a delicious six-pack and pecs under that thin cotton.

"Reanna? What's going on? I thought you'd be satisfied with your performance."

Closing the space between us, I drop my bag into the empty chair where Sharon sat last time. "I'm sorry to bother you. I wanted to thank you for giving me an *A* on the assignment."

"I didn't *give* you an *A*. You earned it."

"I'm not sure that's entirely true, but I appreciate you saying it. I appreciate you believing in me. No one ever has before."

The muscle in his jaw moves, and concern is in his pretty hazel eyes. "I'm sorry to hear that."

"It's not your fault." I look down at my hands, walking slowly past him into the smaller office with the desk I dream of defiling. "During your lecture, I was wondering if that's why I struggle sometimes with my grades. I'm like the children who only see violence growing up. I've learned to only expect failure."

He follows me into the small room and stops at my back. The heat of his body lights up every part of my core, and when he lifts his hand, my eyes close at the thought he'll touch me. At the last minute, he seems to think better of it, going around the desk instead.

"In this field, we know not to say that things are all in your mind." He takes a seat, and I sit across from him frustrated by his restraint. "However, I can tell you as a teacher and an experienced professional, you demonstrated an understanding of the concepts that surpassed your classmates."

"My nightmares have returned," I blurt, wasting no time. "They started the first night I was back on campus, and they're getting stronger. I'm afraid I won't be able to keep up with my assignments if they don't stop."

The more I say, the tighter his brow grows, the more

concern brims in his eyes. "I'm sorry to hear you're having nightmares. Are they about your father?"

Dropping my eyes to my lap, I nod. "My father, my cousin, the violence I endured after he was killed when I was sent to live with my uncle."

He flinches as if from a memory. "Childhood trauma can be difficult to overcome. Mental health services are included in your tuition. I could help you get an appointment with a counselor, maybe you could try sleeping pills."

"Pills don't work for me."

"I'm afraid that's the best I can offer."

Blinking up at him, I hesitate. "I always have trouble when I'm alone at night. I don't think humans are meant to sleep alone. We're social creatures, aren't we?"

"We are."

"Do you sleep alone, Professor Winston?" My question is quiet, a shared secret.

"Again, this isn't appropriate—"

"It's not right for a man so strong and virile to be celibate."

He rises from the chair, walking around to where I sit and holding out his hand. "I'll help you get an appointment with a counselor. I'll email you the information. That's all."

"Are you sleeping with her?"

"Who?"

"Your graduate assistant." A bite is in my tone. "She's totally into you. I could see it last time I visited."

"No." He's angry now, and I meet him with my own frustrated anger, taunting him.

"She's just giving you blow jobs?"

"Stop it, Reanna." His eyes flash.

Stepping closer, I put my hand on his chest, loving the heat of his body through the thin cotton. "You're the first man who's ever seen me."

"I doubt that." A harsh laugh scrapes from his throat.

"It's true. You understand how I feel because you've lost

someone, too. You know how hard it is to trust, to believe you won't get hurt again." Again, speaking the words, I realize how true they are. "You could teach me that."

Two hands grip my upper arms, and he moves me away. "I'm not doing this. I'm not risking my reputation or my job for this."

Falling back, I pull my lower lip into my mouth, studying his eyes. Reaching out, I take my bag and slip it over my shoulder, walking slowly to the door.

I unlock it, but before I open it, I look back at him. "You might like me if you stop fighting."

Clenched white teeth are visible behind his parted lips, and his eyes drink in my body. The cropped sweater I'm wearing leaves little to the imagination. I'm not wearing a bra, and my nipples are pointed. Straightening, I slide my hand over the bare strip of exposed skin, wishing it was his hand.

Without another word, I leave his office and exit the building, falling back against the limestone exterior as energy hums in my veins. He didn't give me much, but he showed me more than he ever has before.

He doesn't just like me, he wants me, and I wonder how I'll survive until I see him again.

CHAPTER 9

Dirk

GRABBING MY COAT OFF THE BACK OF MY CHAIR, I HEAD OUT INTO the waning twilight, hands shoved in my pockets, thinking I'll have a drink at the Den then head to my place and pack. I don't have classes tomorrow, and I've decided I will take Hana up on her suggestion that I drive back to Hamiltown this weekend.

It'll be good to be around family, get some perspective, have a few familial hugs. Perhaps this is homesickness.

"We meet again, Professor Winston." Sharon jogs up to my side. "You seem pissed. Don't tell me, Dr. O'Toole is being a tool again?"

A tight laugh huffs from my chest. "I thought I was the only one who called him that."

"It's a rare thing when someone's personality so closely matches his or her name. It definitely adds credence to the theory that one's name impacts one's social development."

"I think this is a topic best left to the linguistic anthropologists."

"Really? I thought it fell more along the lines of nature versus nurture."

"You never told me the topic of your graduate thesis." We're at the Husky Den, and I hold the door for her.

"The role of sex and perceived opportunity in the career choices of men versus women."

"Phew, that's a mouthful," I chuckle. "So Jung versus Freud?"

The bar is crowded for a Thursday evening, and I follow her to our usual spot, waving to the student bartender. "A double bourbon on the rocks, and a…"

"Dog Pack Pale Ale," Sharon calls over the noise, and the guy nods, turning quickly to fill our order. "To answer your question, more like Freud and Jung working together to demonstrate to what extent both theories play a role in the choices we make."

"Sounds interesting."

"It's mostly surveys, trying to get students to remember messages they received in childhood and comparing that to their choice of major."

"Still, interesting." A tumbler is placed in front of me and a pint glass for Sharon. I pass my card to the guy. "Leave it open."

Sharon lifts her glass, turning her back to the bar and surveying the crowd. "Every semester it's the same. The more weeks pass, the more crowded it gets in here. I stop coming after fall break."

"Good to know." I raise my voice, thinking I won't have a voice by tomorrow.

Lifting the tumbler to my lips, the warm liquid hits my tongue and high-pitched cheers and clapping draw my attention to the back area of the bar where pool tables are arranged.

I almost choke when I see her. She's still dressed in those

tight jeans and that short sweater, and my mind goes instantly, rebelliously to lifting her round tits.

She's holding a short glass of clear liquid, and that fucker Evan is beside her, holding a pool cue and leaning in to whisper something in her ear. She waves him away, going to stand beside a smaller girl with light blonde hair.

Red floods my vision, and I turn to the bar, taking another, longer sip of whiskey. Sharon said he's harmless. She claims the girls all know he's a player, but still, jealousy fires in my blood. The thought of his hands on her bare skin nearly sends me over the edge.

Sharon turns to the bar, leaning into my shoulder. "Freud would have a field day on college campuses."

I huff a bitter laugh. "He had a field day in Vienna."

"Yes, but this is the perfect setting to validate all his wildest theories. It's a hotbed of sexual desires and frustrations."

She has no idea, and I polish off the last of my drink, signaling the bartender for another. Driving music overhead sounds like "Everlong" by the Foo Fighters, and my insides rage in time with the drums. I can't punch a student unprovoked.

"That thing you said earlier about Landon, what did that mean?" I don't even care how O'Toole acted like a tool, but I need to distract myself.

"Oh," she laughs, finishing her beer. "He's just a hypocrite, bringing up all that shit about Efington at your party when I'm constantly turning him down for dates."

Distraction accomplished.

My chin pulls in, and I have to clarify. "What happened to the invisible line and 'one loses and we all lose'?"

"Exactly." She shakes her head, rolling her eyes. "He acts like I'm in some gray area because I'm a grad student. I wish he'd take a hint and leave me alone already."

"Would you like me to say something to him?"

"You are such a hero." She places a hand on my forearm. "Thank you, but I'm a big girl. I can handle a pushy professor."

"Still, if he gets too pushy, you let me know."

At that moment, a body pushes up to the bar on my opposite side, and I turn, ready to snap when the words die in my throat. Reanna is standing beside me with an empty pitcher and an angry expression.

"Dog's Den," she calls to the bartender, and he takes it from her, propping it under the tap and flipping the handle down.

"Reanna." Her name is lost in the noise of the bar.

She leans closer, her full breasts practically pressed against my forearm, the heat of her body tightening my muscles.

"I see you're here with *her*." Her accent is more pronounced, and her ice-blue eyes flash with cold fire.

I shouldn't like it that she's jealous. This afternoon, when things got tense in my office, I almost broke. I'm a physical guy, and the idea she could hold her own is as much a turn-on as her fuck-me body.

"Just having a friendly drink." I should let her think I'm with Sharon, but I can't stop playing with fire, this blazing inferno I'm ready to dive into headfirst.

"Oh, hello!" Sharon leans around my shoulder holding my arm. "You did really well on that paper, by the way. Totally deserved the *A*."

The bartender slides the pitcher to Reanna, but her eyes are fixed on Sharon's arm clutching my bicep. They slowly rise to hers.

"You're too kind." It's not entirely sarcastic, but it has an edge.

Reanna turns, carrying the pitcher back to the pool area, and I can't take my eyes off the sway of her hips in those tight jeans. I can't make my brain stop thinking how easy it would be to get beneath her sweater, ravish her breasts then come all over them.

Fuck me.

"Well, I hate to leave you this way," Sharon teases, breaking my fantasy. "I've got an early class with Pamela in the morning."

"You're kidding." I hold up the full tumbler of bourbon I'm holding. "Stay for one more."

"Sorry, Prof, can't." She gives my arm a squeeze. "I'll see you next week, don't do anything I wouldn't do, and all that jazz."

With a small wave, she plunges into the growing crowd, heading for the door and leaving me at the bar to finish my drink alone. Automatically, my rebellious eyes go to the pool area, where Reanna stands behind her friend, with her arms crossed, watching me.

The other boy, the one who looks like a football player, says something, and the blonde laughs. Then that asshole Evan walks up to Reanna again, sliding his arm around her waist and speaking in her ear. His lips curl in a slimy smile, and I'm about to come off the bar when she elbows him away impatiently.

If that motherfucker thinks he's going to touch her… Her eyes haven't left mine, and I lift my chin. I want her to come back to me.

I tell myself it's because I want to warn her about his reputation, make sure she's aware he's a player, but a dangerous hum low in my stomach says it's a lie. It's way more than that.

She's already on the move, making her way to where I'm standing at the bar, moving through the crowd as if cutting through still water. Students drift out of her way, parting before an invisible force, the undeniable pull of our attraction.

I can't take my eyes off her as she gets closer, coming straight to where I stand and stopping directly in front of me, daring me to do something.

"You flick your chin, and I come." Her voice is smoldering. "Even when you hurt me, I'll come to you."

"How did I hurt you?" My face is lowered, and my voice cracks.

"Lying to me, telling me she means nothing to you."

"She's my assistant, nothing more. I bumped into her on my way here."

My elbow is propped on the bar, and she looks to the bar-tender. "Stoli, neat."

He nods, moving into action, placing a small glass on the polished wood and turning over a tall bottle of vodka, quickly filling it.

"Put it on my tab," I say as he slides it across, and he nods.

"Thank you, professor." She shoots the glass, setting it down without a flinch. "What do you want from me?"

"I don't like you being here with Evan."

"I don't like you being here with Sharon."

My jaw clenches, and I put my hand on her elbow, pulling her closer. "Sharon isn't a danger to me. I want to break his hands every time he touches you."

She flinches, but her eyes are locked with mine. "Maybe I should go back and let him touch me some more if this is how you respond."

"He's a player." It's practically a growl. "He'll mistreat you."

"I have no interest in him." She slides her eyes down to my lips. "You, on the other hand…"

My grip tightens, and I lower my chin to her ear. "I would never hurt you."

"You're hurting me now."

I release her arm at once. "I'm sorry. I didn't realize."

"It's too loud in here." She takes my hand briefly, tugging me away from the bar. "Follow me."

I hesitate, finishing the last of my drink, while she cuts a path along the bar to a side door and quickly exits. Lowering my tumbler, I glance around to be sure no one is watching before I retrace her steps, jerking open the metal door and leaving the noisy room.

Rusty hinges squeak loudly as I step into a narrow alley. The silence is deafening after the roar inside, and the metal door closes with a bang.

The space is empty. Two dumpsters are against the opposite

wall, and the ground is damp with the occasional puddle dotting the brick pavement. The only sounds are the scree of cicadas and the occasional shush of a car passing on the street. A light at the end of the alley provides dim illumination, and it smells like wet asphalt, old beer, and garbage.

"I'm here," her voice calls softly, like a siren in the sea.

Turning, I find her standing against the brick wall. Her hands are behind her waist, and she's breathing rapidly, her full breasts rising and falling. I've had too much bourbon. My control is frayed thin, and I close the space between us without hesitation.

"Oh, God," she gasps as I catch her face in my hand, holding her cheeks with my fingers.

Leaning closer, our noses brush. "What do you want from me?" I'm breathing fast, and it's my last chance to turn back.

Turning her face in my hand, her pink tongue slips out, and she sucks my thumb into her mouth. I hiss, allowing her to do it, to pulse her tongue against the base as she holds my gaze.

Jerking my hand away, I seal my lips to hers. A moan slips from her throat, and I push her mouth open, plunging my tongue inside to taste her. She meets me halfway, curling her tongue with mine, straight vodka.

Her fingers thread in my hair, tugging me closer, and our faces turn, lips pulling as we consume, chasing each other's mouths in ravenous kisses.

My hands start at her waist before sliding higher, cupping and lifting her bare breasts under her sweater. My thumbs circle her hardened nipples, and I want to rip the fabric away and consume her soft flesh.

Breaking apart, my face is in her hair, and I'm breathing fast, inhaling her scent of jasmine and rich woods. She's decadent and delicious.

"I want you to touch me," she purrs, and the inferno inside me destroys the last of my resistance.

My brain burns remembering how she left my office, and

my hands quickly move from her breasts to her waist. I quickly unfasten her jeans, shoving them low enough to allow my hand inside her panties.

Lifting my face, I meet her eyes as my hand cups her bare pussy. Her head drops back as her lips part, and she moans deeply as I trace my fingers along her slick core. Sliding two fingers inside, I curl them as I circle her clit with my thumb. Another moan, and her hips begin to rock.

I'm hypnotized by the sight of her, riding my hand as I touch all that's forbidden. With my free hand, I grip her face, pulling her mouth to mine again.

Her fingers curl and pull my hair as her hips rock faster. Little whimpers escape her throat, and every noise makes me want to be inside her. I'm not stopping until she comes. I have to hear her come.

"Fuck, it's so good," she gasps.

"Come for me," I growl, and she makes another soft noise, nodding her head fast.

My thumb moves faster. The two fingers inside her curl and massage the place that will push her over the edge. Lust and desire are fueled by anger. I'm furious she has this power over me. I'm risking everything to do this, but there's no way I'm stopping.

"Oh, God, oh, fuck, oh…" In that moment, she climaxes on my hand.

Her nails scratch my neck, falling to my shoulders as her knees buckle. I lift her up, plunging three fingers into her slippery depths, feeling the squeeze of her core, the spasm of her orgasm, cupping her wetness with my hand.

She moans and shudders, bucking with every touch of my thumb against her clit. My arm is around her waist, and I hold her body tighter against mine. She's quivering, grasping at my shoulder, and my dick is so hard in my jeans. I want to fuck her right now. I can't fuck her right now. I've already done too much. Anyone could catch us in this alley.

Still, I'm hypnotized by the sight of her, her hand sliding lower, palming my hardened cock through my jeans.

Leaning forward, my lips are at her ear, my nose in the side of her hair. "You feel what you do to me?" My voice is hot, hoarse, and angry.

"Yes," she whispers, quickly unfastening my pants, allowing the pink tip of my erection to stretch free.

"Fuck," I hiss as she pushes the fabric lower, wrapping slim fingers around my shaft and pumping up and down.

Without a word, she drops to her knees, teasing me with her tongue just before taking my cock fully into her mouth.

"Shit," I groan, knowing I should stop this, knowing this is wrong.

She's on her knees with her back to the wall, and I'm facing her, my pants lowered just enough for it to happen. She's hidden by my legs, and at a glance, it probably looks like I'm hiding in the alley to take a leak.

In reality, I'm losing my mind.

She's sucking me like she did my thumb. Her head bobs faster, and she pulls me deeper, all the way to her throat, watery eyes blinking up at me.

Stop this, stop this, stop this, my conscience is screaming, but my body won't let me. I want this. I want her. I want all of her. There's no way I'm stopping now.

My hand is in her hair, and I growl, "You like sucking my cock?"

She manages to nod, and it's my fucking fantasy. Her hot mouth is on my tip, and her hand grips the base of my shaft, jerking it in time. Then she pops off, flickering her tongue against the ridges of my dick, and my vision fails.

My orgasm is a runaway train, a steady urge growing stronger in my belly as sparks flood my veins. Heat is in my thighs, tightening my balls.

Her other hand slides around to grip my ass, holding me steady as she sucks and pulls, dragging me to that explosive edge. One more grip, one more plunge to the back of her throat, and I barely grind out a warning.

"I'm coming." I'm going to pull out, but she holds my hips with both hands, holding me steady as her lips touch the skin of my belly, as my cock pulses, shooting jets of orgasm down her throat.

"Fuck," I groan, holding the back of her head as she blinks up at me, swallowing greedily, round eyes watering.

My knees almost buckle as my fingers curl against the damp bricks. My face is against my arm, and my hand slides through her soft hair, cupping her cheek. She takes every drop, not releasing me until my shudders subside, my pulsing stops.

Then she rocks back on her heels, holding my waist as she slowly rises. "I've wanted to do that since the first day of class."

She slides her hands up my chest, and my arms are around her waist. Her body is flush against mine, and I confess, I don't want to let her go, even if she is a student, even if she is ten years younger than me. I want to hold her, take away her pain, the loneliness I know too well.

Lifting my head, I meet her stunning blue eyes. "Reanna…" I don't know what to say. I'm not sorry.

"That was amazing." She places her palm against my cheek.

"It was wrong." I start to release her, but her grip on me tightens.

"It was not wrong."

"I crossed the line." That fucking invisible line between professor and student. "Not only that, but we've both been drinking…"

"I'm not impaired, and consent is not an issue." An edge is in her voice. "I want you to fuck me."

Need flashes in my chest, and my barely sated lust for her flames back to life.

"I can't do that." I've got to grab the reins and be the adult here. "I've already done too much."

"We're both adults. Where I come from, that's all that matters."

"That's never all that matters. I'm your professor. I'm in a position of trust."

She hesitates, blinking into my eyes, then she steps to the side, out of the dominating cage of my arms. I drop them to my sides, and her lips curl into a knowing smile.

We restore our clothes, and she nods briefly, turning away from me towards the entrance to the alley.

"In that case, I'll see you in class, professor."

"Will you be able to sleep?"

"I don't know."

She takes that first step to leave me, and it aches not to stop her, not to take her in my arms and carry her to my bed, fuck her all night, and protect her from the nightmares.

Instead, I hold myself in place, focusing on my job, my reputation, my position. "When I can't sleep, I watch *The Goblet of Fire*."

I don't know why I say it, why I can't just let her go.

"Good to know." Her back is still turned, but she nods, walking away from me, leaving me scorched and raw inside.

I thought I was off-course when I came here, but now I can't even find the fucking map. And standing here in this dim alley, watching the sway of her hips as she leaves me, remembering the sounds she makes when she comes for me, all I can think is when can I do it again?

CHAPTER 10

Reanna

ENERGY FLOODS MY VEINS, AND I'M BUZZING WITH THE ANTICIPATION of seeing him again.

It's especially thrilling after weeks of building tension to have it all pay off so spectacularly in a dirty alley outside a college bar.

Oh, that alley. It was the perfect place to act out our forbidden desires. Heat floods my veins when I remember his hands desperately grasping between my legs, his filthy words as I took his dick in my mouth. We were hungry and raw, and I want to do it again. I want to do everything with him just as ferociously.

For years, I've been so focused on research and finding clues and getting revenge for my father's murder. It's nice to have some fun for a change, and Professor Dirk Winston is *very* fun. Bonus? I slept like a baby when I got home.

Too bad the afterglow fades, because now I'm ready to go to his house and knock on his door. Preferably with as little clothing as possible.

Ali is on a date with Ryan and said not to expect her home tonight, so I'm alone in the dorm, staring at my phone, tossing and turning in the bed and wondering why I don't have his number. I could text him… I could *sext* him. Heat lights between my thighs, and I curse my lack of forethought.

Pulling out my tablet, I search for *The Goblet of Fire* movie on a streaming app. He was so adorable worrying about my nightmares immediately after dominating me, fucking my face, then pushing me away. I'm definitely sick, because I kind of loved him for it.

Could it be possible we might have something once I've found my revenge? Could we build on the foundation we've laid here? Maybe he could see past the lies I've had to tell, the double-life I've had to live. Maybe he would like me for me.

Clicking play, I wait as the story begins with a giant snake and a murder. I've never been into normal, popular things—I've never had a normal life, so watching these magical children, I'm surprised by the darkness and relatability here.

Snuggling deeper beneath my blankets, I imagine him unable to sleep, watching it with me, tracing his fingers in my hair. Now that he's finally touched me, more like now that he devoured me with his hands everywhere like he couldn't get enough—thumbs circling my nipples, fingers in my mouth, inside my pussy. Now that I know being with him is even hotter than my imagination, I want more.

My toes curl, and I'm ready to shut off the movie, slip my hand in my panties, and have a new sexy fantasy with him when my phone buzzes. Turning on my side, I lift it to see another annoying text from Natasha. *Do you have it yet?*

I can picture her thin lips pressed into an impatient line, and I quickly reply. *Should be close enough in another week.*

Just typing the words sends a thrill through my chest. One more week, and I'll have him. He's so close to losing control right now. I have one last card to play, and he'll be mine.

Pressing my lips into a smile, I will miss his sexy internal battles. Such a good professor.

WTF is taking so long???

Her reply makes me sit up and growl, tapping furiously. *It'll take as long as I need. This was your GD idea. I don't even know if it's here.*

211 Faculty Road. GO FIND IT.

Grinding my jaw, I toss the phone on my bed, pissed at her bossy text, her shouty caps. If she wanted the book so badly, she could've come down herself or hired a thief to steal it back. Oh, wait, that would require money and manpower, two things she has in short supply right now.

Sitting on my hands, I resist shooting back a snarky reply. Instead, I consider her order. I would like to see him before Tuesday. Glancing at the clock, I see it's almost midnight…

Hopping up, I pull on black sweatpants and a black hoodie. I'm a professional. I can sneak over to his house in the dark and tell him I couldn't sleep. Maybe we'll watch *Goblet of Fire* together. Maybe we'll make our own fire.

The fact I have no idea how it will play out squeezes my stomach, making me smile.

Tennis shoes on, I head out the door, jogging down the stairs and out into the night.

Students are milling around the quad, so I stick to the trees, hanging back when a couple or a group of friends passes on the wide sidewalk lining the lawn in front of the fraternity houses.

Faculty housing is further back, behind the academic buildings, with a row of Bradford pear trees lining the sidewalk that runs in front of them.

Rick sent me the details on this small block of private residences the week I arrived. Two of the houses are empty, as most of the faculty lives in town or on Miranda Beach. The one on the end belongs to a professor in the history department. The one beside it is a married couple who have no children, and on the end is Dirk's, 211 Faculty Row.

Hesitating at the tree line, I look up and down the street. It's pretty late, and all the lights are off, which makes this even better for me. Hustling into the trees, I quickly slip around to the back of Dirk's residence, to a small, fenced-in yard.

Hopping the fence, I duck into the shadows under the covered patio, pressing my back to the wall and waiting. I'm breathing fast, but I don't hear a sound. No one is stirring or seems to have noticed. Why would they? It's a college campus on a Friday night. Nothing to see here.

A metal door with a window is in the back, and I carefully place my hand on the knob, turning it slowly and hoping he doesn't have a house alarm activated. As I expected, it's locked, and I chew my lip, thinking.

Straightening, I pull the hood off my head and just knock. Seconds slip past as I wait, and I cup my hand to peer through the glass. A single lamp is on beside a leather couch, but it appears no one is home.

Sneaking around the side of the house, I check the driveway. *Empty.* Stepping up on a box, I look through the windows on the garage door. *Empty.* My brow furrows... *Where is he?*

I didn't expect this, but it's actually a golden opportunity. If I do manage to get through these doors with him, I'm not going to want to spend time searching when I could be fucking him. That means I have to break in and do my searching now.

Hesitating a moment, I scratch my neck as I think about the kind of man he is. Defying external appearance, he's supposed to be a computer geek, which means he might have security cameras, an intricate system protecting against intruders. At the same time, he's on campus, in this cloistered environment.

He's not expecting me.

With that in mind, I go to the door, reaching overhead, feeling all around the jamb. Nothing. Stepping back, I chew my lip, looking for unusual ornaments. Not even a plant. He does, however, have a mat, and lifting it up... *Voila!*

"Oh, Professor Winston," I shake my head affectionately, picking up the hidden key. "You know better."

It slides easily into the lock, and in one turn, I'm in his world. It's like walking into your teenage crush's bedroom for the first time, getting to know if he's a clean freak or a slob, learning if he puts his dirty clothes in the laundry bin (*almost—a small pile is on the floor*), learning if he cleans up after himself in the kitchen (*yes—I'm impressed*).

Walking down the short hall, I go to his bedroom, straight to his closet. His clothes are arranged on hangers or folded neatly on shelves. The faint scent of his citrusy cologne hangs in the air, and I pull off my hoodie. Taking a thin, navy sweater off a shelf, I pull it over my head, burying my face in his clean scent. His closet is too neat, and I have the devious urge to re-arrange it all.

Instead, I fold my hoodie and put it where the sweater was, then I drop to my knees, feeling around behind his shoes, searching for a safe or a fireproof box. Nothing.

Standing, I turn and scan his room, looking for a desk or a filing cabinet or any type of place books might be stored or hidden.

Despite Natasha's insistence I do this, I don't believe the ledger is here. It's most likely at his office in Hamiltown or at Hugh van Hamilton's estate. When she suggested this plan, I already knew I'd have to find some way to get there and search those key places without being caught.

Still, I'll do my diligence. I'll search this residence the way I've been trained to do, and if it is here, I'll find it.

His bed is a queen size, which doesn't surprise me. This house is one step above student apartments. Still it's neat, with a simple, off-white duvet and a collection of matching pillows. Sitting on the bedside, I pull one onto my lap and hug it to my chest, burying my face in the cover and inhaling deeply.

Is this the one he sleeps on? I pick up another, sniffing, then another, searching for that distinct fragrance that makes it feel like he's here with me. I wonder if his scent is really enticing or if I'm obsessed with him or is he legitimately obsess-inspiring? (*Is that a thing?*) Chasing these thoughts in circles makes me smile like a teenager with a crush.

What I'm doing is dangerous. I'm hugging his pillow like I'm falling for him, like he's not a mark. I'm ready to shake myself and continue looking for that book when my eyes fall on a battered paperback sitting on the nightstand.

I pick it up, and an old photograph falls to the carpet. Leaning down, I hold it under the light, and a smile curls my lips. It's a picture of an adorable blond boy standing beside a taller teenage boy with dark hair and a lowered brow. The younger boy is holding up a large paperback, and the older has his hands behind his back like he's a soldier at attention.

It's clearly Dirk and Hutch, and it looks like they're in a bookstore or a library. I wonder who took this… One of their parents? A teacher? Hutch's expression is focused, disciplined as always, but I see that flicker of mischief in Dirk's grin. My lip catches between my teeth, and I trace my finger over his image. He's perfect. I'd have had a crush on him even then.

Turning the battered paperback in my hand, it's an old-school copy of *The Goblet of Fire* with the original, cartoonish picture of Harry holding a shiny bowl and waving his wand on the front. It's the same book in the photograph. He must be using this as a bookmark, but I've lost his place. Slipping the photo into a random spot, I hope he won't notice it moved.

Lying on my side in his bed, I open the cover and read the first line, *The villagers of Little Hangleton called it "the Riddle house…"*

Dirk Winston is strong and dominant. He won't let me get away with shit, and yet he has this soft side, this connection to nostalgia. I want to know why. I want to know what draws him to this story.

Pulling a blanket over my shoulder, I roll onto my back and

continue reading, wanting to know what secrets about him are hidden in the words of this book…

"I'll protect you, Rainey." He reaches out, cupping my face in his hand. "You don't have to fight alone anymore. I'm here, and I've got people to help us."

Straining for his touch, the cold bands surrounding my heart are slow to break. It's hard to believe someone might care for me, might really want to help me.

"I dreamed you would say this." My voice is strained, wistful. "I never thought it could happen…"

His words are lost in the fading mist. Pale light glows in the windows, awakening me with a start. Dirk is gone, and I'm alone, but his voice still feels so close. I sit up fast, looking around the empty room, my heart beating out of my chest. No one is here to help me. I fell asleep reading, and dawn is breaking.

Hopping up, I do my best to shake the dream away. I place the book on the nightstand and quickly straighten the bed and the pillows. I've got to get out of here before I'm trapped in his empty house, and I didn't even finish searching it. I quickly circle the room, methodically searching drawers, feeling behind books in the bookcase. Nothing.

Returning to the living room, I scan the space quickly, looking for any type of hiding place or study area. It's pretty sparsely decorated, and he doesn't have many personal items here. It makes sense with him being a new professor in temporary housing.

The daylight is growing brighter, and I'm out of time. Dashing to the bedroom, I quickly strip off his sweater and put my hoodie back on. I straighten the stack of clothes, making sure everything looks as it did when I arrived.

Grabbing the key off the kitchen table, I head out the door, quickly dropping it under the mat again. Then I sneak to the edge of the house, my back to the brick wall, and peek around the corner. No one appears to be awake yet, so I hop over the fence and dash right up to the sidewalk, walking confidently to my dorm.

The more steps I take, the less suspicious my presence becomes. I'm an early-morning jogger or a student up early, going for coffee. I feel so refreshed I could go for a jog, and I realize I did it again. I slept like a baby, wrapped in Dirk's blankets, wearing his clothes, dreaming of him. No vodka to kill the nightmares, because there were none, only his voice offering to help me.

I don't have time to think about what it means. I need to get back to the dorm before Ali does. She won't believe I'm out of bed this early, and I don't have an alibi.

CHAPTER 11

Dirk

BIG BROWN EYES GAZE INTO MINE, AND I SCRUB MY FINGERS UNDER the curtain of white hair hanging down her neck.

"I think Dancer misses you when you're gone." Hana walks up to where I'm standing at the stall, a Palomino horse's face in my arms. "Blake rides her, but she never hangs over the door like this for us."

"It's because I rode her when she was a yearling. Hugh asked me to take her out for him when I was home from college for the summer." Sliding my hand down her nose, I remember those days.

My father was pressuring me to join his investment firm, but I didn't like the vibe of Wall Street. I didn't like their greedy world of hard parties, cocaine, and high-end hookers.

My college girlfriend was pressuring me to settle down. She wanted to get married, live in the suburbs, have babies, but I didn't share those feelings. She would tell me her plans, and the back of my neck would grow tight. I felt the distinct urge to run.

I wanted to be free, and that summer, riding all over the county on this golden horse, I did what I wanted. I slept under the stars, I cooked over a fire, and I had no commitments or rules, for a few weeks at least.

"That's the reason." My little sister-in-law tilts her blonde head. "You were her first love."

That makes me chuckle. "You think horses fall in love?"

"I think everything falls in love, including you."

"I just wanted to be a cowboy." Me in another life.

"You've been different since you've been back. Something happened at school—is it your graduate student?"

"No," I answer too quickly, and Hana laughs, poking my arm with her finger.

"Got you—so there *is* someone?"

"There's no one, Hana."

I push the memory of Reanna and the alley from my mind. It's been a struggle since that lapse of judgment happened, waking up with a tent in my sheets, the echo of her moans in my memory. I've been in relationships before, but this feels like obsession. I'm not sure how I'm going to finish the semester.

You and I are adults. That's all that matters… Her words torment me. It's *not* all that matters. My reputation matters, the school matters, my position.

"Well, something is definitely on your mind, and I can tell it's got you on edge. If it's not a woman, I can't imagine what else it could be."

"It's so good to be home." I slant an eye at her. "Always love playing twenty questions."

She holds up both hands. "Fine! No more questions. You should go for a ride, though, since I can't do it now. Dancer needs the exercise."

"I think I will." Giving the horse a pat, I start for the tack room.

Hana stays at the stall, calling to me. "Blake thought it would be fun for us to do a little girls' weekend before I'm too big to enjoy myself."

I toss a bridle over my shoulder, lifting a saddle and blanket off a wooden sawhorse and carrying them back to where she's standing. "That so?"

She lifts the latch, opening the door for me, and I put the blanket and saddle on top.

"I think it's the same weekend you have fall break. Maybe you could come home and check on the horses while we're gone?"

"Where will Hutch and Scar be?"

"Scar thought they should tag along in case I go into labor. You know how he is."

"And Hugh?" Not that her elderly uncle rides much anymore.

"He's visiting his friend in North Carolina—the one with a place near the Biltmore."

The one he ran off to when we were first pulled into this mess. Sifting through the dates in my head, fall break is a few weeks away, and I don't have anything on my calendar, no reason to stay on campus… *besides her.*

"Yes, I'll come back."

"Such a good brother." She gives my arm a playful squeeze. "Thank you."

I give her a tight smile. She has no idea. I finish dressing the horse, and lead her out of the barn. Once we reach the open field, I give her an encouraging nudge, and she takes off at a brisk canter, covering the lush pasture at a smooth clip. It's not long before we reach the backwoods of Hugh's immense property.

Dancer and I know these grounds so well. The value of a good horse is lost on most people these days, but Dancer was my faithful friend. No one could steal her. She wouldn't go anywhere with anyone but me or Hugh.

Harry had a broomstick, but growing up with an absentee dad and a mother who tried very hard, I felt like I had a lot in common with that boy wizard. My problem was I didn't have any magical powers. Still, we could ride fast and far, and it felt like flying.

A narrow creek divides the pasture land from the start of the denser trees. When we reach it, I slide off and allow her to drink while I glance up at the surrounding foliage. It's a beautiful setting, and without warning, I imagine bringing Reanna here. It's peaceful, a little like she described her life before her father was killed. I have no reason, but I think she would love it like I do. I think she would understand why I want to share it with her.

It's when I know this is not simply an obsession. Her intelligence appeals to me. She's beautiful, yes, and sexy as hell, but she's also determined and strong. We've both lost loved ones, but I had Hutch. I wasn't completely alone. I don't want her to be alone.

Climbing onto the large beast, I return to the barn at a more leisurely pace. I remove Dancer's saddle and blanket in the breezeway, and I carry the bridle and all the tacking to the storage room, grabbing a brush on the way out.

Hugh has a groomsman who cares for the horses, but I like to brush them down. It's calming, almost like meditation. I slide the coarse bristles over her body, and with every stroke, the tension in my mind relaxes.

"You headed back this evening?" Scar's low voice breaks the silence.

"Yeah, I gotta get back for class." Glancing up, he's looking over the horses, hands in his pockets like he's concerned. "Something on your mind?"

Straightening, he holds the door as I exit the stall, fastening the latch behind me. "I didn't expect you to come home this weekend. I thought you might pursue that other interest."

Scar moved here not long before Blake and Hana came into

our lives. He showed up needing a place to live, almost like he was on the run, and it was a long time before we knew why. "That other interest is like playing with fire."

His arms cross, and he nods. "I'm familiar with the feeling."

"I haven't felt this way in a long time."

"Have you decided if she's the real deal?"

I consider the question. I consider my thoughts while riding, and I try to classify what's happening as concrete or ephemeral. Our sexual attraction is undeniable, the unmitigated possessiveness I feel towards her is inexplicable. I want to rip the arms off any man who touches her—and it seems I'm not the only one. She was furious when she saw me with Sharon.

A half-smile curls my lips, and I glance up to see my over-sized partner watching me. "That was a long pause."

Clearing my throat, I look down. "It's a lot, and I'm not sure I trust it. It's too fast and too..." I can't say too primal, so I go for the obvious. "I'm her professor."

"A temporary setback." A tease is in his tone, but he has a point. "Like I said, if it's the real thing, it's worth giving it a chance."

But how can anyone know what's real? Only time can prove if something is worth fighting for, and we only have a few months. "The risks are all I see at the moment."

He nods, and we walk to the house. "You've always been good at managing risk."

It's true—when it comes to concrete things, facts, figures, bad guys. Relationships on the other hand are uncontrollable, and there's never a guarantee you won't lose everything.

Reanna Lorak might be a sensual distraction, but I'm not ready for that kind of loss.

"A common element of criminal psychology is working with law enforcement." We're back in class, and I'm doing my best to keep my eyes on my work, not Reanna in the center row of the middle risers.

Today, she's in a short skirt. Her blue blouse makes her eyes seem to glow, and the scoop neck gives a hint of her cleavage beneath. It's not a provocative outfit, but I've tasted what's under that fabric, and my dick is semi-hard.

The few times my eyes drift to hers, she smiles knowingly, and heat simmers in my veins. It makes me angry, which makes me fantasize about spanking her round ass, which makes me lose my train of thought.

Luckily, we've reached the part of my course I'm most familiar with. "As someone who works with law enforcement, I can tell you, the role of a criminal psychologist can be invaluable. Not only can they guide questions, they can give important insight."

A hand rises in the group, and it's a female student who doesn't talk much.

"Yes, Miss…" I don't remember her name. "You have a question?"

"You were a member of law enforcement?" Her voice is breathy, a little gushing.

"I'm actually a partner in a private investigative firm in Hamiltown."

"Oh…" She sits back in her seat, her face turning bright red.

I'm not sure why she's blushing, and I hesitate, glancing around the small auditorium. Naturally, Reanna's waiting to meet my eyes, and her eyebrow arches.

Fuck it. I've fought with my brain the entire ninety minutes of class, and now I'm ready to be done. I quickly announce the writing assignment and turn to unplug my laptop from the overhead projector, collecting my things so I can head back to my office and take a long drink of cold water.

Students file out, and the girl with the question slowly passes, batting her eyes at me. I want to laugh, but the truth hits me like cold water in the face. Other female students flirt, hell, some of the male students flirt, but I'm not tempted by any of them.

Reanna triggers something more urgent in me. Her touch activates a need I can't deny—even though I must.

"Did you have a nice weekend?" My back is turned, but her low voice sets off electricity in my skin.

She places a small item on the desk. A card is attached, and when I pick it up, I see it's a green Jolly Rancher.

"My favorite," I say quietly, unsure if this is a coincidence.

Lifting the card, she's written in perfect penmanship, *I trust you.*

My eyes meet hers. It's a reference to what I said Thursday night. *I'm in a position of trust...* "Are you mocking me?"

"I mean it with all my heart."

Her blue eyes are so round, her lips so full, her hair so silky, that cleft in her chin... her beauty makes my chest hurt. I want to touch her so badly, and it's so wrong.

Students filter past us, heading for the door, and I snap out of it. Our sexual tension is blatantly obvious, and it has to stop.

Reaching out, I touch her arm. "Wait."

She doesn't move, and finally, the last student leaves. The door closes with a loud click, and I scan the room to be sure we're completely alone. Sharon wasn't here today, and the next classes are starting soon. I have to make this fast.

Meeting her gaze, my tone is fiercely low. "You've got to stop this."

She slides her hand over mine, looking up at me with wide eyes. "But your voice was so hoarse when you came in my mouth. I was worried about you."

My dick hardens, and I growl. "You can't give me gifts in class. People will notice."

Lifting her chin, she steps closer. "I'd like to give you more."

My skin tingles, and I want to grab her face the way I did in the alley. I want to kiss her hard and fuck her harder. I want to spank her until her ass is red and painful. She's a fiery pool of temptation, and I want to dive in and burn to death.

Through clenched teeth, I try to stop it. "No gifts. No touching. No *more*."

"Last one…" She nudges my hand, and I look down to watch her slide a scrap of red lace into my palm. It's her micro-thong, and I freeze as it enters my fist. "I'm sorry it's damp. I couldn't stop thinking about your mouth on my pussy in class."

She walks to the door, leaving me alone, and I lift the scrap of lace to my nose, inhaling jasmine, deep woods, and the unmistakable scent that drives me wild. *Fuck.*

Shoving her thong in my pocket, I snatch up my bag, holding it over my erection as I quickly make my way back to my office, to the small bathroom.

CHAPTER 12

Reanna

"THE DIFFERENCE BETWEEN FORENSIC PSYCHOLOGY AND CLINICAL psychology is best understood if taken in terms of setting…" Professor Winston's glasses are firmly in place, his voice low and controlled.

We're back here again, and my vision has tunneled.

I pretend to go to Spanish. I pretend to go to English. I pretend to do my assignments, study for quizzes, fret over reports due by the end of the week, but none of it matters. Nothing I do here matters except this man.

Ali says it's time to eat, and I follow her to the dining hall where food is placed in front of me. I go through the motions of feeding myself, of washing my body and my hair, of putting myself to sleep, but my mind never stops.

The nightmares have stopped—because of him.

I don't wake up in the middle of my bed searching the empty sheets for everything I've lost anymore. I don't wake up screaming because everything I love has been ripped from me and I'm alone and afraid.

I'm not alone anymore, and I'm definitely not afraid.

He's the first thing that has ever been almost mine, and all I can think about is getting what I want. All I can think about is him.

Natasha is bearing down hard, but I don't care about her either. I'm the lioness stalking her prey, the cat waiting for the mouse. I'm perfectly still, laser-focused, watching for the moment his weakness is exposed, and it's happened.

I'm his weakness. He tries to pretend it's not true. He tries to hide it, but his efforts only whet my appetite for him. They only tease my muscles tighter.

We've reached the part where I pounce.

"Clinical psychologists want to build a trusting, empathetic alliance with their clients, but forensic psychologists cannot ethically nurture or act in a helping role." Dirk is in the front of the class, sliding his finger down bullet points on the screen.

Shifting in my seat, I wish his finger was sliding down my bullet point. A laugh sniffs in my nose, and I cover my lips with my hand. His eyes flicker to mine, and it's a flash of heat in my chest. It almost feels like he knows what I'm about to do.

I'm in the middle row, directly in his line of vision, vibrating like a sinner in church. My heart beats so fast, and my mouth is dry. If what I'm planning for the end of class doesn't work, nothing will.

I'm betting all my money it will.

He switches off the computer and goes to the door to turn on the lights in the room. The sudden wash of fluorescent white makes everyone blink hard. A few groans break out around me, and a student across the aisle rubs his eyes like he's waking from a nap.

Evan isn't in class, which is a stroke of luck for me. I lift the desktop in front of me and slide it into the arm of my chair.

I'm not sure my heart can beat any harder as I wait for it...

Wait for him to finish giving us the assignment…

Wait for him to place the bag on his desk…

Wait for him to glance in my direction again, and I make my move.

Lifting my leg, I uncross, widen my knees to give him a clear view of my bare pussy, and watch as the heat explodes in his hazel eyes, as light pink lust creeps from beneath his collar, as his Adam's apple bobs, and the muscle in his jaw clenches. I cross my legs again, and when his eyes lift to mine, they've gone dark.

Students stand and funnel down the aisles, but I wait, sitting in my chair in the shortest skirt I own with nothing underneath it. Once the last person is at the door, I stand, lifting my bag onto my shoulder and walking down the steps slowly.

He doesn't look up. His eyes are fixed on the items he's shoving roughly into his backpack, and I continue to the exit, going into the hall and walking the short distance to his office. Clusters of students filter past, laughing and making plans for the weekend.

When I reach his door, I turn my back to it, slipping my hand behind me to turn the knob. It's unlocked, and I go inside when no one is watching. The room is empty and the lights are off. Only the dim light from the hall filters through the frosted glass. I go into the smaller, private room in the back of his office, placing my bag on the floor by the filing cabinet.

The sound of his door opening is as loud as a clap of thunder in the quiet space. He doesn't turn on the light, and I know he knows I'm here waiting. I hear the click of the lock, and adrenaline floods my veins.

Without a sound, he enters the smaller office where I wait, and he closes the second door, turning to face me.

"I asked you to stop." The anger in his voice clenches my core.

"I can't." My breath catches, breaking my voice. "I want you too much."

Crossing the space, he grips my arm so fast, a yelp jumps from my throat. "What's it going to take for you to stop?"

We're so close, I step forward so our bodies are touching. I rise on my toes, sliding my fingers in the side of his thick, wavy hair.

My lips brush his ear as I whisper. "I think you'll have to fuck me."

The room tilts, and he spins me around so I'm facing the mahogany desk of my dreams. My hips hit the dark wood, and his hands move quickly behind me, unfastening his pants.

"Oh, God," I whimper.

A tear of foil, the snap of a condom, and wetness floods between my thighs, my stomach twists in anticipation.

"Hold onto the desk." It's a low order, and I do as he says, sliding his things out of the way and lying on my stomach before him, lifting my bare ass for him.

Cool air drifts across my flesh, and goosebumps break out on my skin. His hand grips my hip so suddenly, I let out another little cry of surprise, but it changes instantly to a low moan of satisfaction when he thrusts his cock inside so fast I rise off the desk.

He's so big, I gasp audibly.

"Fuck…" His groan is loud, and my pussy tightens at the thought someone might hear us in the hall. "It's so good."

Lying on my stomach, I arch my back up rocking him deeper into my slippery core. "No… I'm bad. You have to punish me."

"You are. And I will." It's a low growl, and his fingers thread in my hair, holding my cheek against the pad on his desk. "Don't let go."

The warning in his tone squeezes my stomach, and I grip the wood, closing my eyes as he starts to move.

After the first thrust, his groans turn ragged, and he picks up speed, fucking me like he's lost control. My feet rise onto my toes with every punishing thrust, and high moans jerk from my throat as he hits me harder, over and over, scooting the desk and blanking my mind. He's got the biggest cock I've ever had, and he's using me in the most delicious way.

"Is this what you want?" It's practically a growl. "You want me to fuck you this way?"

"Yes," I moan, lifting my ass so he can drive deeper. "More…"

His hand on my hip grips and pulls me to him as he complies, releasing all the anger, need, and frustration we've battled for so many weeks.

"You like my dick in your pussy?"

"Yes…" I'm practically sobbing. "I love it."

His hand goes around to my front, cupping between my thighs as he locates my clit. Rough fingers press and circle that hypersensitive spot, and my eyes squeeze as pleasure radiates in my inner thighs. I'm moaning and gasping, rising higher…

"Come," he orders.

"Oh, God…" I'm going blind as he massages my clit, his unrelenting cock driving deeper. Wetness spills onto my thighs.

"I said come." His voice is stern, and I cry out, shooting to the top so fast, I'm afraid I might die when I hit it.

Orgasm radiates in my stomach so hot, it burns in my veins. I stiffen, another hard thrust, and I break into shuddering wails. My muscles contract wildly, shaking and buckling my legs, my toes on pointe.

The impact is almost overpowering, then he slaps my clit sharply, repeatedly, and I scream. He continues slapping harder, and I hear the smack of wetness. *Did I just…?*

"Fuck," he groans as he comes, his cock pulsing inside me. "Fuck, Reanna."

His pelvis presses against my backside, and his stomach trembles against my ass. His voice shudders as he holds deep inside my clenching core.

His groans are as thrilling as the rules we've just shattered. We're both leaning forward on the desk breathing heavily, and his chest is against my back, one large hand cupping my pussy possessively, the other threaded in my hair.

The pressure of his weight holding me down is amazing. I'm surrounded by his heat, the scent of citrus and jasmine, sweat and sex. We're slowly coming into focus, and I'm pretty sure I just had the best fuck of my life.

With a low groan, he releases my hair, placing his hand on the desk and pushing his body off me. I don't move. I don't open my eyes, listening as he enters the small bathroom, disposes of the condom, and turns on the sink.

I miss him already. I want him to come back and hold me. He does come back, but he doesn't hold me. He touches me gently with the damp towel, cleaning my legs before lowering my skirt and taking my arm.

"Stand up." His voice is gentler now, although still quiet.

I'm wobbly like a new foal, and I lean my face against his firm chest, sliding my hand up to his neck. "I think you made me squirt."

Air rushes from his lips, and he threads his fingers in the side of my hair, wrapping his other arm around my body at last. It feels so good to be in his arms. He truly is my safe place. I actually do trust him.

A bitter thought cramps my stomach. *What does it mean if he can't trust me?*

Stop. I shove that unwelcome thought aside, remembering what I need to do. Stepping carefully out of his arms, I go to his bag and dig around, searching.

"What are you doing?" His sexy voice tickles my stomach, and I switch on the small lamp on his desk.

"Getting this." I hold his phone up to his face, a clench in my chest at the sight of his hazel eyes. Everything about him is different to me now. "Look."

The phone unlocks, and I quickly open his Messages app, entering my number and sending a text to myself.

He takes the device from my hand, studying the screen a moment. "This is your number?"

"You were gone this weekend, and I didn't know where you were."

Placing it on his desk, he straightens, sliding his hand around the back of his neck as he walks away from me to the filing cabinet where my bag is on the floor. Silence falls over the office, and I study his sexy back, his broad shoulders, his strong hands in his hair.

Heat warms my belly, and I wonder how fast I can make him hard again. Now that I've had a taste, I'm so hungry for more.

"We can't be together, Reanna." He speaks the words slowly, in a low voice, like he's reading a verdict.

I'm not sure I'm breathing. The words are a sucker punch. "But... How can you say that after—"

"What happened just now?" Turning to face me, his brow furrows. "I'm your professor. I could get fired, you could be put on probation or worse."

"I don't care about that." I take a step closer, but he puts a hand on my shoulder to stop me.

"You don't know how something like this could affect your life, your future."

Anger flashes in my throat, and I want to scream.

Instead I take a beat.

I'm a soldier, a master of controlling my feelings. Even if he did just fuck my brains out, I'm a professional. I have to play it cool.

"How might it affect my life, professor?" Curiosity is in my voice, and perhaps a touch of sarcasm.

His eyes narrow, and I'm glad to know both our tempers are still intact. If he weren't angry, he wouldn't care.

"In a few months, you'll graduate and move on with your life. You should spend this time getting to know your peers."

Not so long ago, I found his restraint sexy. Now I'm pissed, but I hold onto my calm. "Are you saying you want me to date someone my own age?"

His jaw tightens, but he looks away, trying to cover. "I think that's probably for the best."

And in that simple response, the tension in his jaw, the way he forces the words, my fury melts into satisfaction. Pushing off the desk, I have a new idea as I pick up my bag, slipping it over my shoulder.

"Thank you, professor. This was a very inspirational visit." I stride out of the smaller office into the main one and unlock the outer door.

I don't even stop when I hear him say my name. He wants to pretend this didn't mean anything, but I felt his desire. It's ravenous and possessive.

Perhaps I've grown a little obsessed with him, but the soreness in my core, the ache when I walk from how he fucked me like a beast, tells me he's equally obsessed.

The game continues, Professor Winston.

CHAPTER 13

Dirk

I MADE A MISTAKE. I MADE A BIG, TERRIBLE MISTAKE.

A phantom image of her bent over the desk in front of me drifts through my mind, and my dick hardens. *Fuck*, I screwed up bad… but I tried to make it right.

Standing over the sink in my kitchen, I brace the sides of the counter with my hands as I try to decide what to do. I came here wanting to be a part of something better. I thought sharing my knowledge, shaping young minds would be a way of giving back. I thought teaching would be a meaningful profession.

Then I found her.

Then the earth moved.

Reaching up, I scrub my hand across my eyes. I can't get the vision of what we did out of my head. Her long hair spread around her on my desktop, her eyes closed as she wrapped her fingers around the edges of the wood. Her narrow waist, her heart-shaped ass, uncovered and lifted to me.

I can still hear her pleas for more. *Punish me…* The noises she made, the little gasps and moans every time I pounded into her, fucking her relentlessly, violently, slapping her pussy until she lost control.

I did punish her, and it was hot as fuck.

"What have I done?" Lacing my fingers behind my neck, I growl, walking from the kitchen to the bathroom and turning on the shower.

Her scent is all over me, driving me crazy, and as much as I want to go to bed smelling like sex with her, I have to wash it off. I have to be better than this. My head has been so far up my ass with this girl, I never considered how damaging it might appear to an outsider. Now that's all I can see, and it has my insides in knots.

Closing my eyes under the hot spray, my memory is relentless. Her number is on my phone, and I want to text her.

I want to be sure she got home safely. *Of course, she did.*

I want to know if she's having trouble sleeping. *It doesn't matter.*

I want to take back everything I said in my office. *Don't do it.*

You want me to date someone my own age? Yes, that's what I want.

It was a lie.

It's for the best, but it's going to *kill me.*

Shutting off the water, I quickly towel dry and pull on my boxer briefs. I've got to stop chasing her around in circles in my mind. I've got to focus on my work here and spend time with the faculty. It was my whole purpose for living on campus, to engage with my colleagues.

Climbing in my bed, I pull the blankets around me and pick up my dog-eared copy of *Goblet of Fire*. It's the original paperback Hutch took me to Barnes & Noble to get the day it was released. He took me right after school, and I was so excited. It was the biggest release of the series to date.

It was the biggest book I'd ever tried to read, and I remember holding it, thinking it was something amazing. Hutch didn't understand why I liked to read these books so much. I couldn't explain it, but being there with him meant so much to me.

Opening the book, our photo falls out, and I smile. Our mother took this picture. She was so happy to be with us, even if our father preferred to stay in New York. She moved us out of the city, all the way to Hamiltown, so we could have a different life, a small-town childhood.

She taught us to dance with her in the kitchen on Saturday nights, and she never missed a baseball game or a football game or a science fair or whatever the hell we did. What would she say about what I'm doing now?

Burying my head in my pillow, I can't believe I can still smell Reanna all around me. It must be in my hair, but I don't know how. I give up. Taking my phone off the side table, I stare at the screen for a long time.

Don't do it. The things I said to her weren't cruel, they were honest. She should be spending time with her peers. We shouldn't be doing what we've been doing. We can't be together.

Tapping quickly, I can't stop myself. Despite it all, I care about her. **I hope you're able to sleep tonight.**

I hit send before I have time to reconsider.

Several seconds pass, and the guilt of what I've done presses inside my temples. I should have said what I ought to say. *I'm sorry.*

Only, it's a lie.

I'm not sorry at all.

The only thing that makes me sorry is the prospect I might never get to do it again.

"It's so nice to have you join us for dinner." Dr. Bowerman passes a dish of dark-brown roast to me, and his wife smiles from across the table.

"Emile has told me so much about you. He said your brother is Hutch Winston."

"Yes, ma'am." I smile, taking an appropriate serving of the meat before returning it to the center of the table.

Dr. Bowerman passes me a bowl of mashed potatoes as his wife continues. "He's sheriff of Hamiltown?"

Exhaling a short chuckle, I shake my head. "No, ma'am. He owns a private investigation firm, which might be confused as a sheriff, but it's not affiliated with law enforcement. It's where I worked before I came here. Still do, actually, part time."

"Oh, I'm sorry." Mrs. Bowerman places a hand on her chest. "I don't know how I got that all mixed up."

"It's easy to do."

"I imagine in these small towns, one wears more than one hat on occasion." Her husband grins, giving me a wink. "Sarah likes to keep up with all the local gossip."

"I do not!" she cries, shaking her head and laughing. "I'm just interested in learning about our new faculty members, especially the young, handsome ones."

Dr. Bowerman leans towards me and stage-whispers. "If you were a woman, you might file a complaint about being objectified."

"I have no problem being complimented by such a lovely hostess." A tease is in my voice.

Sarah laughs, narrowing her eyes. "You're dangerous, Professor Winston."

Dangerous to myself, I think.

I didn't sleep after my massive indiscretion Thursday night, so I decided to take Dr. Bowerman up on his standing offer for me to have dinner with him and his wife at their home in Miranda Bay proper. I couldn't think of anything worse than spending a Friday night alone attempting not to think about Reanna.

She never replied to my text, which is for the best. I can't let myself think she might be angry or hurt. I can't let myself think about her at all, so I'm here in this safe house with these safe, paternal figures, trying to convince myself I don't have an unhealthy obsession with a student.

"Well, tell me how it's going so far." Dr. Bowerman sits back, sipping his glass of red wine. "I expect it's quite an adjustment going from the excitement of your work to the quiet life of a professor in this sleepy college town."

Exhaling a laugh, I shake my head. "Hamiltown's pretty sleepy 90 percent of the time."

"Yes, but you boys had a pretty big case not too long ago from what I understand. Organized crime, Russian mafia… I heard there was even a murder?"

"What?" Sarah gasps. "A murder in Hamiltown?"

I've just taken a bite of meat, which buys me a little time. The only murder that happened in Hamiltown was committed by Hugh van Hamilton's bodyguard. Hugh agreed to pay Andre Bertonelli to steal a ledger of all the transactions carried out by RDIF-Kazan. It was quite the get, their leader Simon's exclusive dishonor roll, but when it came time to deliver, Andre wanted more than the agreed-upon price.

None of us were there when it happened, but Hugh claims Andre became violent, and Hugh's bodyguard subdued him a little too roughly. Hutch was furious, but he kept it off the record. One less criminal to worry about, one more piece of their puzzle in our hands.

Sometimes our family operates in the gray zone, but it's what you have to do when taking down high-stakes criminals with vast networks and billions of dollars.

"That was a very long pause, young man." Dr. Bowerman chuckles, and I straighten in my chair.

"I'm sorry. I was just trying to remember. The murders happened in New York, and from what I've been told there's no actual Russian mafia…"

"Surely you don't believe that?" My mentor's brow furrows, and I shrug.

"I only deal with them state-side, and from what I've observed, there's a lot of in-fighting among the groups. No one's particularly loyal to anyone."

"Well, it sounds very exciting." Sarah smiles, taking a sip of her wine.

"To be honest, my role is almost exclusively sitting behind a desk, researching information we find, monitoring the chat rooms where suspects hang out on the dark web, hacking into street cams or security cameras or using AirTags to track them across the city."

"Is that legal?"

"Mostly, if you have the right license." Taking my final bite of dinner, I smile. "This is really good, by the way. My brother's housekeeper Lurlene makes dinner like this, and I've been missing it."

"Oh, you're too kind. It's just a simple pot roast."

"Simple to you." I wink, and she waves me away.

Dr. Bowerman stands. "It's that type of real-world experience that gives our students a view of the criminal mind they can't find in a textbook."

Standing, I follow him into the living room. "It's true. The books make our work sound very simple, follow the steps and find the solution. In real life, it's a lot messier, a lot more guesswork, more unanswered questions."

I don't add it's exactly where we left that case, once Hugh declared it closed—so many unanswered questions.

A warm fire is in the hearth, and while it's early in the season for a fire, it's a homey touch. He offers me a brandy, but I decline. I have to drive back to campus tonight. He offers to let me sleep in one of his sons' old rooms, but again I decline.

We spend a little while longer discussing my adjustment to campus life and the rewards of shaping young minds. The more we talk, the shittier I feel. He's so proud of me, and he has no idea I've royally let him down.

After an hour, I'm ready to drive home. He walks me to

the door, offering more words of encouragement as a new faculty member.

Driving back to campus, I commit to making a change. No more fantasizing about her or allowing myself to fixate on her body. During class, I'll keep my mind on the subject matter. I'll think of her as a student in need of guidance.

Yes, pity is a good counterbalance to lust. You can't want to fuck someone you feel sorry for.

The flaw in my plan is I don't buy it. I've already acknowledged a big part of my attraction to her is her strength. She had to be strong to survive losing her family, moving here alone, working to make a life for herself.

I'm back on campus, so I drop my speed. It's dark, and pedestrians tend to wander into the streets on campus. I'm waiting for a group to cross when my phone lights up with a text. Lifting it off the seat, my chest tightens when I see it's a photo of Reanna.

The angle is from above and she's looking up, her head tilted to the side. Her dark hair is loose and wavy around her cheeks, and she's fucking gorgeous, full lips crimson red, blue eyes taunting.

It's the motherfucker behind her that grinds my jaw. Evan is holding a shot glass over their heads, and his eyes are not on the camera, they're on her breasts. I want to grab him by the neck and slam him against the wall.

What are you doing with him?

The jealousy churning my stomach is unreasonable, and her reply makes it worse. *I'm doing what you said, professor. I'm out with a boy my age.*

"Not him." My voice is tight, and a horn blares behind me. "Fuck."

I toss the phone on the seat and move my vehicle out of traffic, pulling into a parking spot facing the residence halls. *Where are you?*

Gray dots float as she composes her answer, and I'm

growing more furious the longer I wait. *I'm having sex on the beachesss...*

My jealousy morphs into overprotective rage. *Are you drunk?*

Her answer is fast. *Not your businessss...*

I'm on the verge of tapping the call button. *Tell me where you are.*

The phone goes silent, and I wait.

When she hasn't responded after a minute, I slam the Jeep into drive and pull out into traffic with a squeal of tires.

I'm going to my place to find her mobile service, run the code, and track her down myself. I do it all the time when we're on a case.

Anger knots in my stomach, and I whip into my driveway as another text lights the screen. Snatching it up, it's another photo. Evan is behind her, and it looks like they're dancing. Her eyes are closed, her mouth is open, and she's sticking out her tongue like she's fucking Miley Cyrus.

She's clearly drunk, and if that little punk touches her, I will beat him to a grease spot.

Opening the door of my vehicle, I'm about to head inside to follow my plan when her answer appears, *Ray's on the River is the best place to dance.*

Closing the door, I type the name into my GPS, and it pops up quickly. Five miles away. I back out quickly, covering the distance at a rapid clip. It's an off-campus bar, which makes it worse. At least on campus we have safeguards in place.

Pulling up, the place is lit, and half the crowd is outside. I slam the door, stalking to the entrance, where a beefy guy with a bald head and tattoos stops me.

"Five dollars." His hand is in front of my chest.

"I'm picking up someone."

"Not without the cover." His brow lowers, and I size him up.

We're about the same height, and with the fury I'm feeling

right now, I'm pretty sure I could take him. My nostrils flare, but he's not the target of my wrath. He's just doing his job.

Taking out my phone, I quickly text, **Come outside. Now.**

Hanging back, I assess the crowd of sloppy, mostly drunk college students. Loud music beats overhead, a mixture of rock and hip-hop I don't recognize, and the crowd inside bounces in time.

A girl staggers past me on the porch, bumping my arm and spilling her beer on my hand.

"I'm sorry!" Her voice is too loud and pitched too high, and when our eyes meet, she blinks fast. "Let me lick it off you…"

She leans down as if she'll actually lick my hand, but I quickly lift it out of her grasp. Turning her away from me, my eyes land on Reanna at the entrance. She's wearing a short dress with a cropped cardigan on top, and her long hair lifts in the breeze.

Crossing the space quickly, she stops right in front of me smiling. "You're here."

I'm not smiling. "Get in the Jeep. I'm taking you home."

"To your home?"

"No. You're drunk." I catch her arm, leading her to my vehicle, where I help her into the seat and strap the belt over her shoulder and lap.

She puts her hands on my shoulders as I make sure she's secure in the seat. "You do care."

"I never said I didn't care. I said we can't be together."

The happiness in her eyes vanishes, and my stomach cramps. I climb in on my side, pressing the ignition button and doing my best to focus on the road. For several moments, the only sound is tires on pavement. I flick on some music, and she rouses at the sound of an old Hole song, hitting the button to lower her window.

She unfastens her seatbelt and climbs onto her knees, yelling, "You really made it!"

I glance at her bare legs, the hem of her skirt swirling in

the wind, rising dangerously high on her thighs. "Sit down, Reanna."

"This night is perfect!"

Checking my mirrors, I pull the Jeep to the side of the road and put it in park. "You're freezing."

"I was born in the cold." She tries to push my hand away, but I evade her grasp, pulling the belt over her shoulder and fastening her in the seat again.

Sitting back, I study her face. Her cheeks are pink, and she's breathing fast. "Sharon told me Evan's no good. He'll hurt you."

"You're worried about me?" She takes my hand, threading our fingers and dropping her head against the headrest and smiling. "No one ever worries about me."

My stomach tightens, and I take my hand away, fastening my seatbelt and pulling on the road. "I want you to be safe."

"That's not all you want," she laughs lightly. "Remember?"

As if I could forget how fucking hot it was to have her at last, what a fucking relief to sink my dick violently and repeatedly into her hot little body. A grin fights with my lips, and she arches an eyebrow nodding like she won some kind of truth prize.

She's playful and beautiful, and I want to kiss her. I want to pull her into my arms and tell her this night *is* perfect. I want to tell her I think she's the sexiest thing I've ever seen, and she fucking blows my mind, and if everything were different…

Reaching across, she takes my hand again, and the music changes to some old U2 song about wild horses and being dangerous.

The skin on the back of my neck tingles when she places my palm on the inside of her bare thigh. Her skin is so soft, and I don't remove my hand. I can't remove it. I can barely breathe.

Clearing my throat, I try to ignore her fingertips tracing mine. "You have to be more careful with men."

"Not with you." Her voice turns sultry, and my dick hardens immediately.

My fingers tighten on her thigh, and all of it is back, all the heat and desire I've struggled to lock down. She's here, the object of my lust, the woman who awakens my senses. Her fingers curl over mine, and she slides my hand higher.

"Reanna…" The warning is lost in the wind swirling around us from her cracked window.

I'm no longer cool. Heat burns in my belly and need seizes my cock. Her fingers leave mine, but I don't remove my hand from her leg. On my own, I slide it higher, until I reach the place I crave, tracing my fingers along the thin scrap of silk covering her cunt.

"Do you feel how wet I am?" She places her fingers behind my neck, sliding closer to me.

She's dripping, and my hand knows what to do. I'm inside her thong, cupping her. My two middle fingers dip into her core, and my thumb circles, pressing and massaging her clit faster.

"Yes…" she moans in my ear, her body moving like waves on the ocean as she rides my hand. "Right there…"

She gasps, and my dick is so hard it aches. Her nipples are sharp points in her thin dress, and I almost swerve in my lane.

"That's it," she gasps. "That's it… oh, God, yes…"

My eyes are on the road, but my brain is on her pussy. I want to put my mouth there. I want to slide my tongue all over her, licking every drop of her essence.

She's writhing, pressing her lips close to my ear so I can hear her breath shudder and hitch. I can hear as her whimpers turn into moans. Her hips start to buck and her head drops back with a louder groan. Her back arches, and her breasts rise tantalizingly close to the top of her dress.

Curling my fingers, I thrust them as I would my dick if only I could. She moves in time, holding my wrist and jerking as she comes, as her pussy clenches around my fingers.

I'd give anything to have her on my lap right now, riding my cock.

We're on campus, moving slowly, and thankfully, the crowd has faded. Only a few pedestrians linger, none of whom seem to be interested in what's happening in a passing Jeep.

I slowly take us up the long drive to Amanda Egret Hall. Reanna has returned to her seat, holding my hand, which is still lodged between her thighs. Her breathing slows, and her come is all over me.

I stop at the entrance, wondering if I dare walk her to the door. I want to. What would people say? Fuck it. I unfasten my seatbelt and go around the car, holding both her hands as she steps down on wobbly feet, leaning into me.

"Thank you." Her lips pout, and her eyes are woozy with afterglow. "Boys my age don't give me orgasms."

Fuck. My body is on fire, and my hands are on her waist. I want to give her more than that, but we're in her fucking dorm parking lot.

Moving her to a breathable distance, I clear the thickness from my throat. "You need to sleep."

My hand lingers on her lower back as I guide her to the entrance of the residence hall. Hesitating outside, I really don't want to go in where students will see us together and see what I'm sure is clear on both our faces. "Can you get to your room?"

She nods, looking up at me. Then leaning closer once more, she whispers, "I'd like to kiss you goodnight."

My lips part, and she seals her mouth to mine, plunging her tongue inside, and without thinking my fingers slide lower, tightening on her bare ass beneath that skirt. She fans the smoldering need in my veins to burning flames, and I slide my finger along her crack dreaming.

Stop this… I need to stop this, but I can't stop tasting her. A soft noise slips from her throat, and she holds me, lips chasing mine. How has she managed to destroy my will, to wrap me around her finger this way?

Releasing her ass, I grip her arms, obeying my screaming brain and stopping us. "Goodnight, Reanna. Go to sleep now."

Her eyes shimmer with joy, and she nods, turning away from me and stepping through the screen door. "Sweet dreams, professor."

She's gone, and I glance around the empty parking lot. *Shit.* Anybody could be out there watching. I lift my hand to slide my hair off my face, and I catch the scent of her orgasm on my fingers.

I'm sure I'm losing it, because I slip my fingers into my mouth, and she tastes like the most addictive drug on the planet.

CHAPTER 14

Reanna

ALI IS ASLEEP WHEN I ENTER OUR ROOM, SO I DON'T TURN ON THE lights. I do my best to clean up and pull on a sleep shirt by the glow of my phone and the streetlights through the window.

Lying on my back, I place both hands over my face, covering my smile. Rolling onto my side, I hug a pillow to my chest reliving every moment from when he ordered me to come to him to his fingers between my thighs in the Jeep.

I confess, I was trying to make him jealous by sending those pictures, but I never thought he'd show up the way he did, such a possessive badass. I had to kiss him, and my stomach flew when he kissed me back with so much force and need, gripping my butt and drawing more wetness to my core.

Anyone could've seen us, and he didn't stop.

Glancing at the clock, I see it's been long enough for him to be home, and I don't want him thinking too much about what we did.

Scooping up my phone, I send a quick text, *I can still feel your fingers inside me.* Seconds tick past, and my heart beats so fast, I feel light-headed. Tapping quickly, I add, *I wish it was your dick.*

Gray dots appear on my screen, and my breath stills. When I see his message, I almost squeal. *The sight of you coming on my hand...*

Pressing my lips together, I finish for him, *Is an express ticket to heaven?*

Gray dots bounce, and he answers, *Every time you look at me or stand near me, all I can think about is your soft, pink pussy swallowing my cock.*

Fuck me, professor! Biting my lips to hold in a laugh, I quickly reply. *Does that include class?*

Class is impossible.

Squeezing my eyes shut, I internally squeal. *When you say words that begin with L, all I can think of is you licking me to ecstasy.*

Lorak begins with L.

Butterflies flood my stomach. *More, please...*

When you put that pen in your mouth, my dick gets hard.

The space between my thighs aches, and I go there. *I'll swallow your dick if you push me to my knees and grip my hair.*

It takes a moment, but his reply appears. *We can't go on this way.*

"No!" I whisper-wail. My brow furrows as I text, *What can we do?*

A moment of silence. Seconds tick by, and I think I'm going to cry.

Finally, he answers, *Let me think about it.*

The fear breaks in my chest, and I breathe. Rolling onto my side again, I'm unsure whether I should laugh or cry. Ali makes a noise, and I set my phone aside, pulling the blankets over my shoulder.

We're in a holding pattern, but he's mine. What's more

complicated is I'm his, and I'm not sure what that's going to mean when it's time to walk away.

"Are you staying on campus for fall break?" Ali's fingers are laced with Ryan's, and we're walking across campus to the large, grassy fields used for soccer and intramural sports.

It's Friday evening, and we're headed to what I've just learned is an annual pre-fall-break tradition at Thornton, the Pi Kappa Rho Haunted Hay Maze to raise money for St. Jude's. After dark is supposed to be the prime time to attend, so we're heading out at twilight for our last activity before everyone goes home, or almost everyone.

I'm running out of time, and Dirk hasn't said a word about his plans, but I expect he's going home.

He hasn't looked at me in class all week, and Sharon the cockblocker has been in his office every day helping him grade midterms. Still, I know he's with me in this. We sext at night, and now I'm horny and antsy and really needing to be with him in private.

Natasha demands daily status reports, most of which I ignore. Somehow I've got to get to his place in Hamiltown, or to Hugh van Hamilton's study so she'll get off my back.

I've considered inviting myself to go with him for the break, but it would be a huge risk. He might ask me to meet his family, which would include Hana and Blake, and then everything would be ruined.

My stomach cramps at the thought of him finding out who I am before I'm ready. I don't want to imagine his words, his expression… It's like the shock of ice water over my head.

I have to control the release of information. I have to explain this to him in my own way and hope I can make him understand.

The dream I had when I fell asleep in his bed gives me hope. *You don't have to fight alone anymore...*

"Re-re?" Ali still calls me that, and I blink out of my distraction.

"What?"

"Fall break," Ryan laughs. "What are you doing for fall break?"

"Oh, I'm not sure. I might go to New York." *Right.* That's something I would never do.

In Natasha's last text, she threatened to send Rick to check on me, and I actually answered that one immediately. *Sending Rick would be the fastest way to ruin everything.*

"Another year with the Pi-Rhos." Evan is following behind us a few paces. "I wonder if this year it will catch fire."

"Funny." Slowing my pace, I walk beside him. "I thought you were sick. You haven't been in class all week."

His brow arches, and he steps away from me. "Yeah, I'm going to drop professor dickhead's class. I can't have a *C* on my transcript."

Twisting my lips, I glance down at my feet, glad the fading light means he can't see the annoyance on my face. *You're a dickhead*, I don't say out loud.

Evan stops short, glaring at me. "Why did you ditch me at the bar?"

"I'd had too much to drink, and you weren't ready to leave."

"You could've said something. I'd have taken you home."

My eyebrow arches. "I've heard you have a reputation."

Shaking his head, he walks ahead of me. "Whatever, Reanna. I thought we could have some fun, sorry for misreading the situation."

Crossing my arms, I'm glad to be rid of Evan, but I'm still frustrated. I want to have some fun with Dirk tonight. I miss him after our hot kisses and even hotter sex.

"This is it!" Ali trills, and I look up to see a giant killer-clown head with its open mouth as the entrance like we're in a rap video or something.

"I hate those things."

I shrink back, but she bounces over to grab my arm. "Don't be a baby. Think of it as a big balloon. You can always prick it with a pin."

"I think it would take more than a pin."

Ryan walks around between us, putting his hands on both our shoulders. "I'll protect you from the scary clown. Don't worry."

He has no idea I could take him and all these fucking clowns out if needed—and there's no reason for him or anyone to know.

Instead, I lean in to sweet, tall Ryan escorting us. "Thanks, Rye-boy."

Once we're through the creepy clown's mouth, we're in front of a basic hay maze, only it has the addition of actors dressed in zombie costumes lurking around and giving us disturbing smiles. Beady black eyes peep out from behind skull makeup, and a black light turns everything white into purple, including Ryan's perfect teeth.

Ali leans into my ear. "Don't be afraid. The student-actors aren't allowed to touch you."

A tremor is in her voice, and I wonder if she's saying it as much for herself as for me.

"Good to know." I slip my hand in the crook of her arm. "I hope I don't forget myself and punch one of them."

A large hand clutches at my ribcage, and a raspy whisper is between our ears. "Let's go, girls." Spinning around fast, I grip the hand, twisting it up behind the attacker's back, causing him to yell. "Uncle! It was a joke!"

"I'm sorry…" I release Ryan at once, rubbing his shoulder. "You shouldn't sneak up on people in a haunted house."

"Hay maze, and what the hell, Reanna?" he groans. "Are you some kind of self-defense expert?"

Ali hurries over to put her arm around my waist. "Stop it, Ryan. She had a difficult childhood, growing up in a war zone. Maybe this was a bad idea. Do you think it might trigger your PTSD, Re-re? We can go."

Again with the war zone. "I'll be okay. Let's just get it over with."

The maze is well-constructed with stacks of hay so tall, we can't see over the tops. Overhead lights illuminate the center of the paths, but the corners are dark as are the curves and dead ends.

"You've done this before?" I lean into Ali's ear.

"Oh, yeah, it's my fourth time."

"Is it the same every year?"

"Every year!" She laces her fingers with Ryan's again, who walks on the other side of us now, giving me plenty of space.

She's enjoying this too much, and my eyes fly to a dark corner where subtle movement precedes the appearance of a burned-faced hobo dressed in rags with stringy hair and blood-shot eyes.

We pick up the pace, dashing further into the grassy labyrinth. "I hate these actors."

Voices are on the path ahead of us, and when we take the next corner, we encounter a group of four adults who seem to be arguing playfully.

"I'm telling you it's right turns the whole way." I recognize that annoying female voice, but it's the male who answers that sets my heart racing.

"That doesn't make sense." Dirk is standing with his hands on his hips scanning the top of the walls.

In addition to Sharon, two women and a little girl are with him, and as we get closer, I recognize one as a psychology professor.

"Hi, Dr. Chase," Ryan calls out, and the group turns to face us.

Dirk's sexy hazel eyes land on mine, and all my twisted

emotions melt into hunger. He's gorgeous in a thin navy sweater stretching over his muscled chest. His dark hair curls are unruly, like he pulled the sweater over his head and walked out the door, and I want to drag him in for a kiss.

His lips part as if he'll say something, but Evan walks up behind us. Dirk's mouth closes as his dark brow lowers, and the anger simmering in his gaze has my stomach buzzy, my core slippery.

"Hello, Ryan," Dr. Chase has a smooth, maternal voice. Her hand is entwined with the other woman's, who is also holding a long strap attached to a wandering toddler with dark brown ringlets all over her little head. "Any luck navigating this maze?"

"We just started," Ryan smiles, his hand in Ali's.

"I knew we hadn't made it far." Dr. Chase turns to her group. "We convinced Professor Winston to join us since he has experience in tracking. You'll all be sorry when Amelia is ready for her dinner."

I assume Amelia is the little girl, who I further assume is her daughter.

"Blame your graduate student," he argues. "She insists we keep going right."

"I don't think that's the way." Ali's eyes are round, and she shakes her head.

Dirk gestures to her. "This is what I said."

"Come on!" Sharon grabs his arm, pulling him in the direction of a path to the right, and the sweater she's wearing dips dangerously low over her ample cleavage.

As they walk away, her tight jeans hug her ass, and jealousy burns in my blood. In addition to slutty, Sharon is pushy and very obvious.

"Have fun, guys." Dirk glances back, his frustrated eyes meeting my furious ones.

"Hopefully we'll see you soon." Dr. Chase sets off after them.

"Good luck," Ryan calls as Ali pulls him straight ahead on the path. "That's not the right way…" She sing-songs as we part.

We're halfway down the path when loud screams and zombie growls echo from the direction they went.

Ali's eyes light, and she jerks Ryan's hand, making a sudden right turn. "Run!"

We all take off after her, with me calling, "I thought you said right was wrong!"

Another actor leaps out from the shadows and Ali screams so loud my ears crackle. She scampers up Ryan's back, and I burst into laughter.

"It's a dead end," Evan calls from ahead of them, and I turn.

Just then another growling zombie actor charges out of the shadows at me. Rather than drop-kicking him, I let out a scream and run the way we came. It's dark, and I'm disoriented when I round the next corner.

I know it's wrong because there's no light. Only the main path is illuminated. Heavy breathing and the swish of feet on grass drives me on, and I take another left turn, trying to find my way out. I only end up at another dead end.

My heart beats too fast and adrenaline surges through my blood. I'm about to double back when strong arms surround my waist. A large hand covers my mouth, muffling my scream, and I'm ready to go full Krav Maga on this person when his low voice is at my ear.

"I've finally got you alone."

Clean citrus mixes with the earthy scent of the hay, and I spin in his embrace. "Dirk…"

It's a heated whisper, and I thread my fingers in his hair, rising on my toes and searching frantically for his mouth in the darkness.

Full lips crash into mine, and my moan is swallowed in the

desperation of our reunion. It's only been a few days, but I'm ravenous like it's been years.

He lifts me off my feet, pressing my back against the hay wall, and we nip and pull each other's lips before our tongues slide and curl together. Holding his cheeks, I kiss his jaw as his lips move to my cheek, then to my closed eye.

"Fuck, I can't believe you're here." His voice is warm honey, and I'm the bee salivating for more.

My mouth is on his neck, moving higher. "Why are you here with her?" It's an angry pout, and he chuckles.

"Are you jealous? Would you feel better knowing all I could think about this week was your juicy little cunt?"

Electric butterflies dive bomb from my chest to my stomach, and I rise higher in his arms. "I hated this week."

"Longest week of the semester." His voice is hoarse with desire.

I've never felt this way. I've never longed for someone so much, to the point where physical pain enters my chest when we're apart. His hips are between my thighs, and I feel his erection pressing against my core.

Reaching between us, I caress his cock through his jeans, and he groans. "We're together now."

He kisses my neck, dragging his mouth up to my ear. "I want to fuck you so bad."

"Do it." I stretch higher, searching for another hit of my favorite drug.

His mouth seals on mine, and he releases my legs as we lick and pull each other's lips. Lifting his head, he scans the small, dark area. We're alone in a dead end with only the dim lights from the main path casting long shadows.

They highlight the muscles in his jaw, and I rise on my toes to lick him, dragging my tongue up his strong neck.

"Fuck, Reanna," he groans.

"I love when you groan."

His large hands are on the front of my jeans, unfastening

the button, lowering the zipper and shoving them down my legs. "Turn around."

"Oh, shit," I whisper, doing as he says without hesitation.

The sound of his pants opening, lowering, a tear of foil, and I feel his tip prodding at my backside, seeking entrance. Another whimper slips from my lips, and I lean forward, arching my back to give him better access.

"Fuck, I love those sounds." He finds the place, slamming his cock balls-deep into me.

"Jesus..."

"Fuck..."

We both moan, and he holds a moment, his large hand on my lower belly and his other wrapped around my shoulders.

"I'm so fucking hungry for you." His hot words clench my core, and he groans again. "I want to fuck you so hard and rough you'll scream louder than the zombies."

"Yes..." I gasp. "Do it."

His dirty words, the utter fullness of him stretching me, heating my insides, has me on the edge, and when his hand on my belly moves lower, I moan.

At the first firm pass of his fingers over my clit, my head drops back and I thrust my ass against him, moving his dick in and out as my orgasm flames to life in my veins.

"Reanna, shit," he groans. "I'm going to come."

His other hand is under my sweater, shoving my bra higher and clutching my breast, pinching my hardened nipple.

"Oh, fuck..." I'm surrounded by him, filled with him, and I'm unable to stop the noises slipping from my lips.

"That's my girl..." His lips are at my ear, and he kisses then bites the shell as his hips begin to move.

My hands brace the hay wall, my knees weaken, but he holds me up thrusting harder as he circles my clit. His simultaneous, relentless massaging and hitting that spot deep inside me again and again, fires orgasm through my inner thighs.

"I'm so close." His lips are at my ear, and another shimmer of sensation erupts in my veins. "Come for me."

The order triggers muscle memory. "Keep going," I gasp. "That's the spot…"

I'm bent forward, all my focus on his cock invading my soft parts. Suddenly a *Slap!* His palm stings against my backside, and I fly straight to the edge.

"Fuck," I gasp, clenching, and he spanks me again, another firm smack of his hand exploding heat through my pelvis.

One more, and my orgasm breaks, drawing my insides tighter as a cry breaks from my lips.

He groans deeply, and I feel him break, his cock pulsing against my walls, and it shoots another burst of flames through my core.

"Oh, God, I'm coming again," I whimper.

He holds each thrust a little longer, groaning as his orgasm shakes his pelvis against my ass.

Reaching up, I hold his neck as I ride out the pulses of my second, fast orgasm. Our bodies pull, thrusting, clinging in time like a dance. His hand on my breast squeezes, and he thumbs my tight nipple.

"You feel so fucking good." His hot mouth is on my skin, kissing behind my ear.

Holding my eyes closed, I revel in the sensation of our bodies fused together, our breath slowly coming down as we embrace until the last pulse subsides.

The shriek of voices on the other side of the hay wall ends it all too soon. He releases me, turning me so I'm hidden by his body as he quickly disposes of the condom and fastens his jeans.

"Why can't I stop fucking you?"

"Because we're too good at it." I can't help laughing as I straighten my clothes.

I'm fizzy and happy.

"You're going to get me fired."

"I would never get you fired."

My chin is lifted, and I look up at him as he looks down at me, a smile gentling his frustrated features. He's so beautiful. I slide my fingers across the line of his cheek, lost in the fantasy of us together.

"Are you staying here for fall break?" His eyes travel from mine to my hair, to my lips.

"I don't have any plans." It's true—I only have dreams of what I want to do and orders of what I must do.

"I promised to go back to Hamiltown and check on the estate, exercise the horses. No one will be there, and I was thinking…" Again his chin lifts, and the muscle in his jaw moves as if he's struggling. "I'd like you to come with me."

"Yes," I answer so fast, a sexy smile curls his full lips.

"I'll pick you up tomorrow morning—"

"Not at my dorm. Pick me up behind the psychology building. I'll wait there out of sight."

His lips tighten, and he nods. "Probably for the best."

Rising on my toes, I kiss him again, and he softens, kissing me back, parting my mouth with his before his tongue slips in to taste me. As good as that fuck was, I instantly want him again.

"Re-re?" Ali calls, and I pull away.

"See you in the morning."

As much as it hurts to leave him, I really don't want to get him fired.

His deep voice mutters something about getting out of this damn maze, and I smile, jogging in the direction of my roommate calling me.

"I'm here!" I yell, and she meets me around the next corner.

"That was crazy!" Her voice is loud and excited, and I look in the direction I came, thinking *yes, it was…*

It's so dark, I can't tell if he's still there or if he slipped away. I only know tomorrow can't get here soon enough.

CHAPTER 15

Dirk

THEY'RE GONE, AND I LEAN AGAINST THE HAY WALL, TRYING TO catch my breath. I need to find Sharon and Pamela, Pamela's wife, and Amelia, but for a minute, I'm lost in the crack cocaine that is Reanna Lorak.

I've always been in control. I've never needed anyone. I've worked long hours, stayed awake all night, tracked criminals, found missing persons… But I've never found *the* person.

Then she appeared.

I don't even remember when the change happened. She has me in knots inside and out. She's beautiful. She's strong and stubborn, but she's also vulnerable. When she asked me why I came here with Sharon, my own jealous feelings about her with that shithead Evan were reflected back at me in her eyes.

This has gone too far… She's a wild card. She's lethal to my career.

I can't wait to see her again.

Scrubbing my hands over my face, I've got to get out of

this maze. Taking off at a jog, I listen closely for the sounds of my party. I go a bit farther, then I shout, "Sharon?"

A few more paces and I jump back as an actor lunges from a dark corner.

"Seriously, dude." I put my hand on his shoulder. "You could get punched doing that."

He hisses, not breaking character, and heads back into the darkness. I've decided the last job I'd ever want would be "zombie actor" in a haunted house, when I turn and almost head-butt Landon O'Toole.

"Fuck," I hiss. "Watch where you're going, Toole."

Did I just say that out loud?

Yes, yes, I did, and his brow lowers in annoyance. "Professor Winston, are you here alone? Odd choice."

Not half as odd as you, I do not say.

"I got separated from my party, but are you... alone?" I look behind him, not seeing anyone.

"I'm with my daughter. She's talking to one of the actors."

"Didn't know you had a daughter."

"I didn't really see the need to get chummy, since it's unclear how long you'll be with us."

"Is it?" I start to walk, ready to be done with this windbag.

Naturally, he follows me. "Let's just say I've heard some concerning rumors of late regarding you and a certain female student." He pauses, and a chill drifts down my spine. "Rumors that make me less optimistic regarding your tenure."

That stops me, and I turn to face him. "I'm not sure what you mean."

Her scent is still on my fingers, the memory of her soft body wrapped around mine, of me bending her forward in the hay and fucking her hard from behind. *Did he see us together?*

A humorless smile curls his lips. "I'd be lying if I hadn't noticed her myself. She's a very attractive young woman, and nothing's more appealing than forbidden fruit."

"Just say what's on your mind, Landon." I'm ready to punch this guy in the face.

He's at least ten years older than me, and he's a professor. A point I realize is completely hypocritical. Still the thought of him looking at Reanna with desire makes me realize just how over the line I've gone.

His eyes narrow as he studies my expression. "Just a friendly word of caution."

From someone who claims not to be interested in being friends, I muse.

He continues. "Grad students do fall in somewhat of a gray zone, but it can be problematic if things don't work out."

"Grad student?" My brow furrows, and in my confusion, I don't consider I could be blowing my cover.

"Dirk?" Pamela's voice calls to me from up ahead.

"There you are." Sharon trots up to where I'm standing, slipping her hand into the crook of my arm. "We were about to send out a search party."

Landon's eyes drift down to where she's touching me, and his eyebrow arches. I almost laugh out loud. Instead, I decide he's a big boy. If he's got the wrong idea about me and Sharon, that's not my problem.

"I was actually trying to find you guys." I pat the top of her hand on my arm.

"We made it to the end." Dr. Chase strolls to where we stand. "Then when you never appeared, we figured we'd better come find you."

"Thanks, I got held up."

"Oh, hello, Landon." Pamela lifts her chin as if she disapproves of the delay. "Didn't know you were coming to the fundraiser. I thought you said the hay maze was a smelly nuisance."

"I'm here with my daughter."

"Speaking of daughters," I interrupt, ready to put an end to this. "How's Amelia holding up? She must be getting hungry."

"Joanna has her in the car."

"Come on." Sharon tugs my arm before dropping it and trotting ahead to what I see is the end of the maze.

I also notice the group of kids Reanna came with gathered there, and my eyes strain as I scan the faces for hers. As always, she's standing a little bit apart, a little distant, watching me.

Our eyes meet, and the familiar lightning electrifies my senses. I've never been this way with a woman. I've had relationships, but I've never felt the things you hear about in songs and sonnets. I've never hungered for someone so intensely.

"As I was saying," Tool's eyes are on me, and I tear mine away.

I realize he's watching me as well, but my thoughts are several hours ahead and miles from this place. "Thanks for the warning, Landon. I'll keep it in mind."

Reanna stands slightly behind the round bushes lining the back of the psychology department, not quite hidden, but not immediately visible to passersby. Her dark hair hangs straight down her back, and she's in dark jeans and a red sweater with a low V that hugs her body.

A small bag is at her feet, and as I drive closer, she looks up at me. Our eyes connect through the windshield, and my stomach tightens, heat filtering below my belt. I barely slept last night, the anticipation of this day holding me in a state of alertness.

I wanted to text all night, but instead, I sent one note, *Pick you up at 9.*

Her reply was simply, *I'll be there.*

Now we're here.

I put the Jeep in park, ready to hop out and help her with her things, but before I can open my door, she tosses her bag in the back and jumps in the passenger's side.

"No need to draw attention." Pushing her hair back, ice-blue eyes meet mine, and adrenaline hums in my veins.

I want to reach over and grab her neck and kiss her roughly like we always do, but she's right, no need to linger where we might attract attention.

Turning the wheel, I drive us off campus to the freeway and out to the interstate highway. We're ten minutes down the road with "Take it Easy" playing on the radio, and I glance over to see her watching the scenery pass.

It's the first time we've been out of the pressure cooker. We're free to do whatever we want as much and at any time, and I search for something to say, to break the silence.

"I guess the Eagles never go out of style."

Her brow furrows, and she turns to look at me. "Who are the Eagles?"

Squinting at her, I look out at the road. "You're joking, right?" She doesn't answer, and I clarify. "You don't know who the Eagles are?"

"I take it that's one of your bands." Her brow arches. "Because you're so much older than me."

Cutting another glance, I see her lips press together, and she turns her face to the window again.

Reaching across the console, I poke her side. "I'm so much older now, am I?"

A laugh bursts from her lips, and it's cute and unexpected. I realize it's the first time I've heard her laugh. She threads her fingers with mine, resting them on the console, and warmth filters from our connection, up my arm, to my heart.

It takes me by surprise, and I'm not sure what to say.

"I know who the Eagles are," she says quietly.

Her thumb slides along the skin at the side of my hand, and it's so familiar. "I figured you did."

She presses the button, lowering the window so the breeze blows around us, lifting her hair. "I love the scent of the ocean. I'm part mermaid, you know."

This playful side is new, and I like it. I think about having her in the ocean and decide a beach trip is now on our bucket list. "How do you feel about horses?"

"I can ride a horse." She shifts in the seat to face me, our hands still clasped. "I didn't know you owned horses."

"They belong to Hugh… my sister-in-law's uncle. He has a big estate, plenty of land for them to run."

Her eyes flicker down, and a shadow seems to pass over her pretty features. She blinks it away, quickly smiling up at me again. "It sounds beautiful. Will we be staying there?"

"I figured we'd stay at my place, but we'll go over during the day."

Her smile holds steady, but again her eyes go to our hands clasped on the console. Her thumb slides over my skin, and she almost seems sad.

"Everything okay?" I glance back at the road.

"Of course." Her voice brightens. "I want to see all your things."

"Good, because I'm planning to show you everything." Yeah, there's a hint of innuendo in my tone.

She's right there with me. "That sounds naughty, professor."

"You have no idea."

CHAPTER 16

Reanna

T HE GOLDEN HORSE LIFTS HER HEAD OVER THE DOOR AT THE sound of Dirk's voice. We drove straight from Thornton to what I now know is Hugh van Hamilton's estate, leaving our bags in the Jeep as Dirk took my hand to walk us straight to the stables.

Sliding my fingers through his on the drive over was the most natural thing. It was the first time I'd held his hand, such a simple gesture, yet so amazing. The heat of his palm warming mine, the strength of his fingers against my skin. I never thought much about holding hands until this moment, when my hand is securely in his firm grip. Now we can't seem to stop touching each other.

He only releases me to cup the face of the massive animal rubbing her nose against his chest. "Reanna, meet Dancer. Hugh van Hamilton's prized Palomino."

"Is she prized?" I slide my hand along the horse's velvety neck.

"Hugh loved old westerns, and when he got her, I think he was hoping for Trigger." He squints an eye at me, and adds, "Roy Rogers was a famous old cowboy. His palomino horse was named Trigger."

"I knew that!" *I didn't.*

"Dancer's not a stallion, but she's a good horse."

The mare nods her head at him as if she understands what he's saying.

Wrinkling my nose, I laugh. "Does everything fall in love with you?"

The words jump out, and I bite my lip at how close it sounds to me saying *I* love him. That's crazy, although I'm acutely aware of how close I am to falling for this sexy-ass man right now, especially with him playfully showing me all his favorite things like a little boy.

He doesn't miss a beat. "I am the youngest."

"So I take that as a yes."

"I can't speak for others." He gives me a sexy wink, and it's a sizzle in my veins.

We've been so restrained since he picked me up this morning, almost as if we were meeting each other for the first time, in a new environment, where we can truly relax and be ourselves. We're not stealing moments or hiding from prying eyes.

The tension between us is tight as a drum, but we can take our time.

I slide my hand down the horse's nose. "She acts like she's your horse."

"We have a history."

"You have a history with this horse?" Stepping closer to him, I rest my cheek against his firm shoulder.

"I was the only person to ride her regularly after Hugh brought her here. He asked me to keep her exercised, so we pretty much spent the summer together."

"Mm, lucky girl." I walk over to an empty stall filled

with fresh hay. "Is it just me or does the smell of hay make you horny?"

His low chuckle meets my ears just before his arms circle my waist. "It's not just you."

Turning, I lift my hands to his cheeks, meeting his lips halfway to mine. They bump in a kiss and part, tongues desperate to taste. He drags my body firmly against his, burying his face in my neck and inhaling deeply.

"I love your scent." His low voice filters heat through my veins. "It haunts me when we're apart."

"We're together all weekend… at least?" I'm not entirely sure of the timeline.

"Everyone gets back Sunday night." He lifts his messy dark head, hazel eyes smoldering. "I thought we could hang around and let you meet them if you want."

There's no way I can meet them, but I'll figure that out when the time comes.

"Sure." I smile, kissing his lips again, loving how I can touch him whenever I want. "You don't think they'll have a problem with you being my professor?"

His lips are at my jaw, tracing a line up to my cheek when he stops. "I'm only your professor for a few more months."

Then he goes back to being my enemy. I cringe at the unwelcome thought, barging in on my happy space.

It makes me shiver, and I pull his hand as if we can run away, back in the direction of the horses. "Can we go for a ride? Then we can come back and clean up… or get dirty."

He grins, walking past me. "Sure, help me grab a saddle."

I follow him into the tack room, which is the size of a large utility closet, filled with blankets and saddles of all sizes and shapes, bridles… and gifts, it seems.

"Oh, man," Dirk laughs softly, putting a straw cowboy hat on his head. "Check this out."

He turns, tilting his head so he looks up at me from under the brim, and a flash of desire shoots straight to my core. "That's a look I didn't know I liked."

"You like it?" He pulls me to his chest, tipping the brim back before leaning down to cover my lips with his in a hot kiss.

My knees actually weaken, and our kiss turns into a smile. "I never had a thing for cowboys before."

"One cowboy." He taps my nose, turning back to grab two blankets and hand them to me. "My little sister loves giving gifts."

I'm ready to send her a thank you card for him.

Arching my brow, I study his broad shoulders in that dark green Henley, tight ass in those jeans, with that hat on his head. "But I thought you were the youngest?"

He lifts two saddles with a grunt, muscles flexing, and I almost need to take a seat.

"Hana's actually my brother's wife's younger sister, but we're like siblings." He passes me, heading into the barn, oblivious to my internal turmoil.

Hearing her name plunges me back into the old days of hiding, doing my best to blend in, trying to disappear. It's been four years since I've seen Hana, and the shame of who I was in those days twists in my chest.

"You coming?" he calls, and I push these intrusive feelings away again.

How long can I keep avoiding the truth? I'm here at ground zero. It's all right here—my mission, the answers I've dedicated myself to finding. All I have to do is search, find that book and take it back to New York.

Yet, all I want to do is stay here with him, share this moment where we don't have to hide, where it's still just a fantasy, and I can have a happily ever after.

Dirk leads us at a gallop across a wide, open pasture. The cool breeze is at our faces, and I'm on a large, black Friesian named Regency's Honor. He's powerful with a long mane and tail and large hooves like a draft horse. Still, he's graceful and nimble, keeping up with Dancer.

It's been years since I've ridden a horse, but it comes back quickly. These move like racehorses, but Dirk said Training Day was the only one who was ever on a track. He didn't mention how the horse was retired, but knowing what I know about this family's history, I have an idea.

When we reach the tree line, we slow to a trot then to a walk. Dirk slides off Dancer, walking her to a small creek pushing through the leaves.

"These streams cut all through here, making their way out to the ocean." He waits while Dancer drinks, and I slide off Rege's back. "It can be tricky to ride if you're unfamiliar with the area, but the horses know."

"Would they fall?" I walk to where he's standing, allowing my horse to drink as well.

"Horses are pretty sure-footed. You're more likely to get wet or muddy."

"I'm halfway there." Stepping closer, I press my chest to his, lifting my chin.

Cupping my face, he slides his thumbs over my cheeks. Smoky hazel burns into my cool blues, but depth is behind his eyes. It tickles my stomach and makes my lips heavy.

"It's been a long time since I've brought someone here," he confesses, almost as if he's treading this ground as cautiously as I am.

As if he knows how close we are to something completely different.

Stepping back quickly, my heel sinks, and I realize I'm at

the edge of a mud puddle. Without a thought, I reach down and scoop it up, wiping a line of brown across his cheek, breaking the moment.

He jerks back, surprised. "What the—"

"Gotcha!" I yell, taking off running up the creek bed, my boots crunching on the watery rocks.

"You'd better run!" The sound of his footsteps chasing me, splashing faster as he gets closer, makes my stomach flip.

I scream and press harder, doing my best to stay ahead, but I'm not familiar with this area, and the creek takes a sharp right before dropping into what I see is a small pool below.

"Oh, no!" I skid to a stop, and he has me around the waist, lifting me off the ground.

"I've got you." Lifting his hand, he's got a scoop of mud just waiting for me.

"No!" I laugh, turning my face side to side, but he doesn't stop coming.

I could get out of his hold, but I don't want to. Instead, mud is smeared all over my cheeks and neck, and I'm laughing as he returns me to my feet.

Turning to face him, we both strike wrestler poses, knees bent and circling. Reaching down, I scoop another handful of mud, and his eyes glitter.

"What are you planning to do with that?" His tone is warning, and nervous laughter bubbles in my throat.

"I think you know." I take a quick step forward, and he dodges, lifting his arm and twisting out of the way.

"You're not going to get that on me."

"I might. I have skills."

"I'm familiar with your skills." A sexy smile curls his lips, and a dimple appears.

Laughter, teasing, these are things we haven't been able to do at Thornton, and I love it.

"Then you know I get what I want." Diving at him, I grip his shoulders, pushing my hand towards his face.

He blocks it easily, holding my arm to the side. At this point, I don't really care about smearing him with mud. I only want to feel his strength again. I want his arms around me, him holding me down. It's how we always are, wild and ravenous.

Then he turns my hand to my face.

"No!" I squeal, pressing my nose against his chest as I struggle against the incoming blob.

"Now who has skills?"

I do the only thing I can, hooking my leg around his and taking him to the ground. He lands on his back with an *oof!* and his grip on my arm loosens. In that instant, I've got him, wiping the mud from his forehead down his nose.

"Motherfucker," he growls, rolling me so my back is in the muck.

Ripping up my sweater, he wipes a line of mud over my bare stomach, and the cold makes me yell. Just as fast, he straddles my waist, gripping my wrists so both my hands are locked in his above my head.

We're breathing fast, smiling wickedly as we gaze at each other, sweaty and gross. One blink, and his mouth is on mine. He releases my wrists, and I rip at his shirt, pulling it higher so our bodies are skin against muddy skin.

"Fuck," he groans, and I laugh against his mouth. "This is disgusting."

"There's a creek down there."

He's on his feet at once, catching both my hands and pulling me to my feet. He doesn't stop there, tossing me over his shoulder and slapping my ass.

"Ow!" I laugh, but I don't struggle as he takes off down the side of the hill to where the small pool waits below.

Dropping me to my feet, he catches me by the waist. "Come here." It's a low order, and he lifts my sweater over my head, tossing it to the side along with his discarded Henley.

Our boots are the next to go. He's actually in cowboy

boots, but mine are simple Chelsea ankle boots. One zip, and they're off.

A hand-sized stripe of mud is across both our stomachs, and I laugh. "Look what you did!"

"What I did," he gripes, jerking me closer by the belt loops before unbuttoning my jeans and lowering the zipper as I unfasten my bra and toss it to the side.

Reaching for his waist, I pull the top button open, dropping my hand to stroke the hard length pressing against the fabric. He groans, pulling me closer and catching my face, sealing his lips over mine.

Mouths open, tongues circle, and he steps back to shove his pants off. I do the same. Straightening, we both hesitate. All our other encounters have been stolen moments, hidden in the dark, our clothes yanked down or up just enough to allow our bodies to unite.

It's the first time we've been completely naked, standing in front of each other. Lifting his hand, he slides his palm over my hip, higher to my waist. His touch is so light, so reverent, it floods heat to my core, forcing a soft whimper from my throat.

Blinking slowly, I place my hands on the lines in his hips wrapping over his waist in that mouth watering V. His hand moves higher, his thumb opening over my stomach before rising to cup my breast and lift, squeeze.

Another soft noise, and my tongue slides over my lips as I trace the muscular lines in his ribs with trembling fingers. My other hand teases his cock, perfectly straining, hard and smooth and pointing right at me. I'm mesmerized by the sight of him.

He speaks in a hushed whisper. "You're so beautiful."

It's more than I can take. I step closer, pressing my open mouth to his firm chest, sliding my tongue over his salty skin, kissing and teasing his hard nipple with my teeth. With a groan, he threads his fingers in my hair, pulling my head back so I'm forced to meet his heated gaze.

"I want to be inside you."

Nodding, I place my hands on his shoulders, and he lifts me in his arms. My legs go around his waist, and he walks slowly into the small pool. I'm bracing for it to be frigid, but it's surprisingly tepid. The depth is only to his waist, and he braces the rocky side where the small creek falls over the hill creating a gentle waterfall.

"I don't have a condom, but I'm clean." His voice is rough. "Hell, you're the first person I've been with in…"

Sliding my thumb across his full bottom lip, I want him so much. "You're the first for me in so long. I'm clean, I have an implant."

Our mouths crash, his hand bracing the back of my head, and I reach down between us to grasp his erection, sliding it smoothly into my slippery core. Again, the sensation of fullness is overwhelming.

His forehead drops to mine, and he groans, squeezing his eyes shut. "Feels so good."

We're facing each other for the first time. He's between my legs, his light chest hairs tickling my nipples, our skin is heated and slick from the water and our desire.

Reaching around I pull him closer as I work my thighs, riding his cock, pressing my pelvis to him so the friction radiates to my core.

"Oh, fuck," I gasp, as the sparks of orgasm awaken.

His hands are on my ass, grasping and squeezing, and he thrusts harder, driving deeper. Again our lips seal, tongues caressing. He moves one hand from my ass to between us, stroking and pinching my clit, and the sparkles turn to flames.

We're both moving faster, frantically chasing that fiery release. His mouth moves to the top of my ear, and I hear his hot breath hitch and shudder as he gets closer. It's fucking hot as hell, and one last, firm circle of his thumb on my clit sends me soaring.

"Dirk," I cry as the waves roll through my body, squeezing and pulsing against his cock, coaxing him to join me.

It doesn't take much. Both his hands are on my ass, and he squeezes as he stills. With a pulse and jerk, he breaks deep within me. His stomach muscles tense, and his thighs tremble beneath mine. My arms wrap tighter around his body, and I hold him, riding out this orgasm chest to chest and face to face like it's our first time.

CHAPTER 17

Dirk

HER BODY IS WARM AGAINST MINE, SITTING ON THE SADDLE IN FRONT of me as we ride back on Regency's Honor. I hold Dancer's reins, leading her beside us as we lope back to the barn.

The image of Reanna's body, naked in front of me, burns in my mind—her perfect, teardrop breasts, small but large enough to squeeze, round hips and flat stomach, ass full enough to grip as I moved her up and down on my dick.

She's muscular. I've never asked if she's an athlete, but she's still soft, with those blue eyes and long dark hair… I haven't been able to stop looking at her or touching her.

Holding her against my chest, taking her slow, without the fever and desperation, without the fear of being caught, changed something in me. At Thornton I fought these feelings. I felt like I was failing to be strong against an amorous young student.

Then, when I couldn't stop wanting her, I supposed it could be the danger, the element of the forbidden, making it feel like something more. Now I'm not sure at all.

Our bodies rock together with the rhythm of the horse. Her back is to my chest, and my hand is on her stomach. Our hips move like they do when we're coming undone, and I think I will always get semi-hard thinking of her ass sliding against my crotch.

Back at the barn, I slide off the Friesian to guide Dancer into her stall. We'll have to brush them down and feed them ourselves, since the groom has the weekend off. It's the first time in a long time the estate is almost entirely empty.

Only Norris, Hugh's old butler, remains in the house, keeping things going as he has since I was a little boy.

Reanna slides off her horse, guiding it into the stall and following my lead, unbuckling the belt around the horse's belly, sliding the heavy, western saddle off his back.

"You got that?" I call from across the alley, but when I look up, I see she's walking to the tack room, blanket and saddle in hand.

I'm right behind her, placing Dancer's saddle on the vacant sawhorse and picking up an oval, boar's hair brush the size of my palm. She does the same, pausing to rise on her toes and kiss my lips before taking the cowboy hat off my head and putting it on hers.

A smile curls my lips as I watch her sassy ass sway as she walks back to the waiting horse. It only takes a few moments to brush them down, stow the bridles, and give them feed.

"I've just got to feed the other three horses and we can head to my place."

She glances around the barn before giving me a worried smile. "Is there somewhere I can use the restroom?"

"Oh, sure. Sorry." I feel pretty damn inconsiderate. "If you go right down that breezeway, it'll lead to the kitchen door. It's always unlocked, and there's a restroom just inside, down a short hall past the pantry."

"I won't be long!" One last peck on my lips and she turns, taking off at a trot towards the house.

I step inside Dancer's stall again, patting the front of her leg so I can inspect her hoof for rocks. I take a second to check all four and then Rege's before I decide they're all set for the night.

The other horses are waiting with their heads over the stalls for dinner. I take my time, lingering as I fill their troughs. Training Day watches with big brown eyes as I scrub my hand down his neck. No one rides him anymore, but I'll take him through the paces tomorrow.

Several minutes have passed, and I realize Reanna hasn't returned. I wonder if she got lost in Hugh's big house or if she thought I might meet her there. I could text her, but I figure I'll go and find her instead, say hello to Norris if he's around.

The sun is on the horizon, a full, red-orange sphere outlining the landscape in glowing yellow. I imagine Hana could turn this into a photographic work of art if she were here, if she hasn't already, as I slowly stroll up the breezeway towards the house.

The back door is unlocked as always, and I step into the large, empty kitchen. Only the small lights under the cabinets are illuminated, and I scan the area looking for any signs of Reanna.

Finding none, I make my way down to the small bathroom on the short hall separating the kitchen from the open living room. The half-bath is dark, and I continue, wondering where she might be.

I realize she could be waiting for me at the Jeep, and I place my hand on my phone to text her when my eyes catch a shaft of light coming from an open door on the next hall between the living room and Hugh's large conservatory-greenhouse.

I'm sure it's Norris cleaning or straightening Hugh's office, and I figure I'll say hello and be sure he knows I'm checking on the horses this weekend. I pull up short when I round the corner and see it's Reanna, sliding her fingers over the spines behind Hugh's desk, pulling a thin book out and reading the cover.

"What are you doing here?" At the sound of my voice she lets out a little yip and throws the book in the air.

It makes me laugh, and I walk over to pick it up off the floor. "If that's not a guilty response…"

"You nearly gave me a heart attack." She places a hand on her chest.

Straightening, I notice papers spread across the oversized, carved-oak desk. "That's what you get for snooping."

"I wasn't snooping." Her laugh is wobbly, I assume from getting caught. "I was just looking at this beautiful old house, and I wandered down the hall and saw all these gorgeous books and I guess…"

"It's okay." I walk up to put my hand on her waist, sliding the slim volume of the poems of T.S. Eliot back on the shelf. "I didn't know where you were."

She pushes her hair behind her ears with trembling hands, and her eyes fall to the desk. "I'm not sure where I am."

"Well, be glad Norris didn't catch you. He's the one who protects all of Hugh's things, and he is not very forgiving about books going missing. At least he wasn't when I was a kid."

"I noticed he has this." She walks over to the opposite side of the room and slides a hardcover edition of *The Sorcerer's Stone* off the shelf.

Joining her, I take it from her hands, inspecting the pristine sheets of the unread book. "He has all of them, I think."

She reaches up to cup my cheek before kissing me again. She's been doing that a lot since our ride, and I like it. I like it so much, I shove the book back in its place and catch her around the waist.

"I have my own copies now, too."

Her eyes light with her smile. "I know, and they're well-read, unlike these museum pieces."

"How would you know?" I give her a squint.

"I mean… I imagine them that way." She drops her chin, circling her finger around the button on my shirt.

"Come on, crazy." I take her hand, leading her out of the office and back to the kitchen, ready to show her my place.

"Numbing the pain for a while will make it worse when you finally feel it." We're propped up on pillows in the center of my bed, boxes of grilled bologna sandwiches and mac and cheese from Slim Harold's in Hamiltown on our bedside tables.

I'm reading Dumbledore's famous lines from *The Goblet of Fire* aloud while Reanna leans against my chest listening intently.

"That's so true." Her voice is soft, musing, and I lower the book.

"What are you thinking about?" My fingers are threaded in her long, silky hair, and I've been running them down her back as I read the story.

We came back here after a brief pit stop in town for dinner. Slim Harold's is a knock-off of a popular dance bar in Myrtle Beach called Fat Harold's. The menu is the same, including their signature grilled bologna sandwiches, and the old-timers go there to shag dance on the weekends.

We got an order to go and came back to my place after dark. "It's better to see it from the inside out the first time," I assured her.

"What does that mean?" Her eyebrow arched as we hopped out of the jeep.

I grabbed our bags while she carried the food, and as I led her through the unfinished ground floor, she noted the ancient thread winders, looms, and weaving machines.

"These are incredible. Do any of them still work?"

"I'm pretty sure they're all out of commission at this point."

Taking the lead, we climbed the stairs to the second level, the main living area, and when I switched on the lights in the vast, open warehouse I'd been transforming into a home, wonder filled her expression.

It's the same size as the space below, but the red pine floors have been sanded and sealed. Heavy cypress beams are uniformly arranged throughout the open space, creating a sense of symmetry. The living area is complete with linen couches and chairs, a 72-inch flatscreen television, a gas log fireplace and sisal rugs.

The kitchen and dining area is in the center with a full, gas stove and oven, quartz countertops, and stainless appliances, then behind it is my bedroom and sitting area. A California king is hidden behind heavy beige canvas curtains hanging from the soaring ceilings overhead. I even have a workout area with weights and a bench on the opposite end.

"This is amazing." Her voice was hushed, and I shrugged with pride.

"Hutch keeps insisting I hire someone to complete the exterior and the first floor. Maybe I will. I've just been having fun doing it myself."

I didn't add that I was lonely and bored out of my mind, and now that she's come into the picture, my brother's words are making a lot more sense.

We changed into comfortable, pajama-like clothes, a pair of shorts for me from my closet. A pair of short shorts and a long-sleeved thin tee for her from her bag.

The dark circles of her areolas were visible through the thin beige fabric and almost made me forget how hungry we both were, but my stomach growling told my dick to take a break.

So I parceled out the food and poured us each a glass of white wine. Now our bellies are full, we're a little buzzy, and she's making me read to her my favorite parts of my favorite Harry Potter book.

"Why do you read this when you can't sleep?" She lifts her head, resting her chin on her hand. "It starts with a nightmare of murder."

"Yeah, sorry about that." I trace my thumb across the top of her cheek. "I think because it's the first time Harry faces down the evil who killed his mom. He learns she died saving his life."

Her eyes are warm, and she touches my cheek. "Losing someone hurts so much. For the longest time, I tried to act like my father's death didn't hurt me, that I was strong enough to take it." Her voice lowers, and I tighten my arm around her. "Four years ago, I decided it wasn't working. I had numbed the pain for so long with vodka, and when I finally felt it, I was determined to get answers… and revenge."

She adds the last part so softly, I'm not sure she meant for me to hear it, but I did.

"They say revenge is a poison you give yourself."

"And wait for the other person to die," she sighs, rolling onto her back. "I know."

"When my mother died, I used these books to escape the pain. I think I wanted to live in a place where magic might bring her back." Exhaling deeply, I set the book aside. "I blamed my father for not being there for her. He left her with three kids and moved to New York to pursue his own interests—in every way. I hated him so much for it. I wanted to make him pay for breaking her heart."

It's an old bitterness that burns on my tongue when I speak it, but it turns her to me again, gazing up at me with curious eyes. "What did you do?"

"Nothing… to him." I think about this topic as I have over and over in the last few years as I've watched my brother then Scar find love and happiness. "I simply stopped believing. I stopped trusting anyone. Until I was completely alone."

Her palm is flat on my chest, and she rests her cheek on it, studying my face as if she understands every word I'm saying, every motivation. "But you're so charming and approachable. You're very handsome."

"You're very beautiful." I lean down and kiss her nose. "My problem is subconscious. People get too close, and I create distance."

"Am I too close?"

Lifting my hand, I smooth her hair off her face. "You're right where I need you to be. Except when I need you to be under me."

I give her a teasing wink, and her cheeks flush a pretty shade of pink. Her chin dips, and she presses a kiss to my bare chest. She holds for a moment, almost seeming like she wants to tell me more, but her head tilts to the side instead.

"You have two siblings? Who's the other one?"

"My sister Judy died of ovarian cancer almost ten years ago."

"Oh, I'm so sorry." She sits up to meet my eyes with her round ones. "You've had so much loss compared to mine."

"Have I?" Reaching for her arm, I pull her to me again. "You said you lost your father and a brother."

"I never knew my brother. You had a whole life with your sister. It's so much harder."

"Good news, she left us a baby girl. Well, she's not a baby anymore. Pepper is so much like her mom. It's like having Judy again."

"Where is Pepper?"

"She lives with her dad now in Hamiltown, but she's always at Hutch's place."

"Doesn't she like her dad?"

"Oh, sure, but when Judy died, Hutch kind of became her dad for a little while."

She's quiet a moment. "Is he a good dad?"

"The best. He's been kind of shoved into the role since our own dad left, but he's good at it. A little overbearing at times, but he can hear it when you tell him to back off."

She's quiet, and I trace my fingers in her hair, curling the silky strands around my fingers lost in thought. Her chest is against my chest, and our hearts beat in time. We're sharing so much, it's hard to think of this as something that will naturally conclude at the end of the semester. I can't imagine shaking hands and saying goodbye.

At the same time, she has no reason to stay, and I'm committed to Thornton. She's supposed to launch, pursue her career, start her life. The thought twists in my stomach. It's a bitter pill I don't want to swallow.

The brush of her lashes tickles my chest, and I wonder if her mind is following the same path as mine.

"What are you thinking?" My voice is solemn, and she lifts her chin.

"The way you describe them makes me miss my dad. I always wanted a family."

I could give her that...

"I didn't mean to bring us down." She sits up in the bed, eyes sparkling with mischief, and my hands fall to her waist. "What?"

"I know how to get you up." Her hand slides to the side, reaching down to stroke and cup my dick, which surges instantly at her touch.

My heated gaze lands on her breasts in that thin top, and I reach out to cup them, circling my thumbs over her hardening nipples. Her blue eyes darken, and she leans forward to kiss me.

"I can make you come first." Turning, she straddles me backwards, leaning forward and pulling my dick all the way into her mouth.

"Fuck..." I groan, pressing my back to the headboard and lifting my hips instinctively as she grips the base of my shaft.

Looking down, her ass is right in my face, and I can take a challenge. "We'll see about that."

Lifting her thighs, I slide lower, shoving her booty shorts aside and dragging my tongue up and down the slippery seam of her pussy.

"Oh!" Her hips jump, and she pops off me with a soft moan.

It only helps me position her higher, my tongue moving swiftly, circling and pulling at her swollen clit.

"No..." She scrambles, reaching for my legs and pulling my cock into her mouth, all the way to her throat again.

"Shit…" I press my head against the pillow a moment at the force of her suction, at the insanity of this competition.

I've never been with such a tomboy, always wanting to wrestle and compete, but I confess, it's hot as fuck in the bedroom, especially with her making my dick so hard it's pointing straight up.

Catching her hips, I roll us so I'm on top, biting at her inner thighs and sucking at her belly, leaving a red mark before I return to her clit. I didn't anticipate she'd be ready, dropping her jaw and taking me all the way back to the back of her throat.

My head lifts with a groan, and the fire in the base of my spine is undeniable. It's too good, and she's not stopping. I can't let her win…

Pushing off the bed, I come out of her mouth with a pop before climbing back just as fast to flip her over quickly. She struggles, laughing as she tries to escape my grip, but my hands are on her waist. She's not going anywhere.

Dragging her down to the end of the bed, I rip her shorts down, lining up my cock before sinking it deep and hard into her hot cunt.

"Dirk…" she gasps, stilling beneath my dominance.

I start to pound into her feverishly from behind and her hands stretch and claw at the sheets as she moans. Her ass rises to meet my thrusts, and the heat of orgasm surges to wildfire in my veins.

Sliding my hand around, I find her clit, massaging firmly as her knees buckle and a whimper comes from her throat.

"That's right." Bending forward, my voice is at her ear. "You like this?"

She nods quickly. "Harder…"

Her body is soft beneath mine, and we're working in time, thrusting and pulling. She turns her face, and I cover her mouth, driving my tongue inside to taste her. Her hand reaches up, fingers threading in my hair, and pulling. Our lips slide and bite, and with another hard thrust, the surge of orgasm rips through my body.

"Fuck!" My mouth breaks away, and I drop my head on her shoulder, holding as the pulsing rocks me, as my own knees bend.

We collapse onto the bed, riding out the last waves, holding, clenching, until the shudders pass, and the room returns to focus.

I roll to the side. She's on her stomach, her arms bent and her head turned to face me. Reaching out, I trace her hair away from her eyes with my finger, and she blinks up at me.

A naughty grin curls her swollen, bruised-red lips. "I let you win."

Exhaling a laugh, I scoot closer, rolling her onto her back and covering her upper body with mine. "I'm stronger than you."

She gazes up at me with those stunning eyes, and I slide my hand across her forehead, moving her hair back.

"I love your strength." A slight rasp is in her voice. "I love knowing you could hurt me, but you're holding back because you can't live without me."

"I would never hurt you."

Quiet falls between us. Our eyes hold, and the pull between us is undeniable, like it always has been since that very first day. Leaning down, I kiss her slowly, gently, sliding my lips across hers before opening her mouth and finding her tongue.

She feels so good, and with every beat of my heart, I'm calm, sure. They say when it's right, you just know it. The words are right there, but I won't say them. Still, it's here, waiting to be plucked from the air like the apple on an ancient tree.

The one we were warned not to touch.

CHAPTER 18

Reanna

THE LIGHT OF MY PHONE ILLUMINATING THE DARKNESS ROUSES ME. I'm curled up next to Dirk in his enormous bed, and his arms are clutched tight around me.

It's the most divine heaven until I read my phone, and it all goes to hell. ***You're in Hamiltown. Do you have it?***

Natasha. *Shit.*

I was hoping to keep her in the dark as long as possible, but of course, she's tracking my phone. ***Started in HVH's study. At DW's. Will return soon.***

That should shut her up for a while. Last thing I need is her bugging me or worse, Dirk seeing one of her texts and asking questions.

Putting my phone away, I trace my fingers along the lines of his forearm wrapped around my shoulders. We're sharing so much and growing so close. I want to stay here with him, know him better, share everything… or as much as I can. I'm having a hard time staying focused on my goal, and searching for the ledger is slipping in my priorities.

Could I let go of trying to find my father's killer? Give up on trying to find out if my brother is still alive? Don't I owe them that? Would Dirk understand if I told him why I'm really here, that I'm not really a student at Thornton?

Every time I close my eyes and imagine saying the words to him—that I was planted in his class to get close to him, so he would bring me here where I could search for a ledger of criminals for an organization he's been fighting for years—paralyzing fear shoots down my spine.

Would he believe I fell in love with him despite every self-protective instinct and order not to do so? It wasn't even an order. The idea I might fall for him never entered the realm of possibilities.

I could make it up to him. I could give him something he wants. I could go back and bring them down myself...

"Are you awake?" His husky voice startles me, and I turn in his arms.

"My phone woke me up."

Even with sleepy eyes and messy hair, he's still so damn gorgeous. Then he leans down and kisses the top of my head, melting my heart and making me want to cry.

"I'll make some coffee." He slides out of bed and walks to the kitchen bare-assed naked, and I lean my cheek on my hand, watching his muscles flex as he moves.

Less than an hour ago, that sexy body was above me, inside me, surrounding me with his scent, for the who-knows-how-many-eth time. I do love his strength, the weight of him holding me down, his mouth opening mine, our tongues curling as our bodies become one.

I can't imagine that strength turning on me in anger. *What have I done?*

Sliding out of the bed, I scoop my shorts off the floor and pull his navy Henley off the chair and over my head. It smells so good like him, clean, fresh, with a little undercurrent of something deeper. I walk up behind him and wrap my arms around his waist, resting my cheek against the firm muscles in his back. I can hold him a little longer... before I have to run.

"Shit, I'm out of coffee." He turns, wrapping me in his arms. "Hang out, and I'll run up to Steamy Beans and grab us a go-order."

I freeze. It's the perfect opportunity to search his place, and he's dropping it directly in my lap, with total trust in me. I remember his words from last night, how he stopped trusting anyone, and I look up at his open smile, his hazel eyes brimming with something so close to...

"I'll go with you." I plant a quick kiss on his lips. "Let me put on some jeans and you can show me the town."

I'm brushed and ready, still wearing his Henley, now paired with fresh jeans and boots and a light canvas jacket. A swipe of lip gloss, and I catch his hand, leaving his apartment and my task behind.

Just before we head out the door, he stops and puts his arm around me, pulling me close to his side. "I like seeing you in my clothes."

Reaching for his cheek, I kiss his lips briefly. "I like so many things right now." I can't begin to tell him all of them.

Steamy Beans is a cute little coffee shop with black and white mosiac tile floors and dark wood cases filled with pastries. They have a delicious house blend, coffee made with cinnamon, and we sit at a black metal table in matching metal chairs with the scent of fresh baked bread and sugar floating in the air around us.

Dirk has a cup of coffee as well, and we split a plate of scones with jam. He's wearing a navy ball cap, and that dimple I adore is in his cheek. I love watching him. He polishes off two scones while I'm still working on my first.

"I have to get over to Hugh's and exercise Training Day. Otherwise we can do pretty much whatever we want."

Leaning closer, I lower my voice. "I like what we've been doing."

"Same here." He kisses my lips. "We'll do plenty more of that. Still, I can show you around. We'll stop by my office, so you can see how exciting my work is here."

A touch of sarcasm is in his tone, and I tease, "Shall we christen your work desk as well?"

"Depends on how much of an exhibitionist you are. Our front walls are glass."

"Sounds like you need some curtains."

When we've finished our coffee and breakfast, he takes my hand, and we walk across the street to a glass-front office with a door that reads *Winston and Lourde* in old-school hand-painted lettering. At least it looks hand-painted. I suspect they're stickers.

"It's like something out of an old film noir." I trace my finger over the words.

"All we need is a femme fatale."

"Yeah." My voice trails off as I consider the femme fatale, the seductive woman who leads the hero into a trap.

Dirk turns the lock, and I follow him into the heart of their operation. The one they used to take down almost all of the organization four years ago. Natasha would be turning herself inside out at the thought of me being here. It's a sparse, open space with three desks, a few filing cabinets, two desktops, and a large computer server.

"I call this the brains of the office." He pats the server. "Although it took my brains to set up the network."

"Are you saying you're the brains of the office?"

"Yes," he laughs. "I am."

That makes me smile, but my tension won't ease. I step over to the desk I'm pretty sure is his. It has a photo of him crouching behind a little girl in pigtails and a softball uniform holding up her hands like she's catching a large, sprinkled donut instead of a softball.

"Cute—are you calling a fair catch?"

"In softball it's a foul-out." He takes the frame. "Hana staged this. She's always coming up with fun ideas. She has a show in New York every other year at the Milo gallery. Blake organized the first one, and it was such a success, they keep having her back."

I knew this about her, but I nod, raising my eyebrows. "Cool."

"This is cool." He sits at a computer and taps a few keys.

Pictures pop up on a computer screen, and my breath stops as the images appear. It's surveillance footage from inside Gibson's. One feed is in a dark room with black leather sofas and no windows. It's one of the small, back rooms where any number of dirty deals take place.

The other is the main office, where Natasha is sitting at her desk and Rick is standing with his arms crossed in front of her. It's a low-resolution, black and white image, but I recognize them immediately.

The small hairs on the back of my neck prickle as I watch him watching them, knowing I could've been on this screen at any time. My fingers tremble, and I'm not sure my voice will cooperate.

Clearing my throat, I ask carefully, "Is this something you're working on?"

"Not really. Just keeping an eye on things. These guys gave us a lot of trouble a few years back. They're sophisticated criminals, true evil."

"But they're not in jail?"

He exhales, tapping another button that pulls up more surveillance of the street outside the club.

"We could never pin anything on those two. Doesn't mean they're innocent. Just means they're better at covering their tracks. And others are still out there. We're waiting to see who joins the party, or my partners are."

Filtering through my memory, Natasha wanted to meet at

the firing range to discuss sending me to Thornton. Was this the reason? To keep me off their cameras? Did she suspect she was being watched?

The muscle in Dirk's jaw moves as he types on his laptop. I study his profile, but there's not a bit of evidence he connects me to the scene in front of him.

"All done." He closes the laptop and stands. "Pretty boring, yeah?"

Not even a little bit.

Blinking up at him, I force a smile. "It's amazing what all you can do from this small office." Stepping closer to his desk, it's completely bare except for a Bluetooth speaker. "You don't have any papers or books here?"

"We keep local police reports in the filing cabinet, but nothing sensitive is stored here. Too easy to break in and steal."

Lifting my chin, I nod. "You keep stuff like that at your place?"

"Scar has a secret room."

A secret room where a book might be hidden?

"And you can track anyone from right here?"

"Pretty much. Hutch and Scar can log into this feed from any networked computer, but I'm taking a break." He catches my hand. "Ready to exercise some horses?"

Glancing around one last time, I feel confident what I'm looking for isn't here. If I don't find it at Hugh's, that leaves Scar's secret room, wherever it might be.

"Sure." I manage a smile, feeling mildly uneasy. "Let's get out of here."

I stand on the wooden fence resting my chin on my hand as I watch him lead the gorgeous, chocolate-brown thoroughbred around the paddock. He's wearing that sexy cowboy hat again, and he's holding a rope attached to the horse's bridle.

Training Day runs in one direction for several minutes, then Dirk nods his head and makes a clicking sound. The horse immediately changes direction and runs the other way for a little while.

After a few more exercises, he removes the rope and loops it around his arm, allowing the horse to lope freely around the arena with the other horses.

"He's so well-trained." I look up at my handsome cowboy.

"He's a thoroughbred. Hugh rescued him from some pretty bad stuff."

My brow furrows. "He rescued him?"

A frown twists his lips, and he looks down. "His nephew, Hana and Blake's dad, was into some bad shit, and Hugh stepped in and paid a lot of money to fix it."

That sounds like the story I remember. My past gave me a front-row seat for most of the van Hamilton indiscretions. I was there for almost all of Hana's, and I can't help wondering what it took for her to find redemption. What would it take for me to find it?

Dancer trots up to where Dirk stands, and he slides his hand along the horse's neck. "That's my girl."

"I think she's jealous." Watching him with these animals, his expert hands and mastery of the training, fills me with unexpected pride.

He's so much more than I was led to believe when I was sent here looking for a computer nerd.

"She's spoiled is more like it." The horse lifts her nose and snuffles at his head, knocking off the cowboy hat.

I laugh, picking it up and putting it on my head. "I like you as a cowboy."

He gives the horse one last pat and climbs the fence, tossing a leg over and dropping to stand beside me. "Better than a professor?"

"Hmm..." Twisting my lips, I study him here, leaning

down, caging me with his arms. "That's a difficult question, Professor Winston. Can I choose all of the above?"

"Actually, you can." He flicks the hat further back on my head before covering my mouth with his, flooding my insides with need and drowning out my fears.

Was it only a few days ago we were sneaking around on campus, stealing moments in his office, in his Jeep, in that hay maze? Now it feels so natural, so easy and free.

Sliding my hands up his chest, I curl my fingers, pulling him closer. I want to keep him in this place with me. It's so safe and good.

His lips move to my brow, and large hands slide under my shirt, thumbs circling my hard nipples. A sigh aches from my throat as heat floods my core, and he exhales a groan.

"I love that sound." His mouth covers mine again, sliding over my lips. "Come on. I'm taking you home."

Fire hums under my skin as I watch him round up the horses. His expression is focused, brow lowered as he gives them a sharp whistle, and they begin to trot to their respective stalls.

Excitement makes me laugh. "They know when you mean business."

He cuts me a look that shoots fire to my core, and I know when he means business, too.

Thirty minutes later, I'm straddling him in the bed, holding his arms over his head as we moan in time. I'm riding him, and with every thrust, I touch stars. I can't hold out much longer, working my hips, clenching my core.

At last he shoots between my legs, groaning deeply as he comes. I drop my head, letting my orgasm take me. Pulsing and shuddering, it's another insane high, sparked by a friendly wrestling match. *So hot...*

The deep-red signs of a hickey are on his collarbone and another is on his chest. Biting my lip, I grin thinking I did that.

Sweeping my hair back, I lean down and nip his jaw with my teeth. His hands are on my ass, squeezing and caressing.

"I won," I purr, but when I sit up again, I catch him smiling. "What?"

"I let you win."

"Bullshit, you did not!" I push against his chest, and he flips me onto my back, holding me down.

"I love watching you ride my cock." In a swoop, he covers my mouth with his, swallowing my protests, then melting them with a hot swipe of his tongue.

"I made you come first!"

"And it was fucking hot." He collapses onto the bed beside me. "I really like this game. Thank you for introducing it to me."

Rolling into his chest, I laugh. "I made it up."

His hand is on my back, stroking and lifting my hair, twisting it around his finger. "I am here for all your made-up games. In fact, you should write them down. They're way better than Quidditch."

"Quidditch." I scoot higher in the bed beside him, and he wraps the blanket around us. "You never told me why Goblet is your favorite Harry Potter book."

"Well…" He hugs me tight against his chest in a possessive way I love before reaching for his battered paperback. "It's probably not the best one in the series, but when I got to it, Hutch took me to the store to get my very own copy."

Sitting up, I take the book from him and shake it so the picture falls out. Lifting it up, I study his adorable little boy face in glasses, holding the giant book.

"Is this the day?"

His eyes warm, and he takes the photo from me. "That's the one."

Holding it a moment, he studies the faces in a way that makes my chest ache.

"It made an impression on me. It was the first one that

went really dark," he explains. "It was almost 700 pages long, which blew my mind. I'd never read a book that long—I didn't even know they existed. Everything about it was just… big."

"Look at you in your glasses." My voice is soft. "I bet you were the cutest little boy walking around with that giant book. Adorable little nerd."

"Hey," he laughs, rolling us over so he can hold me down again. I don't protest.

Again, our lips unite in hungry kisses. We can never get enough. We can't stop touching each other, and even with that last fantastic fuck, I feel his hardness against my leg. It stokes the fire simmering in my lower belly, the one that never goes out for him.

Lifting his head, he looks deep into my eyes and asks the one question I can't answer. "What are we doing? I went to Thornton to teach, not to find this… with a student."

I know he didn't, and my eyes slide closed. An invisible hand closes around my neck, but I answer truthfully. "I want this so much."

He hears the hesitation in my voice. "But you're just getting started with your life—"

"No," My eyes meet his again. "It's not that. It's just… old business I need to settle."

"Is it about your father's death?" His brow lowers.

Blinking away, I nod. "And some other things. I can't really talk about it."

"Okay." The tension leaves his voice, and he bends down to kiss me again. I love his kisses. "When you're ready… maybe I can help you."

Chewing my lip, I trace my fingers through his soft hair.

When I'm ready.

CHAPTER 19

Reanna

DIRK IS LYING ON HIS BACK, FAST ASLEEP WHEN I AWAKE WITH A start. I know my phone went off, and I know what it means. I lie still a moment longer, making sure he's completely out. His hands are on me, but it's not hard to slide from under them and off the side of the bed.

Hesitating, I study his profile in the dusk, straight nose, full lips, square jaw dusted with a light scruff that drives me wild when his head is between my thighs. How I wish I could stay here and forget everything that brought me here.

He's my dirty professor, my gorgeous nerd, my sexy cowboy, and another buzz on my phone tells me our time is up. Pushing my infatuation to the back burner, I carefully step into my black leggings and a long-sleeved navy sweater. Socks are on my feet, and I close the curtains around his bed.

Using the light on my phone, I tip-toe across his enormous loft apartment to his desk. It's an incredible risk, but I have to search here. Sliding my fingers over the stack of papers and books on his wide-plank desk, I lift and open covers, read briefly and set aside, doing my best to search quickly without making any sound.

It doesn't take long to go through everything on the desktop. Another, careful glance over my shoulder, and I have to go for the drawers. One on each side and a narrow one in the middle.

Holding my breath, I slide the first drawer open, only to find an assortment of wires and computer adapters. Shining my light to the bottom, nothing more is there. The narrow, middle drawer is essentially empty but for a stack of Post-Its, a few check stubs, and several twist-ties. I slowly open the last drawer, and my shoulders drop.

Power strips, a discarded keyboard, and two portable hard drives are inside. I'm sure they have valuable information on them, for someone or something, but none of this is the book I need. I slide the drawer closed and crouch lower, crawling beneath the desk and shining the light all around in case there's a secret compartment or something taped under the desk.

Nothing.

I crawl out again and inspect the surface to be sure everything looks the same as it did when I got here. Returning to the bedroom area, I cross my arms, trying to decide my next move. It's 4:00 a.m., and I have an idea.

Moving fast, I pack all my things in my bag and grab one of the Post-Its out of his desk. I quickly write a note saying I had to leave early and stick it on his phone. No texting—I don't want to wake him.

I take one last look at him sleeping so peacefully. My fingers curl with longing to touch him, but I can't lose any more time. My brief visit to heaven is over, and the devil is waiting for me.

Carrying my boots, I creep to his door and open it slowly, slipping out to the stairs leading to the first floor where I step into my boots and go around to the back where a golf cart is parked behind a motorcycle.

It's a gamble, but it pays off. I press the power button on the cart and silently cruise out into the night, headed for Hugh van Hamilton's estate.

A full moon is out, but occasionally a cloud will drift by and obscure it, sending the narrow, country roads from brilliant, silvery light, to dark shadows. Still, I'm confident of the route, and it's not long before I reach the long circular driveway leading to the mansion.

Avoiding the gravel, I take a sharp curve, following the path around to where the stables are located, and I park near the barn behind an enormous rhododendron bush.

The metallic scent of dew hangs in the air, touching my tongue, and the thick, carpet grass is coated in a haze of moisture. Looking behind me, the tracks leading to where I hid the cart are unmistakable, but it's too late to turn back now. I can only hope no one notices until after the sun rises and melts away the evidence.

My boots make soft thudding noises on the dirt as I dash up the alley in the center of the dark barn. The horses are asleep in their stalls, but one brown head lifts over a door to see what's happening. I'd like to stop and pet Training Day, but everything has changed, and I'm playing beat the clock.

On a hunch, I creep across the short yard to the kitchen door at the rear of the house, silently climbing the back steps and holding my breath. He said it's always open. I turn the handle, and…

It opens.

A knot twists in my throat, and a pit is in my stomach. I'm somewhere between relieved and miserable, and I reach down to quickly remove my boots. The house is dark, and the only signs I've seen of Norris the butler are the fresh plates of sandwiches in the afternoons when we've been here.

I don't have time to wonder as I make my way rapidly to the large office I partially searched two days ago.

Bursting in, I quietly shut the heavy oak door, then I round the desk fast, pulling the drawers open and moving papers aside, not worrying about the mess. The pressure of time passing weighs on my shoulders, and I'm as worried about losing this chance as I am about getting caught.

My heart is a steady drumbeat in my ears, and I hear myself breathing fast. When Dirk caught me last time, I had searched all the bookshelves and found nothing but leather-bound classic literature and the occasional law book.

This desk is my only hope. All the drawers on the left side seem to be tax documents, deeds to the house, appraisal forms, receipts for repairs, no books. The narrow center drawer holds pens, paper clips, Post-It notes, all the usual office supplies, stamps, binder clamps. I shove it closed and go immediately to the right hand drawers.

Top drawer, more papers. I shove my fingers down, lifting them up like flipping pages in a book. Nothing. I slam it closed and move to the second and last one. It's a deep drawer, with several items stacked on top of each other.

A cigar box is on top, and I lift it, opening the lid and checking the contents. Three Don Arturo cigars remain inside, which I know from Gibson's sell for $15,000 a box. Setting it on the desk, I take out the next item. It's a very thin volume with a pale blue and cream cover. Opening it, I see it's a hand-written edition of *The Tales of Beedle the Bard*. A little stab pierces my chest, and I wonder how his uncle has this rare edition... Looking up, I see pale blue light warming the edges of the trees through the small oval window. Time's up.

Setting the special edition Harry Potter aside, my fingertips tingle as they slide across the next book in the drawer, and lifting it out, I swallow my breath. A long, thin volume with a dark brown leather spine and beige fabric cover is in my hands.

Opening it, I see in the top right the initials VP-K, and I stand, shoving it in my bag and quickly returning everything to the drawer. I'm moving so fast, I don't give myself time to react. I only know I've got the ledger, and I've got to get out of here now.

The sun is getting closer to breaking over the horizon, and I need to be far, far from here when it does. Everything is returned to the desk, and I open the door slowly. The house is still dark, and I take two steps in my socked feet, retracing the direction I came, when a creak of wooden floor freezes me in place.

My fists tighten on my bag, and I'm stock-still with my back pressed into a corner behind a wingback chair. Silence falls in the dark living room. My heart beats so hard, it nauseates me, and I hold my breath. The vibration of another human's presence is intense.

It's not Dirk, and I'm sure it's not the butler, who would most likely walk without hesitation to the kitchen to begin the day. Dirk mentioned a bodyguard, but wouldn't he travel with Mr. van Hamilton?

Dirk's family was supposed to arrive back today, but I'm pretty sure he said it would be later. Is it possible someone came back early? I'm doing my best to shrink smaller into the darkness when another creak of wood flooring lights every nerve in my body.

Whoever is in here is moving slowly, cautiously towards the office, where I just was. From the sound of it, they're on the other side of the bookcase, and I don't move. As soon as the door opens, I take off fast as a rabbit, not stopping for anything.

When I get to the kitchen, the door stands open, and I fly through it, scooping my boots up on my way down the short flight of steps, and running as hard as I can for the tree line.

I don't stop running until I'm a good distance away from the house, and then I pull up my ride-share app, ordering a car and quickly following my map to the highway. Fifteen minutes of hiding in the woods later, a lone Chevy Equinox appears, and I dash out of the woods to hop inside.

The driver gives me a mildly suspicious glance, but I smile brightly. "Heading back to school!"

With a shrug he turns the wheel, and we're headed back to Thornton. After a few miles, I open my bag and take out the book. All this work, and it's right here in my hands.

CHAPTER 20

Dirk

THE NOISE OF MY PHONE VIBRATING PULLS ME FROM A DEEP SLEEP. At first I'm disoriented. The bed is empty, and looking all around, I see no sign of Reanna anywhere. Then I notice her bag is gone.

My phone continues to vibrate, and I pick it up, expecting to see it's her.

It's Scar calling.

"Hey, bro, what's up?" I turn in the bed, putting my feet on the floor.

"You still in town?" His raspy voice is low, and I can tell something's up.

"Yeah, I've got the week off, but I was planning to head back…" *Now*, looking around and finding Reanna gone.

"I need you to come to Hugh's as soon as you can."

I'm out of the bed at once, pulling on my boxer briefs and scooping up my jeans. "I'm on my way. Is everything okay? Is Hana…"

"Hana's good. She's coming back this evening with Blake and Hutch."

"What's going on?" Walking to my armoire, I notice a yellow Post-It on the floor beside the nightstand.

Picking it up, I see a note, *Something came up. Had to head back to Thornton. Will text asap. -R.*

"Come over, and I'll fill you in."

Frowning at the note, I nod. "Give me five minutes."

We disconnect, and I tap out a quick text. **Don't like waking up alone.**

I hit send and pull a brown sweater over my head before stepping into my boots and scooping up my keys.

Scar's in the kitchen with Norris when I arrive, and a platter of fresh scones is on the bar.

The old butler is flustered, but he's a pro at taking care of this house and Hugh and Hugh's guests. "Would you like some coffee, Mr. Dirk?"

"Sure, thanks." I don't even bother asking him to drop the Mister for the hundredth time. "What's this all about?"

Scar steps forward, placing his phone on the cypress bar between us. "I came home early this morning, and I was headed to my place when the motion detectors went off."

He taps the screen, and Hugh's golf cart appears, driving away from the front of the house towards the barn.

Frowning, I back it up and lean in to try and get a better look, but it's too dark to make out the driver. "Someone took a joy ride on Hugh's golf cart?"

"That's what I thought, so I came to investigate."

"Where is it now?"

"Parked behind the barn."

"So they didn't steal it." I glance from him to Norris and back again. "It could've been teenagers pulling a prank. If they returned it, no harm done, right?"

"Except I noticed the back door wasn't closed all the way.

So I came in the house to check on things, and someone was inside."

"Oh!" Norris emits a terrified sound. "I can't even think of such a thing!"

"You saw someone in the house?"

"I didn't see them. A pair of Doc Marten boots were at the back door, so I came in and when I entered Hugh's study, the intruder took off running for the back door. It took me a minute to realize where they were, and by the time I caught up, they were gone, boots and all. Still, I could probably pick up the trail."

I cross my arms, leaning against the bar. "You've got to start locking that door, Norris."

"Mr. Hugh is going to hate that. He likes Hamiltown being the kind of place where doors don't have to be locked."

Scar and I both shift our stance, and I know we're thinking the same thing. It's my six-foot-four, Viking of a partner who states the obvious. "Hamiltown might be that kind of place, but with all the shit we've been through, Hugh's property is not."

"Was anything missing?" I step from the kitchen into the living room, where nothing appears to be disturbed.

"So far I haven't detected anything missing." Norris scurries around topping off everyone's coffee cups. "I'd like to think it's just mischievous teenagers, bored on a Saturday night. Perhaps they were drinking alcohol or smoking marijuana. They're all doing that now."

Scar's brow lowers, and I know he's not about to let it go. My phone buzzes, and I take it from my pocket. When I see the message on the screen, my stomach tightens. It's Reanna.

Sorry to leave. Hope I can explain soon.

I wait for more, but nothing comes. I'm not sure what to make of this message, and after the last few days, I don't like this change, this withdrawal.

"Doc Martens are preferred mostly by young people, but adults also wear them. They were a smaller size, but the brand

has unisex sizing, which again, points to a teen. Or a female."
Scar's still going on about whoever broke in, so I slide the device back into my pocket and try to focus on what he's saying.

When I look up, he's watching me. "You good?"

Forcing my face to relax, I nod. "Yeah, it's all good." It's not, but I can put my concerns on hold.

"Oh, Mr. Dirk," Norris suddenly joins the conversation. "Weren't you supposed to have a guest for the weekend? Shall I make more coffee? Breakfast?"

"Ah, no, that's okay, not necessary." I slide my hand over the tension in my stomach. "She had to head on back, so it's just me."

"I'm sorry to hear that." The older man gives me a sympathetic face.

"Yeah, me too." Scar gives me a knowing grin. "I was looking forward to meeting this mystery lady."

"No mystery. Just bad timing." Even I'm not convinced by my tone.

Reanna is surrounded by mystery.

"Well, if you won't be needing me," Norris straightens, tipping his chin, "I have to prep the house for Mr. Hugh's return."

We assure him we're fine, then head out the back door.

"They waited until everyone was gone, which means they're watching us." Scar has become hypervigilant since Hana became pregnant. I know it's rooted in his past, but I think he might be overreacting this time.

"I've been over here every day working with the horses. It was probably kids playing a prank, maybe truth or dare."

"Check it out." He gets down on one knee, pressing his fingers to the tracks left in the soft ground. "They ran straight to the woods, like they knew where they were going."

More indication to me it's local kids. Everyone is familiar with the woods around this area—either to meet up for keggers or to make out or just to make mischief. I know he won't sleep until he has the answer, so I half-heartedly play along, my mind an hour up the road in Thornton.

While Scar takes off into the woods, I take out my phone, studying the screen. I could tell something was troubling her last night. My mind drifts to my question, *What are we doing?*

Did things get too close? I told her I could help her.

Chasing has never been my style, and I'm not a high-pressure guy. As much as I hate it, the right thing would be to give her space.

The day passes slowly with no text, no word. I humor Scar in his search for clues. The intruder took off on foot and ran through the woods, where he or she took a break to change clothes or retrieve a bag. The array of leaves tells him they searched for something here.

It's pretty amazing the way he can piece such things together from sticks and leaves, scuff marks on the lichens growing on exposed tree roots. I can find just about anything or anyone on the web, dark and light, but Scar's part bloodhound.

Hutch always bragged about his abilities when they were in the military together in eastern Europe. My brother was a Marine, and Scar was his assigned translator and scout. He never said it, but when Scar showed up in our office wanting to join our team, it was the best day of my brother's life, until Blake entered the picture.

The sun is lowering when Hutch, Blake, and Hana arrive, and they come straight to Hugh's. Scar filled him in on what we've been able to uncover so far.

"I think we might be overreacting," I suggest gently.

Hana waddles up to her broody husband, and he relaxes for the first time all day. "I can't even remember the last time I drove that golf cart," she says. "Where did I leave it?"

"It should've been parked in Hugh's garage." A touch of scolding is in Hutch's tone.

Blake puts her hand on his arm as if to say it's okay. "Wherever it was, it's here now. Isn't that the important thing?"

"Except someone was in the house." Scar's deep voice is ominous, and Hana's eyes blink wide.

"That's a little terrifying. Should we have Uncle Hugh stay with us a few days until we're sure it's not... someone bad?"

Her dark blue eyes flicker from her husband to me to Hutch, and my brother shifts in his stance. "Hugh has a body-guard. I can call the sheriff and see if they've had any reports of breaking and entering around town lately. We could put them on alert to what happened."

They're doing everything right, and my restlessness has reached an all-time high. "I've got to head back to campus for the night."

"What?" Hana's the first to complain. "We just got back. You can't leave."

"I'll be back tomorrow." *Maybe.* "I just remembered... I forgot to do something."

My brother and Scar are watching me like they know I'm full of shit, but I kiss Hana and Blake's cheeks and jog out to my waiting Jeep.

Before I get on the road, I send one text. ***Miss L, Report to my office at 8 tonight. Don't make me come find you. -Professor***

CHAPTER 21

Reanna

CAMPUS IS EMPTY WHEN I ARRIVE, AND I DON'T STOP UNTIL I'M locked in my dorm room, completely alone. I sit on the bed and carefully take out the book that's been burning a hole in my messenger bag the entire drive home, the entire trip across campus, to here.

It's almost anti-climactic when I open the cover and music doesn't play, lights don't shine from the pages. To the average observer, it would appear to be a simple list of names with numbers in columns beside them, a basic accounting record.

The difference is I know all of these names by heart, starting with the most significant, *Petrovich*, owner of all the accounts and recipient of the deposits. *VP-K* is written small, in ink on the inside cover, which means Victor Petrovich kept the records. Simon gave the orders.

Sliding my finger down the rows, I read their assets, their deposits, their withdrawals, and their payments. Sidorov, Devney, Ivanov, Lourdnikov, the names continue, page after page, spanning a period of more than twenty years, until my heart stops at the letters ZP, Zander Petrovich.

Natasha thinks I don't know who he is, but I've been sneaking into the office at Gibson's for years, searching through documents, reading and trying to find this information. I've seen the birth certificates, and I know what I have in my hands.

The dates line up, along with the word *Terminated*. It's an enormous sum of money, property, assets, and it was simply moved in two bullets and two strokes of a pen to *VP* and *SP*. Right here in his own ledger, he had the nerve to record what he did.

Victor Petrovich was a monster, but he was the uncontrolled, ragey type of demon. Simon Petrovich was Satan, calm, always in control, the leader.

I know Zander was part of it, whether by choice or by coercion. I don't know if he was trying to get out, trying to get clean. I only know we were hiding, living a different life far away from their evil. We lived quietly, simply. We had a happy home, full of love, until they gunned him down in cold blood, before my eyes.

I have the proof he was part of it now, the proof they terminated him and took everything he had, including me. All that's left is to prove they lied. They were thieves stealing their brother's birthright, and as much as I hate it, I have to go back to New York to finish this.

Lying on my side, the memories of that last day wash over me again, playing with my nesting doll, lining up all the pieces, the grandma and the mamma and the sisters, all the way down to the little baby no bigger than a grain of rice. I was so terrified I'd lose her. Then the shooting broke out, and I scooped them up so fast.

I ran as hard as I could on little child legs, but when I got there, it was too late. He was gone, and I was taken like so much collateral to that enormous house in Minsk then to New York. I was property, a pawn in their game. I'm still not sure why they didn't kill me, too. Is it because I was a little girl? Is it because they thought I'd never find out? Is it because they believed I was too weak to matter?

Closing my eyes, I remember his dark hair and ice-blue eyes. He had the kindest smile. He taught me to sand and paint the furniture he made. He taught me to hunt and to track and to build a fire. I can still feel his large hands guiding my small ones, his patient words as I learned. We would sit, and he would tell me about my family of strong men and women, conquerors who helped settle that brutal terrain. He told me I was like my mother, fierce and protective, a fighter who loved with all her heart. He told me she loved me. He told me I could survive anything.

My phone buzzes, waking me, and I realize I fell asleep.

I'm not in the mood for Natasha's crap, so I leave the device on the bed and walk to the window, gazing out at the lavender twilight settling on the horizon. I'm cold, and my chest aches. I want to see Dirk.

Resting my forehead against the windowsill, I try to think of a way I could ever see him again. We didn't get a proper goodbye, but I don't want that. I never want to tell him goodbye. I still cling to that dream like a subconscious wish. *You don't have to fight alone anymore...*

If only that were true, but it's not.

My heart hurts, and I know the way my story ends. I'm always alone.

Opening my laptop, I book a plane ticket to New York departing early in the morning. I know I won't be coming back here, and sadness is a hollow space in my chest. The confirmation comes through, and I send the boarding pass to my phone. It's when I finally pick up the device and see two notifications.

One is the ticket and the other tightens my stomach. *Miss L, Report to my office at 8 tonight. Don't make me come find you. -Professor*

I have just enough time to shower.

Damp wind sweeps the dead leaves across the sidewalk, and I'm in a low-cut sweater, short skirt, and thigh-high tights as I race across campus. A cold change is coming, and the swirling air is driving rain ahead of the front, but I'm not even wearing a coat.

My body is flushed with the heat of anticipation, lust, and need. I move like a woman obsessed, my vision focused on the tall building ahead and all the dirty, wicked, forbidden delights waiting for me inside it.

I shouldn't do this. It'll only complicate things, but I'm an addict. Rational thinking has left my mind, and my body demands my drug, his strong arms, his full mouth, his rigid cock.

Lights are scattered along my route, but small patches of darkness remain under trees and near bushes. I'm oblivious to all of it. The campus is deserted, and I have no fear of being caught flying to him, no need to sneak.

I'm across the central lawn when I notice a dark shadow moving near a tree a few paces ahead of me. The hair on my arms prickles, and I have a flashback of the hay maze when student actors lurked in the dark corners waiting to rush out and scare us.

Only those were actors with rules and limits, and I'm alone on an empty college campus in the middle of the night.

Slowing my pace, I fall back on my self-defense training. I know the best defense is avoiding danger, and I shouldn't race up on a lurker hiding in the bushes. It could be nothing, or it could be someone with bad intentions. Still, I'm not about to turn around with satisfaction so close to my grasp.

I'm breathing fast, walking slowly, when an involuntary shiver moves through my limbs. I have to pass that tree in order to enter the building. Squaring my shoulders, I decide to go for it, holding my head high and walking fast, purposefully to the door that will lead me to him.

I don't get five paces when the figure steps out in front of me, directly in my path. Blackness shrouds his features, but even obscured, I know who he is. His long hair is pulled back, and I manage to get out a short scream before the cloth is over my mouth and nose, and the world goes dark.

When I open my eyes again, I'm alone in a small room with a desk and chair facing bookshelves. My head hurts, and my vision is foggy. My mouth is dry and tastes like a penny. Silence surrounds me.

It takes several seconds of blinking to make out this place. A narrow, black filing cabinet stands beside the desk and bookshelves. The opposite wall is covered with maps and pictures and letters. It reminds me of something out of a crime movie where clues are arranged on top of notes, and everything is tied together with yarn wrapped around thumbtacks.

Shaking my head, I try to stand, but only rise an inch before being jerked back down by my wrists. I'm handcuffed to the chair, and I have no idea where I am.

The last thing I remember is...

The doorknob rattles, and a key is inserted. A click, and the wooden door opens inward, revealing Scar Lourde standing in the doorway, scowling. I'm not afraid of him, although I suppose I ought to be. It's hard to be afraid of anything with the pounding in my temples.

"Did you drug me?" My voice is sandpaper.

He lifts his chin, walking in and going to the desk, where he crosses his arms, studying me. Fine, he doesn't have to answer. Seconds pass, and he doesn't speak. His wolf eyes narrow, and I can't tell if he's trying to decide what to say or if he's waiting for me to confess.

"Where are we?" I ask.

"Somewhere no one knows to look." His voice is rough and smokey, and I remember. *Scar's secret room…*

He places a hand on the desk beside him, lifting the ledger I stole and holding it in the air. "What do you want with this?"

My eyes narrow, and I purse my lips. Now it's my turn for silence, primarily because I'm not sure the safest answer. Also, because I'm not a snitch. Not that I'm loyal to Natasha. I'm simply not sure I'll get what I want by cooperating with this guy.

He slaps it down on the desk again, rising to his full height. "You lied to my partner. You spent six weeks running a con. What do you have to say for yourself?"

"It's not what you think."

"It's exactly what I think. I know who you are, Rainey Sidorova."

Nodding, my eyes fall to the floor. Guilt by association. No matter what I say, I'm the enemy, so I might as well show my cards. I'm not getting out of this chair without his help.

"You think you know me, but you don't. I'm not part of their criminal organization. I was brought into it as a child, against my will, just like you were, and I want to get out like you did."

"I wasn't brought into it against my will." His tone is sharp. "I joined Simon because I lost everything. Then I learned who they were and what they did, and I walked away. But I was never free until he died. Now you're here. Why? Are you trying to drag me back?"

His eyes are deadly serious, and I know his story. The last time I saw him, I was hiding in Gibson's, trying to fade into the curtains, and he was making a deal with the devil.

"I'm trying to find the people who killed my father. They took everything from me, and I want to bring them down. If you would be willing to come back, I could use your help."

"Sounds like a convenient lie to me. You broke into Hugh's home, stole this ledger, and booked a one-way ticket to Manhattan. You expect me to believe you want my help?"

"No." My chin drops. He's right. There's no way he should believe me. "I can only tell you the truth."

"The truth." He huffs a laugh. "Pretty sure you never learned the meaning of that word, little girl."

My stomach sinks. "Then what's the point in holding me?"

"For starters, you've evolved into a clever spy as well as a liar, and I want to know why. I want to know what Natasha is after in this ledger, and I can't have you running back to warn her."

"Natasha is trying to revive their operation. She wants to be the leader, and she thinks that book is going to help her do it."

"Their operation is dead. The men are all gone, and nothing is going to bring it back."

"She's determined to try. She wants to be the leader, and she thinks that book will give her legitimacy."

He's silent, pushing off the desk and walking to the wall, where pictures of Victor and Simon are marked off in red. For a long while, he studies the photographs as if he's thinking about my words. He was in this world long before me, so perhaps he's remembering something—or reliving it. Finally, his chin drops, and he exhales deeply.

"I want them to stay dead." He's chillingly calm. "I'm done looking over my shoulder. I want peace. I want to live my life and raise my family without fear."

"You'll never have that as long as any of them remain. Neither of us can." I study his massive frame. Even with his strength, he can't stop a bullet, and he knows it. It's the only leverage I could possibly have. "Simon killed my father, and I'm trying to prove it. Help me."

"Simon is dead." He turns to face me. "It doesn't matter if he killed your father; he can't be punished anymore."

"But the machine is still in place. It's damaged, but Natasha is more dangerous than you think. She will put it back together, and they will come after you."

"I know what Natasha wants." Scar's voice is grave. "She

wants the same thing as you. She wants the man who killed her father."

"That's not all she wants. She wants everything, the money, the power, the glory, all of it. Nothing is going to stop her."

"Something will stop her." His ice-blue gaze lands on mine, and I know what he means, or more precisely who he means. "I'll return this ledger to your boss. In the meantime, you're not going anywhere. I have someone coming to keep an eye on you, and he won't let you get away with shit."

"Who..." The question slips out on a nervous whisper.

He continues, "I know your type. I know you're trained to lie. Now he'll know it, too."

"Scar?" A male voice echoes from the front of the house, and my heart freezes.

No...

"Back here," Scar calls.

I'm not ready.

Panic grips my throat, and I can't breathe. Fear shakes my ribs like bars on a cage, and I jerk against the handcuffs as the low thud of boots grows closer in the hall, as dread rises like bile in my stomach.

"Don't. Please..." It's a desperate plea for mercy, a supplication from the bottom of my soul as my shoulder rises, and I shrink lower. "Please please please..."

My voice cracks, and my vision blurs as the door shimmers and starts to move. An invisible sledgehammer swings as it opens, and when our eyes meet, it slams into my heart, smashing it into a million pieces.

CHAPTER 22

Dirk

IGHT O'CLOCK CAME AND WENT, AND REANNA NEVER APPEARED. Scooping up my phone, I sent a short text. ***I will come to your dorm and get you.***

Hunger drove me, and my dick demanded satisfaction. Campus was empty, and a fantasy of storming into her room, throwing her over my shoulder, and carrying her to my bed made me smile. She does like it rough...

The text I received next wasn't what I expected. It was Scar. ***I need you to get back to Hamiltown now. I caught the intruder.***

"Fuck," I growled, typing a fast reply. ***Tonight's bad. Can it wait until tomorrow?***

Gray dots, and his reply is short. ***Need you back here now.***

In any other situation, I'd argue I'm off the clock, I have prior commitments, but in spite of his overprotective tendencies these days, when Scar says it's serious, it is.

Exhaling heavily, I send her a final text, ***Must go to H'town, but want to see you tonight.***

I don't even bother packing a bag. I head for my waiting Jeep and floor it down the empty highway. Traffic is light, and in less than an hour, I'm pulling up to Scar's house.

The one-bedroom cottage is usually open and well-lit. He built it in a clearing on the edge of town near the woods, and just about everything in it is hand-made by him. Tonight, as I park in the driveway, it looks like no one is home.

Stepping out, a chill is in the humid air, and the damp makes it feel colder. The clouds are growing thick, and the weather is changing. Dry leaves fall in the occasional, sudden gust of wind, and my boots crunch as I walk up the gravel drive. It smells like fall, and the metallic taste of rain is on my tongue.

I'm frustrated to be back here without seeing Reanna. I'm worried that she hasn't replied to any of my texts since yesterday. I don't think she's in trouble, but she did mention unfinished business and revenge. The idea something might have happened has me on edge, and I want to wrap this up here and head back ASAP.

The front door is unlocked, and I open it slowly to a dark kitchen. "Scar?" I call, stepping inside and looking all around.

"Back here." His low voice echoes from the small room in the middle of the short hall.

It's a secret office he keeps locked at all times. It contains his old files from when he wasn't on the good side of the law. It also contains records we've collected, items we hold onto for leverage, and maps of the cases we've worked on as well as other things. Hell, there's no telling what all is stored in there.

Reaching for the doorknob, I turn it, opening it quickly and stepping inside. "What have you got to show me…?"

My voice dies, and I feel like I've stepped through the looking glass. I see what's before me, but my brain won't make it make sense.

Scar is leaning against the small desk with his arms crossed and his brow lowered. He's holding the slim ledger Hugh got from Simon's rat, the same one I spent weeks researching at the start of that twisted case.

I don't know why he has it, and I don't care. It's the person sitting in front of him, the woman handcuffed to a chair, I can't understand.

It's Reanna.

Her head is bowed, her long, dark hair hangs in silky curtains past her cheeks, and she doesn't look at me when I enter.

"Scar, what…" I take a staggered step forward. "What the hell?"

"Recognize this?" He holds up the book.

"Of course. What about it?"

He pushes off the desk and walks straight to where Reanna sits, gripping her chin and lifting her face to me. Our eyes meet for half a second before she closes hers, and a lone tear hits her cheek.

"You've never met this one in person—at least not using her true identity." Scar's voice is a rough growl, a hint of his almost-gone Russian accent lacing the words. "Dirk Winston, meet Rainey Sidorova, Natasha Petrovna's right hand. She was sent here to retrieve this book and bring it back to her boss in New York."

My stomach twists, and disbelief fights against his words. "Rainey?"

"She's not my boss." Her teeth grind. "I'm not her right hand, that's Rick Ivanov."

The sound of his name flashes rage in my chest. "Rick Ivanov is the guy who blackmailed Hana." My muscles shake. "The one who drugged and abused her."

"It would seem they're comrades."

"We're not…" Rainey snaps, and Scar releases her chin with a flick of his wrist.

"I'd advise you to speak carefully."

Turning away, I heave out a breath. Fury knots in my throat, and humiliation burns my chest. My fingers curl into fists, and I'm struggling for control. I'm struggling not to turn around and slam her against the wall.

"I'm going to New York to get to the bottom of this. Hutch is coming with me. He's already ordered the private jet." Scar takes a key out of his desk and hands it to me. "I need you to keep her here while we're gone."

"Wait… I can't stay here," Rainey's voice is desperate. Her eyes flicker from him to me, but I turn away from her. "I need to go with you."

"Your butt's not going anywhere." Scar collects his phone, his handgun, and the book before going to the door.

"Weren't you listening to anything I said?" Her voice breaks.

"Yeah, I was listening. It's a good story. It makes a lot of sense, and it sure lets you off the hook."

"No." She struggles against the cuffs, but I follow Scar into the hall, shutting the door.

He pauses, speaking low. "Keep her here, or she'll jeopardize everything. Don't let her out of your sight, and don't listen to her. She'll lie. It's all they know to do."

Through the door, I hear her yell. "It's not true. I'm not one of them. I'm trying to help."

My stomach cramps, and I'm so angry, I need to get away from that sound. "I'll keep her here."

"I've talked to Hutch. He's going to bring in Louie."

"The cop?"

"Yeah. I'll arrange a meeting at Gibson's so you'll be able to monitor everything. Listen, and if anything happens, get Louie on the line. He can get there faster than anyone."

"I'm on it." I nod, following him to the kitchen.

"Hana is staying with Blake. We're planning to be back by the weekend, and we'll deal with our captive then." He takes a canvas bag off the bar, and stepping back, he grips my shoulder. "This time we're getting rid of these assholes for good."

He disappears into the night, and I step out onto the back porch. I didn't pack a bag, which means I need to go to my place and gather some things to stay here. Walking back into the house, I assess the situation.

Scar's cottage has only one bedroom, but with the anger churning in my stomach, I have no problem letting her sleep in that chair or on the floor. All of this has just happened, which means he's leaving her needs in my hands. I can't dwell on what I think she needs. She's a prisoner, and I have to think like a warden.

My boots scuff the wood floors as I return to the small office. My brain is slowly piecing together all the ways she used me, from the very first day she appeared in my office pretending to be a victim, pretending to need my help.

She wasn't a student, and she sure as hell wasn't a victim. She was there so she could get here via me. Only, I'm sure *here* is not where she intended to be—according to Scar, she had a one-way ticket to New York.

All the texts I sent, her unfinished business... I was never going to see her again.

Closing my eyes, my jaw grinds remembering how I waited for her in my office, eager, believing, ultimately worrying. *Fuck.* Standing in that hall, those feelings morph into something bitter and raw in my chest. Placing my hand on the door, I hesitate, breathing deeply to fight off my base desire to hurt her for hurting me.

I don't enter the room. I don't want to look at her. I only open the door a crack.

"I'm going to my place to get some things. I'll be back."

She doesn't answer, and I pull the door closed again.

Turning the key in the lock, I place it on the ledge above the door. Walking out to my Jeep, I look across the vacant yard at the tall trees swaying in the wind.

Scar's place isn't too far from mine, and I'd give anything to be wearing running shoes. I want to run long and hard. I want to do something that will burn these feelings out of my chest. I want to get away from the flicker trying not to die, the pain that reminds me I loved her.

Gripping the sides of my forehead, I close my eyes against it. I'm not going there. I'm a professional. I'm trained to deal with all kinds of shit, and that's all this is. More bullshit.

Parking outside my house, I push back on the memory of bringing her here in the dark, the way her eyes lit and she ran around admiring the ancient weaving machines. I walk past them without a second glance, jogging up the steps to the main level. I resist remembering how she turned, amazed at the work I'd done here, sliding her fingers over my furniture as she walked around the place.

Going to the armoire, I take down my bag, stuffing underwear, jeans, and extra shirts for me. I take out a pair of sweatpants and a long-sleeved tee for her. It's getting cold. I take the corduroy blazer I wore home off the back of a chair, tucking my hand in the pocket.

"Fuck," I growl, when I pull out a micro thong.

Fury twists my insides, and my fist shakes as I tighten it over the scrap of elastic and silk. Surges of need knot my stomach, as if my body doesn't understand why this is a bad thing. I throw the offensive undergarment in the small trash can beside my nightstand.

More lies, more manipulation.

The bed is unmade, and my eyes linger on the rumpled pillows and twisted sheets. She played her part very well. I haven't fucked like that in… ever.

Scooping the book off my bedside table, I go to the bathroom and grab my deodorant and toothbrush. I've got to get out of this place.

Maybe later, when all this is over, I'll burn it to the ground.

Scar's place is as I left it when I return, and I drop my bag in the kitchen, reaching inside for the extra pair of boxer briefs, a long-sleeved tee, and sweatpants I brought for her. Seeing her won't get any easier, and I decide to rip off the Band-Aid now.

I take a bottle of water out of the refrigerator and go to the small room. Taking the key off the ledge, I unlock the door and open it abruptly. Her head shakes, and she seems to rouse from sleep. Her eyes are smudged like she's been crying, and I don't care. The pinch in my stomach is a liar. Just like her.

"I brought you some water." I place the bottle on the floor. "And these."

"Thank you." Her voice is raspy, just above a whisper.

The keys to the handcuffs are on the desk, and I pick them up slowly. "I'm going to unlock those, and if you start anything, I will finish it."

Fixing my eyes on hers, she only meets my gaze briefly before nodding. I can only assume the ferocity of my feelings is apparent in my eyes. She'd be a fool to try anything.

Stepping closer, the faint scent of jasmine surrounds me, and I part my lips to breathe through my mouth. I don't need her scent lying to me.

I unlock one cuff, freeing her hand but leaving the bracelet hooked to the chair. Moving to the other side, I do the same, and her arms drop limply at her sides before she lifts them, slowly crossing them over her chest.

Straightening, I step back. "Do you need to use the restroom?"

"Yes." Her voice is just above a whisper, and she reaches down to take the water bottle.

"This way." I wait as she stands slowly, a little wobbly.

She holds a moment, swaying slightly in place, and I do not reach out to help her. When she's ready to walk, I lead her to the small, windowless half bathroom in the hall. Stepping inside, I do a quick sweep, checking for razors or scissors or anything that could be used as a weapon.

Finding nothing, I step back and allow her to go inside. "Don't lock the door or I'll kick it in."

Again, a silent nod is her only response. She closes the door, and I carry my bag to Scar's bedroom. I don't have a choice but to sleep in his bed, and I glance around for what I might arrange for her.

Returning to the living room, an oversize wicker basket sits at the end of the couch. It's filled with blankets, and I lift out all of them. Carrying them to the room, I arrange a pallet on the floor near the wrought iron and stone nightstand.

I'm not sure my partner had this in mind when he chose these furnishings, but it'll do nicely. Returning to the small room, I take one set of handcuffs off the chair then stop at the bathroom.

"Time's up." I knock hard on the door, and it opens at once.

She has changed into the sweat pants and long-sleeved tee. My clothes are enormous on her small frame, and the sight of her peaked nipples pressing through the soft cotton floods my memory with our weekend together. Turning away from that fresh slice of pain, I tell myself I don't care about her body in my clothes.

"This way." I nudge her with my bag in the direction of Scar's bedroom.

We enter the door, and she looks around, her eyes going from the large king-size bed filling the room to the small, makeshift pallet on the floor.

Walking to it, she kneels, moving the blankets aside as if she'll make herself comfortable.

"Just a minute." I step forward with the handcuffs.

Dropping to one knee, I attach one side to the iron base of the nightstand. When I reach for her left wrist, it all goes to shit.

"Dirk…" Her voice is a choked whisper. "I'm sorry…"

All the hurt and anger, the humiliation and loss explode like a gas fire in my veins, and my hand shoots out to grab her face. "Don't speak to me."

She blinks rapidly, fighting tears, but her eyes never leave mine. "I need to—"

Gripping my palm over her lips, I inhale slowly, struggling to calm myself. "If you say another word, I'll tape your mouth shut."

Her eyes slide closed, and she nods, dropping her chin. I remove my hand, wiping the damp stain of her tears off my skin and finish cuffing her to the table. Then I stand, snatch up my bag, and go to the bathroom.

Slamming the door shut, I switch on the shower and turn to lean on the counter. Every time I close my eyes, I see hers. Every time I try to force hate, I want to fall apart. For six weeks she owned me, and I wanted her with every waking breath.

The only thing that can kill it is my anger. I won't be used like that again by her or anyone.

CHAPTER 23

Rainey

YING ON MY BACK IN THE DARKNESS, TEARS COAT MY CHEEKS AS THE
pain collapses my chest. The sides of my cheeks throb from
his hand squeezing them so hard. I closed my eyes, bracing
for the hit I knew he wanted to deliver, the strike I knew I
deserved.

Against all logic, I believed I could have his love and have
what I wanted. I got lost in my own desires, and then I lost control of the narrative. Now I've lost him. The truth of it curls
me into a ball, loss tearing me apart from within.

I've retraced every mistake I made since the beginning. My
assignment wasn't to sleep with him. I said I wouldn't sleep
with him for a book, and I didn't. I slept with him because he
was everything I'd never had. He wanted me, and with him,
I wasn't alone.

He's beautiful and smart and funny and possessive and
strong and passionate. He healed my wounds and stopped the

nightmares. He was the fire burning deep in my soul, feeding me, giving me life.

Pulling my knees to my chest, dressed in his clothes, I'm surrounded by his scent, and it hurts so much. Still, I bury my face in his shirt, needing him more than air.

I crave the barbed wires cutting into my heart and making me bleed. I want to atone for what I've done, even while I know I never will. I'll never stop seeing the betrayal in his eyes when he walked through that door.

If I'd told him before, in his bed this weekend, would I still be here? He would've been angry, but he would've had control. I turn my cheek against my handcuffed arm extended over my head. My heart drains out through my eyes until I have nothing left.

I still want him, but he'll never want me.

Again, I'm alone. Only this time I have no hope.

"Get up." He pushes me with his foot, and I squint against the morning sunlight.

My hand is uncuffed, and I lower my aching arm. I don't care if it hurts. I want to feel pain. Anything besides the numbness of my frozen insides.

He nudges me with the bag into the hall, and I go to the small bathroom to clean up and use the toilet. After five minutes, he's back, and I emerge to be led to the secret room, where again, I'm cuffed to the chair.

He doesn't speak. He doesn't look at me, but my hungry eyes steal glances at him. His dark hair is messy, and he's wearing jeans and his green Henley. His lean muscles ripple beneath the fabric as he pulls out the chair and sits in front of a laptop.

I watch as he types on the keyboard, pulling up the same live feed he showed me in his office in town. He's watching the hidden cameras at Gibson's, but no one is in view right now. I don't know where my phone is, but I'm sure Natasha is blow-ing it up. I'm sure it won't take long before this entire situation blows up, and if it does, I'm ready to be collateral. I want to be taken out of this battle.

A knock on the door out front makes him stand. He looks at me for the first time, and dark circles are under his sexy hazel eyes. I wonder if he slept. I'm surprised I did.

At the clash of our gaze, he winces, and my stomach twists. His pain increases my pain, and my fingers curl. I want to reach for him. I want to bathe him with my tears and vow to make it up to him. I want to tell him I love him.

I thought he might speak, but he only leaves the room, shutting the door behind him. Leaning forward, my chin falls to my chest.

"Good morning, big brother!" Hana's voice comes through the door from what I remember is the kitchen. "I've come for my stuff, and Norris sent a smorgasbord."

"Hey, thanks, babe." His affectionate voice is warm honey in my veins. "Get whatever you need. I'm just keeping an eye on things here."

"Scar said you're watching the bad guys. I told him that was so uncool." Her voice calls from the bedroom where we slept. "You left Hamiltown so you could stop doing all this. And you have a girlfriend now."

Drawers open and close in the next room, and I wince at his rough answer. "It's okay. We broke up."

"Oh no!" Her voice is in the hall again, passing as she re-turns to where he's waiting. "What happened?"

"Ah, you know. Same story, new day. Relationships are al-ways fucking drama."

"Don't tell me. She wanted more, and you ran away again." Her voice turns teasing. "Are you going to play the bachelor forever?"

"No, actually. It wasn't like that." His voice is husky, and through two walls of wood, I can hear his pain. "She wasn't who I thought she was."

Tears sting my eyes. *But I was…*

"I'm so sorry." Hana's voice is kind, and I imagine her hugging him.

"I'll be okay. I'm a big boy. But I have to get back to watching—you good?"

She exhales a little noise. "I'll be better in three more weeks, once this little guy is on the outside."

"Scar's bad enough with only you. Add a baby boy, and I can't even imagine."

"It's going to be wild," she laughs.

"Get some rest."

"I will. Don't work too hard. I'll be back with lunch."

With that, she's gone, and the thump of boots returns up the hall. My breath catches as the door opens, and seeing him is another smack of pain in my face.

His brow is lowered, and he's holding a paper plate with two muffins. "Breakfast."

He sets the food on the desk before leaving again. When he returns, he's holding a paper cup of coffee and a TV tray, which he unfolds and places beside me. Then he leans down and uncuffs my right hand.

The proximity of him leaning over me, his warmth passing by my face, is almost unbearable. I want to rest my forehead against his neck and feel the heat of his skin, but I've lost that right.

He walks to the desk and sits, taking out his phone and checking for texts. I hesitate a moment, but the cramping in my stomach tells me I need to eat.

Using one hand, I break off little pieces and put them in my mouth. It's warm cinnamon and smoky walnuts. The coffee is delicious, and I'm revived by the food and drink.

Dirk is in and out, keeping an eye on the cameras while keeping his eyes off me. His rejection hurts, but ironically, being near him also comforts me. He's the only man I've wanted to be close to since my father's murder.

Before noon, he uncuffs my hands and takes my arm. My breath catches when he touches me. It's the first time since last night when he grabbed my face, and the strength of his anger seems to have eased some.

Still, I don't speak as he leads me to the restroom and pushes me inside, closing the door. It's almost as if he wants the wooden barrier between us, and I wonder if he aches for me as much as I do for him.

I'm washing my hands when I hear voices in the kitchen again, and I shut off the water. Closing the toilet lid, I sit, wondering if I'm allowed to go out there when visitors are here. Am I a secret?

Chewing my nail, I wait, listening as Dirk tells them what's happening. "Scar texted he made contact. He set up a meeting, but they won't see her until tomorrow."

I wonder if Scar told Natasha he's holding me prisoner. He had to have told her about the book. It's the only way Natasha would've agreed to see him. She's afraid of his strength, and her only muscle is Rick and possibly Marco, although I doubt he'll fight for her.

The visitors, who I assume are Blake and Hana, leave, and he returns to the door, tapping shortly before opening it.

"Come and eat lunch."

For a moment, I hesitate. Is he not going to handcuff me to the chair again? Opening the door slowly, I step into the hall and walk to the kitchen. I thought too soon, because as soon as I arrive, he slaps the cuff around my left wrist and attaches it to the arm of a heavy barstool.

"Okay," I whisper, jumping at the sound that slipped out of my lips.

My eyes fly to his, but he walks around the bar, taking out sandwiches and soft drinks. He gives me another bottle of water, and I pick up what looks like a chicken salad sandwich.

Taking a bite, I have the flashback of a memory from when I was a teenager. Blake would make these sandwiches for us when we visited her condo in New York. It almost makes me want to cry, which I don't understand.

He takes his food and leaves me, returning to the small office. My appetite disappears with his departure, and I pick at the bread. After several minutes, he returns, taking my paper plate and studying it for a moment. He glances at me without smiling, and I shrug. I haven't been given permission to speak, and I'm not sure if it would be worse to try and talk to him or to remain silent.

Turning he carries the plate to the refrigerator and places it inside. Again, without a word, he unfastens the handcuff from the chair, leading me by the metal restraint to the bedroom and hooking me to the small table on the floor again.

"I'm going to my place, then I'm going for a long jog."

My lips part, and I'm about to answer when he leaves, shutting the door, and I drop back on my behind. Looking around the empty room, I see a king-size bed with a white duvet and gray sheets. Pictures are on the dresser of Scar and Hana, more of the little girl softball players, and one of Blake with Training Day.

My eyes move to the nightstand, and I see the beat-up copy of *Goblet of Fire*. Crawling closer, I pick it up and open the cover. The picture drops out, and I lift it, studying his young face.

I remember lying in his bed as he read to me, and I remember his words, *I stopped trusting anyone until I was completely alone…*

We were both completely alone, but he trusted me. Hugging the book to my chest, I place my hand over my eyes. I don't want to cry anymore. I want him to hear me. I want him to believe me… and one day to trust me again.

I wake to the sound of water running in the bathroom. The room is dark, and the book is back on the nightstand. Sitting up, I rub my eyes, but I don't have my phone, and there isn't a clock anywhere I can see.

The noise of the shower ends, and I wait, listening until the door opens. He steps into the room and pauses when he sees me sitting up.

"I picked up dinner in town." He looks down, then glances to the bathroom.

The muscle in his jaw moves as if he considers offering me a shower. He must think better of it, because he walks over to where I'm sitting, leaning down to take the cuff off the table. He waits as I stand, and again, he leads me by the restraint to the kitchen.

I'm again fastened to the barstool, and I wait as he takes out containers of cole slaw, mac and cheese, and sandwiches from Slim Harold's. This time he doesn't take his food and leave. He stands at the bar and shovels large bites into his mouth as I sit and watch before lifting the plastic fork and eating a few bites of cheesy elbow noodles with a crispy parmesan crust.

Skipping lunch has me ravenous, and after the first few bites, I'm eating more. I wish I could take a shower, but I imagine that might be a bridge too far at present.

When we're done, he walks me to the bathroom, leaving me alone to wash up, brush my teeth, and take care of business. I hear when he exits the small room to fetch me, and we return to the bedroom, where I'm fastened to the nightstand again.

He kneels in front of me as he attaches the metal to the base, and when he lifts his head our eyes meet for the first time since he returned. Heat burns in my chest, and I see it reflected in his eyes. Just as fast, it morphs into anger.

His jaw tightens and he turns away, walking to the door. I think he'll leave, and swallowing the fear in my throat, I take a chance.

"Are you angry because you fell for me?" My voice is scratchy from lack of use, and I clear it.

He stops, and I shudder, wondering if he'll leave without a

word, if he'll go to the office and return with the duct tape, or if he'll double back and slap me. He does none of these things.

"I'm angry because I was worried about you." His voice has a quiet edge. "I actually wasted time thinking our relationship might jeopardize your future, but you planned it all from the first day. None of it was real, and you were willing to risk my reputation, my livelihood, everything for a list of names."

"I had one job." It sounds so stupid now. "I didn't expect it to be... *you*."

"It was all a lie."

"It wasn't all a lie." He might not believe me, but it's true. "I didn't have a choice—everything I told you about my past was true. My father was murdered, they took me when I was a child. I'm convinced they killed him, and I have to find out why."

He's quiet, and I'm not sure he believes me. "Your people abused Hana, one of the sweetest people I know. They raped her and blackmailed her for a revenge porn film. Made her think she killed a man."

Lowering my chin, regret aches in my chest. My hatred for them, for my guilt by association with them, is an unquenchable source of despair. If I could get out of here, I could do something to help. Maybe then he'd believe me.

"I didn't know about that." My voice is quiet. "I only knew Hana had problems."

He exhales sharply. "You honestly think I believe a word you say? Your fucking heart is as cold as your people. If you even have a heart."

He leaves, shutting the door firmly.

I had a heart. I thought I'd lost it, but he helped me find it again.

Now it's broken.

CHAPTER 24

Dirk

I WAKE IN THE NIGHT TO THE SOUND OF WHIMPERS. THE RAIN IS BACK, and a tree sways violently in the breeze outside the window, casting shadows like arms waving. Sitting up in the bed, I think I must've dreamed the cry. My sleep has been restless since I came here, and Rainey's presence keeps me on edge.

During the day, I do my best not to look at her. My anger is hot as ever, but unfortunately, so is my desire. Her submission crawls under my skin making me want to punish her for what she did. Only I sense she wants to be punished, and the kind of punishment I have in mind involves holding her down and fucking her senseless.

It's messing with my mind, and I need Scar to finish what he's doing and get back here, so I can leave and get my head together. Rolling onto my side, I scrub a hand over my forehead, summoning all the horrible things their criminal band has done through the years. It's my defense against these feelings for her that don't want to die.

Hana is the easiest way to refocus my anger. Victor Petrovich abused her for years, then when he died, Rick Ivanov took up the mantle, drugging her, using her for porn, and then blackmailing her with it. Hana spent years in therapy, and she's still scarred by what they did.

Second best is the horse doping racket, which is why Hugh has Training Day. That beautiful horse was tortured, forced to run on injuries, all so those assholes could line their pockets and pay their bookies.

"Give it to me!" Rainey's voice is a broken cry, and I sit up again, panic twisting my chest.

The sound of rustling sheets, the clink of the handcuff jerking against the table leg, another cry. "No, no, no!"

I throw back the blankets, swinging my feet out of the bed and dropping to my knees on the rug. She's on her hands and knees, eyes closed as she digs in the pallet, throwing blankets aside as she frantically searches for some invisible thing, hampered by her arm attached to the nightstand.

"Please, please…" Her voice is shattered, and in the dim light, I see tears on her cheeks. "It's all I have."

Crawling closer, I put my hands on her shoulders. I've heard it's dangerous to wake people in the middle of a nightmare, but I don't know what else to do.

"Rainey, wake up." My voice is quiet but firm. "You're having a nightmare."

She lifts her free arm, slapping me away. "Don't touch me." Again her voice cracks. "I know you did it!"

She's crying, and my instinct is to pull her close, hold her and tell her she's safe, I'm here. Only, that's not what we're doing now. She crawls to the back wall, scooting as if she'll get behind the furniture, and I decide maybe it is.

Crossing the blankets, I pull her to me, away from her hiding place. I turn her so her back is against my chest, and she shivers in my arms.

Wrapping her tighter in my embrace, I speak in her ear. "Wake up now. You're having a dream."

My voice is gentle, calming. Her body stiffens, another shiver, and I shush her again, sliding my hands up and down her arms. My face is in her hair, and the faintest scent of jasmine still clings to her tresses.

A sob jerks her body, and her head turns to the side suddenly. "What's happening?"

Relaxing my hold, I'm reluctant to let her go. "You were having a nightmare." My voice is quiet. "A pretty bad one from the sound of it."

"Oh, God." Her body goes limp in my arms, her head falling forward. "I'm sorry."

Clearing my throat, I force my arms to release her. "No problem." I push into a sitting position beside her, and she reaches for the blankets.

Thunder rumbles low on the horizon, and I feel the shift in my chest. It's not okay, and nothing is forgotten. I rub both hands over my face before pushing off on my knees.

"Get some sleep."

I return to the bed, but wind and rain rage all night. I don't sleep, and I can't tell, but I don't think she's sleeping either. At some point before dawn, the storm passes, and I manage to nod off for an hour or two.

The glow of the dawn rouses me, and I slide out of bed, staggering down the hall to make coffee. This day is critical. At least this evening is. While I wait for the coffee to drip, I return to the bedroom. Rainey is lying on her side with her back to me, so I decide to let her sleep.

I take out my phone and text Scar and Hutch. *I'll be on the cams. Somebody call me so I'll have audio.*

It doesn't take long for Scar to text me back. *We're meeting at five before customers arrive. I'll call. How's our prisoner?*

My thumbs fly as I answer. *No problems here. All prepped for backup.*

I get a thumbs up, and I walk over to pour a cup of coffee. I'm settling in when I hear a voice calling from the bedroom. Walking down the hall, I push the door open to find her sitting up waiting.

"Sorry to bother you. I need to use the restroom."

Bending down, I unlock the cuff from the furniture and straighten, offering my hand this time as well as holding the other end of the bracelet. I won't let her roam free or give her the chance to bolt. I'm not an amateur.

At the same time, I feel certain she's not going to run.

When I hear the flush and the noise of the sink in the half-bathroom in the hall, I return to meet her. Then I lead her to the kitchen and lock her to the chair.

"Coffee?" I hold up a mug, and she nods. "Sorry, we're all out of cinnamon."

A cautious smile presses her lips together. She blinks down, taking the mug and pouring a dollop of cream in it before taking a sip of the warm liquid.

"It's good," she nods, lowering the mug.

I return to the basket, retrieving a couple of muffins. "They're day-old, but they should reheat okay."

"I liked the walnut ones."

I dig a little deeper and pull out a few of those, putting them all on a plate and nuking them for fifteen seconds. When the bell dings, I take them out, putting the dish between us and sitting beside her to eat.

Her eyes are fixed on the muffin as she struggles to break it apart with one hand.

"Here." I reach over and cut it into bite-sized pieces with my fork.

She waits, watching me with her hands in her lap. "Thank you."

A pit is in my stomach, and I stand, going around the bar for more coffee, using the wooden barrier as a form of defense against the pull between us.

Holding the cup, I look out the kitchen window. Several limbs are down in the yard from the storm that passed last night, and the air is clean and chilly. I have several hours to kill before Scar needs me, and I can't spend them in this house fighting these feelings.

When I turn to face her again, her eyes are on her fingers turning a piece of muffin on the plate, but she's not eating. She's blinking in a way that seems like she's fighting some internal battle, and my stomach twists. I tell myself I don't want to know, but she's so small sitting at the table in my shirt and sweatpants. For the first time, she seems ten years younger than me. She seems vulnerable—a view I know is dangerous.

"Everything okay?" I ask, unable to stop myself.

Her lips press together before she lifts her blue eyes to mine. "I'm really sorry about last night. That hasn't happened in a while."

I nod, not sure what to say. She told me she had nightmares, but she didn't tell me how severe they were. She also hadn't told me they'd stopped. I guess that part wasn't a lie.

Setting my mug down, I straighten. "I'm going to clean up some of the mess outside. Would you like to sit out there or... in here?"

"I'd like to sit outside if that's okay."

Wiping my hands, I take a Carhart jacket hanging on the rack and toss it over my arm. She stands, one hand still attached to the barstool, and I slide the right coat sleeve up her arm. Taking out the key, I unhook the cuff from the chair, and she slides her arm in the other sleeve.

Pulling the lapels, I straighten the jacket over her shoulders then fasten the button at her neck. Her eyes lift to mine again, and we're so close. The heat of her body warms mine, and I could dip my face down and kiss her the way I used to do.

Taking a step back, I clear my throat. "Come on." I guide her by the handcuff, not touching her skin, to the porch. "Would you prefer the bench or the swing?"

"Swing, please."

My jaw clenches at her small voice, but I lead her to the wooden swing hanging from the porch ceiling. Locking the cuff around the chain going through the armrest, I turn and walk out to the covered patio. Scar has several small hand tools, a rake, and a large pile of limbs and leaves in a clear spot for burning. I pick up a hatchet and a pair of tree loppers and get started. Nothing's better than manual labor to burn off bull-shit feelings.

Hours later, I'm sweaty and energized, and Scar's yard is completely clear. Throughout the morning, every time I glanced over, she was quietly gliding back and forth on the swing, her blue eyes fixed on me and my progress.

Returning to where she sits, I wipe the sweat off my fore-head with the back of my glove. "I'm heading in to take a shower. Do you need the restroom or anything?"

"Yes, please."

I'm not sure why her soft, simple answers piss me off. It's like she's taunting me with compliance, submission, penance. I roughly unhook her and lift her a little too hard out of the swing. This time I grip her wrist, dragging her across the porch and into the house behind me.

I don't stop until we're at the bathroom, where I open the door and shove her inside. "Don't take too long."

I pull the door closed then go to the kitchen where I take a long drink of ice-cold water, but it only cools my anger slightly. I need a shower. The sound of the toilet flush makes me turn, and I go to the bathroom, banging on the door with my fist. "Let's go."

The door opens, and her eyes are round when she looks up at me as if she's afraid. I don't react. I take her wrist again, lead-ing her to the bedroom and telling her to sit, hooking her to the nightstand before going to the bathroom and closing the door.

Stripping off my sweaty clothes, I switch on the shower and stand beneath the warm spray for several long minutes with my eyes closed. Scar and Hutch's meeting today has to bring some sort of resolution to all this. I can't keep going this way.

Slamming off the water, I turn, grab a towel, and quickly dry myself, tying the cloth around my waist. When I return to the bedroom, she's holding my book again, reading with my picture in her fingers.

I go straight to where she's sitting and snatch it out of her grasp. "This isn't for you."

Her feet shoot out, and she scrambles, pressing her back against the wall, and I feel like an ass. She's not fighting me. I have no reason to be cruel. Still, I'm pissed.

"I'm sorry." Her voice is quiet. "I was just trying to pass the time."

Without an answer, I take the photo and return it to my book before placing it on the nightstand where it belongs. Going around to my bag, I pull out a pair of sweats and a tee, pulling the shirt over my head before going to the bathroom to hang the towel and step into my pants.

When I get back, she's sitting with her legs crossed, studying her fingers. She lifts her head when I enter.

"Dirk…" Her brow furrows, like she's afraid to ask. "I really need to shower. Would it be possible, please, real quick—"

Inhaling deeply, I bend down to unhook the handcuff. "Come on."

I wait until she stands, then I lead her to the bathroom I've just vacated. Steam is on the mirrors, and I look at the large window behind the bathtub. Scar's razor, a pair of scissors, a hand mirror, a set of candles in heavy, stone containers, hell, the iron sculpture over the tub, all of these things can be used to break out or be used as weapons.

Scrubbing the back of my neck, I don't see another option. "I'll have to stay in here with you, but I'll turn my back."

"I'll be quick." She grabs the hem of the tee I gave her to wear, and I turn the minute it starts to rise.

Last thing I need is to see her breasts with the way I'm

feeling. My hands are on the counter, when I realize turning my back doesn't remove the oversized mirrors directly in front of me lining the two walls behind the vanity.

She steps into the glass shower stall and switches on the water, and my eyes drift from my hands on the counter to the mirror. The steam is dissipating, and I can see her smooth back as she holds out her hand, testing the water. When it's acceptable, she steps forward, and I'm not sure if she intends to moan, but she does. It's a charge straight to my dick.

Reaching down, I slide my palm over my semi to calm the raging need her round ass and soft noises provoke. It's when I realize I've made a critical mistake.

CHAPTER 25

Rainey

T HIS MIGHT BE THE BEST SHOWER I'VE HAD IN MY ENTIRE LIFE. For three days I've been stuck in this miserable prison, and while the temperature has been cool and I haven't done any strenuous exercise, I still feel like I'm wearing a second skin. My deodorant failed days ago, and even the clean, citrusy scent in Dirk's clothes is gone.

Forgetting my promise to work quickly, I close my eyes and let the luscious warm water flow over my dirty hair and face. I've been so miserable, this one small comfort is like a lifeline. It's like the warm muffin or the hot coffee, or the feeling of being wrapped in Dirk's arms in the middle of the night, even for just a few moments.

I'd been in hell in my sleep, running from the men who shot my father, terrified. I'd been clinging to my little doll for comfort when Natasha threw it into the fire. My heart was breaking over and over as I lost all the things I held dear, and once again, he saved me from the nightmares.

Only now he's the thing I hold dear, and I don't think I'll ever have him again.

Reaching for the shampoo, I quickly wash my hair. It smells like honeysuckle, and I realize it must belong to Hana. Next, I take the soap and quickly form a lather, running my hands all over my body, under my arms, over my belly, between my legs.

Automatically, I turn to rinse, and my eyes land on dark hazel watching me in the mirror. It's a strike of lightning from my chest to my core, and I freeze, holding my hands in my hair, my breasts lifted, my lips parted.

He doesn't look away, and I don't either. Moving my hands slowly, I slide my palms down my cheeks, then I slide them lower, over my breasts. My nipples are peaked, and I lift them, keeping my eyes on his as warmth floods my belly.

In my peripheral vision, I see his hand move over his dick. Slipping out my tongue, I wet my bottom lip as I continue caressing my breasts. It's hypnotic watching him watch me. His hand is outside his sweatpants, but the bulge in the thin fabric is painfully obvious.

I take a chance, reaching behind me to switch off the water. I reach up again, arching my back to lift my breasts as I wring the excess water out of my hair, then I step to the door and push it open.

His back is still to me, but his eyes drink in my naked body in the mirror, small drops of water clinging to my skin. Steam climbs the glass, but I've reached him. His muscles are tense, his broad shoulders rising with his rapid breathing. I press my breasts to his back, sliding my hands around his waist and moving one beneath the fabric to caress his hard cock.

Wetness floods my core, and I close my eyes remembering how good it feels, curling my fingers and tracing every line and ridge of his erection. I want him so much. With a start, as if waking from a dream, he grips my wrist, jerking my hand away as he turns in my arms to face me.

My eyes fly open, and when they meet his, he's furious. I'm not sure what comes over me, but I lift my other hand and grip his shoulder, pushing him back as if I'll fight with him. He grips my other wrist pushing me, and I pivot, rotating my body so he slams me against the wall.

I exhale a moan, and his eyes flash. He closes the space between us, caging me with his body, and my lips part. We're not speaking, but a whimper slips from my throat. Every noise seems to enrage him more, and he puts his hand between my legs, cupping my pussy.

"Oh," I gasp as his fingers invade, testing my wetness.

My hands go to his waist, and I push the soft cotton pants lower. I palm his erection before quickly dropping to my knees and pulling it into my mouth.

"Fuck," he groans as I suck deeper, taking him to the back of my throat.

Large hands grip my damp hair, and he guides me, rocking his hips slightly, hitting the back of my throat with his cock. My hands are on his thighs, and I slide them higher, gripping his ass and giving him what he needs, what I need as well, letting him take his anger out on me.

He groans again, and I feel the tension in his legs. I brace for his orgasm, but his hands move quickly, gripping me under the arms. I'm off him with a pop, and he turns me, pushing me forward onto the bathroom counter on my stomach.

I've just braced my hands when he slams into me from behind, and I let out a loud moan. He doesn't stop, driving violently into me. My body quivers, and the heat of his anger, the desperate force of his fucking, triggers a surge of orgasm in my belly.

Rough hands reach beneath, finding my breasts and squeezing, kneading them. He's feverish, taking what he wants, not waiting for me to come. He's punishing me for betraying him, and I press my hand against the mirror. I drive my ass back to meet him. His hands move to my hips, gripping me harder as he thrusts, growling words of anger and need with every hit.

A loud crack echoes in the bathroom and heat blasts across my ass from his palm.

"Oh, God," I gasp as the orgasm rages through my core, clenching my insides with violent spasms.

He slaps me again, and my knees buckle. He lifts me up by my hips, fucking me two, three more times relentlessly, before holding steady, roaring with release as his cock pulses deep inside me. He holds my ass firmly against his body, and his thighs jerk and tremble against mine. Another spasm of orgasm grips my core, and another groaning swear leaves his lips.

Several seconds pass, and he holds me, until he seems to regain his bearings. Then without a word, he pulls out, restores his pants, and leaves the bathroom, slamming the door.

I place my palms on the cool, marble counter, straightening before the mirror. Wetness is on my thighs, and I go to the shower, taking the cloth and running a bit more water to clean myself again. His damp towel hangs behind the door, and I lift it off the hook, wrapping it securely under my arms before opening the bathroom door.

He's not in the bedroom, but a fresh stack of clothes I assume are for me sits on the edge of the bed. I take his boxer briefs and pull them over my hips, then I pull on the new long-sleeved Henley, which smells divinely of him, and the loose, linen pants I think might be Hana's, although she's a few sizes smaller than me. Perhaps they're Blake's.

Taking the handcuff off the bed, I return the towel to the bathroom before walking down the hall to find him. He's in the kitchen when I enter, standing with his hands bracing the sink, facing the window.

It's after lunchtime, and I'm not sure what to do. I decide a peace offering is all I have left, so I sit on the stool and handcuff my wrist to the arm of the stool like he always does.

The clink of metal causes him to turn, and his eyes narrow when he sees me sitting, fully dressed, the good little prisoner.

Clearing his throat, he scrubs a hand over the back of his neck. "Nothing's changed."

I nod slowly, studying my hand on the bar. "When I was given this assignment, they said you were the computer geek, the tech guy, and I expected a nerd, a nobody. I didn't expect what I found. I didn't expect you to affect me. I didn't expect to want you so much."

"It didn't stop you from lying to me."

"No." Inhaling slowly, I steady my voice. "I was too focused on revenge. Then I had this fantasy you might understand. I dreamed of us working together, finding the killer and bringing him to justice together."

"Don't say that to me. I didn't make you lie." It's a low rasp, and I know he's struggling as much as I am.

"Even if you hate me now, I still want you. Could you ever be on my side?"

"No." His gaze levels on mine. "I could never trust you."

"But you can." My voice breaks. "Yes, it started as a setup, the visits to your office, the seduction, it was all a big master plan, but at some point everything changed. My feelings for you became very real."

His hands grip my shoulders, and he gives me a hard shake as he growls. "Stop lying to me!"

"I'm not," I gasp, tears filling my eyes. My head drops, and I whisper. "I'm not."

At once, he releases me, turning away. His breath comes fast, and his voice is low. "Remember when you said you liked to feel my strength, knowing I could hurt you, but I wouldn't?"

"Yes."

"Now I would."

A hot tear spills over onto my cheek, and I wish I had the key to this handcuff. I wish I had taken myself to the bedroom and crawled beneath the blankets before I locked it.

My voice is quiet, as I speak. "Even when you hurt me, I'll still come to you. Remember?"

"I didn't hurt you." His voice is equally quiet. "You hurt me."

"And for that I'm so sorry. You're the best man I've ever known."

CHAPTER 26

Dirk

I T'S FIVE O'CLOCK, AND WE'RE BOTH IN THE SMALL ROOM MONITORING the camera feeds on Scar's twenty-seven-inch desktop computer. Rainey is handcuffed to the chair near the filing cabinet, and we've said nothing more about what happened this afternoon.

There's nothing more to say.

My job is to keep my eyes on what's happening in Gibson's, and I have Louie's number at the ready on my phone. Hutch said he chatted with his old friend with the Brooklyn Police Department yesterday and this morning. Louie knows what's going down, and I'm on the line ready to call him at the first sign of a trap.

Sliding my glasses over my eyes, I lean back in my chair, focusing my gaze on the screen. The quality is grainy and the picture is black and white, but I can make out everyone's faces.

Then a call comes through on the computer. I press accept, and we have sound.

"I see you intercepted my girl retrieving what you stole

from us." Natasha's voice has matured, but it still smacks of entitlement.

Hutch's voice is level. "Simon's own guy Andre stole this book and sold it to Hugh van Hamilton."

"Doesn't make it yours."

Scar cuts in. "Why do you want it back?"

"Because it belongs to me now. It's my inheritance, along with this club and everything else that was Simon's."

In the feed we see her face turn to Scar, and my skin prickles. What is she up to?

"You're not Simon's heir." Scar's voice is dangerously quiet. "His enterprise died with him, and I'm here to see you don't try to revive it."

"Then it seems we're wasting time."

The screen breaks into confusion. A swarm of men fills the office, and the struggle is short. A nightstick flies, leaving Hutch unconscious on the floor, hands locked in zip ties. Scar is bound to a chair with a gun at his neck. I'm on my feet at once, waking my phone, ready to call Louie.

"Wait!" Scar shouts, and his eyes cut straight to the camera, to me.

"Wait?" I yell from 800 miles away. "What the fuck just happened?"

"She hired reinforcements." Rainey's tone is quiet surprise. "She was ready for this."

The other feed, which until now has been black springs to life, and I watch as three guys drag my unconscious brother into the smaller room, deposit him on the black leather, and close the door.

"She could have taken him anywhere, but she brought him to that room," I muse.

"She knows you're watching." Turning my head, I meet Rainey's eyes, and she shrugs. "It's a guess, but I know her pretty well."

My eyes narrow, and I study Rainey's position, leaning

forward in her seat before turning back to the screen. Scar is seated across from Natasha, and a big man with a gun stands behind him. On a hunch, I hit the record button to capture everything that comes next for the record.

"You thought you got away with it, didn't you?" Natasha leans back in her chair, crossing her arms. "You thought you could welsh out of the deal you made with my uncle, but you forgot one thing. I was there. I witnessed your vow to take Hana's place and to pay for what you did to Victor for however long Simon said."

Scar crosses his arms, mimicking her pose. "So this whole thing was a trap, a ploy to bring me here, with Rainey as a decoy?"

"Oh, no. I still need that book, but now that you've caught her, you can do what you will with that little cunt."

"You don't care about your people?"

Natasha stands from her chair, and the smile on her lips is visible even with the poor quality. "Rainey's not my people. She's been waiting to betray me. The only thing Rainey wants is the man who killed her father. Boo-hoo, poor little rich girl, can't live without knowing the truth about her past." She lifts her chin and shouts into the air. "Simon killed your dad, Rainey! Get the fuck over it!"

A shifting noise behind me pulls my attention from the screen. Rainey's eyes are red-rimmed and burning with fury, and her hands are clenched into fists.

"Why did Simon kill Rainey's father?" Scar asks slowly. "Did he owe him money?"

"Hardly," she huffs with a laugh. "Zander Petrovich had all the money. He was the only thing standing in Simon's way, much like his children are the only things standing in mine. Victor and Simon worked hard to get what they wanted. They sacrificed their brother, and I'm not letting their efforts go to waste."

Rainey's voice is low and sinister. "Because you're a vicious, soulless piece of shit."

A shift in my chest forces me to my feet, and I turn to face her. "Simon killed your father?"

Her jaw is tight. "Apparently so."

Scar's question interrupts us. "You want us to dispose of Rainey?"

"Please," Natasha laughs. "Spare me the trouble. I don't want to keep Zander's heirs alive."

"Heirs... as in more than one?"

"Rainey has a brother, but the last time I checked she was still trying to find him, and he has no idea who he is." Her eyes level on my partner. "But I know."

Rainey gasps, standing to her feet, her hand still cuffed to the chair.

Scar's tone is measured. "You think it's me."

"I don't have to think. I own Gibson's now. I have all of Simon's records in the safe."

"Which means you want to kill us both."

"I don't have to kill you, Oskar *Lourde*." Natasha walks around the desk again, taking a seat. "I know exactly how to control you."

"The last man who threatened my family is dead." His tone is lethal, even at 800 miles away.

"Actually, the last man was Rick, if I'm not mistaken, and he's very much alive and working for me." She leans back in her seat, condescension in her tone. "Do you have any idea the vast quantity of wealth we're talking about? Not to mention the property, the political power, oh, and the super yacht."

"You're doing it for the money?" Scar seems to be fishing, and his order for me to wait makes sense to me now. I'm capturing everything she says on video.

"It's always about money, but also the power. Rainey has no use for power, and you've consistently wanted no part of it. I'm essentially doing you a favor by taking it off your hands. You should be thanking me."

Scar continues speaking. "You killed Greg Peters. Did you also kill Debbie Desayda-Rice?"

It's like the last act in one of those Agatha Christie plays. She's spilling the whole story, and he's drawing the story out of her for the record.

"To be fair, I tried to get Greg and Debbie to kill each other. They simply wouldn't cooperate." She laughs, sounding unhinged.

"You're crazy," Scar mutters.

"No, I'm justice." In a flash she's back to evil. "I'm doing what's right and fair. Simon tried to bring Greg in over my head. Me, his own niece who faithfully served him my whole life."

"Simon knew the truth." Scar's voice rises. "The Russian mafia would never let a little girl take over a powerful family like his."

"There is no Russian mafia!" Natasha shouts furiously. "RDIF-Kazan is an investment group! It's completely legal!"

"It's a shell company, and Gibson's is a money laundering operation, and who knows how many other businesses are on record in that book committing white collar crimes. It's horse doping and blackmail, it's murder for hire and every unsolved mystery in the world of vice, and that book is the key to all of it."

Natasha stands, placing her hands on the desk, a wicked hiss in her voice. "And you're the only thing standing in my way."

"That's right, because I'll do everything in my power to make sure none of it ever comes back again."

"You're making me tired." She flicks her wrist at the big guy behind my partner. "Take him to the back room and lock him in with the other one. I'll be finished cleaning out this dump by morning, then it's going up in flames."

The guy jerks Scar up, gun still at his neck, but it's Natasha's final words that send me into action. "The fire won't let you escape twice."

"Then I'll see you in hell."

The phone falls, and we lose sound.

Rainey's head drops, and I take the handcuff keys from my pocket. Standing, I unlock the bracelet from her wrist and let it fall, and she lifts her eyes to mine. I take off my glasses, and she's in my arms.

I press my lips to the side of her head, holding her close as her body tenses and trembles. "It's okay. I've got you."

"She's always hated me, and now she's going to win."

With one last squeeze, I release her, meeting her eyes. "She's not going to win, because I'm going to stop her."

"There's no time!"

"Just leave it to me." Grabbing my phone, I call Louie as I watch my partner stagger through the door to where my brother is still unconscious in the small, black room.

Scar's hands are still bound, but he quickly pulls the zip tie tighter then breaks it apart, freeing himself. Next, he lifts Hutch to sitting against the wall.

"Louie?" Louie Jackson is a sergeant on the Brooklyn PD, and he's one of my brother's friends from before he started the private investigation firm, from when he'd just left the Marines.

"Dirk, what's happening?" His voice is urgent.

"I need you to go to Gibson's. Natasha has Hutch and Scar captive, and she just said she's planning to burn the place to the ground."

"She said that to you?" Louie's voice goes loud.

"No, I have it on video. Give me two seconds, and I'll send it to you now."

Silence fills the line while I type on the keyboard, sending the recording, and Rainey paces the small room, arms crossed over her waist.

"I've located a private jet. It'll take me a few hours, so you've got to get over there now and get them out. Gibson's is underground. Firefighters won't know it's burning until the smoke reaches the ground level, and by then the whole place will be an inferno. It's a tinder box as it is."

"I'll need to obtain a search warrant. Believe it or not, police can't simply storm into a private club without a reason."

Anger tightens my forehead. "I just sent you the reason. It's an immediate threat."

"That you obtained by listening on an unauthorized device."

"Jesus Christ…" I'm one breath from shouting. "We don't have time, Louie!"

"Trust me, I'm moving this as fast as I can. I'm putting the fire department on alert so they'll be there. I've got to follow the rules if we're going to make this stick, but I'll call in some favors."

"I'm on my way." Disconnecting, I shove my phone in my pocket and reach behind the books on the bookcase to take a gun out of Scar's lockbox.

Rainey's phone is inside as well, and I hand it to her. She powers it on, and it immediately begins vibrating with text alerts, all of which she dismisses.

"Take me with you." She catches my arm. "I know where everything is. I know the back entrances. I can help you."

Placing my hands on her shoulders, I look into her blue eyes. I remember her words about us working together to bring justice, and warmth unfurls in my chest as I realize I want that too. I want her on my team, and I want to be on hers.

"You can help me by staying here. I don't know what Natasha has up her sleeve, and I need someone to be with Hana, just in case."

"You think she might try to hurt her?" Rainey's eyes widen.

"I don't know, but I do know Hana's as mixed up in all this as Scar. I also know he'd murder me if I saved him and left her unprotected. I don't know who we can trust in all this."

"You can trust me." Her tone is fierce, and her eyes hold mine. "I'll never lie to you again."

Reaching out, I cup her face in my hand, then without hesitation, I lean down to seal her lips with mine.

CHAPTER 27

Dirk

"I'VE BROUGHT SOMEONE TO STAY WITH YOU." I PUSH THROUGH the kitchen door at Hugh's to find Hana standing at the bar with her sister and Norris.

Rainey is behind me, still wearing the linen pants and long-sleeved tee with my Carhartt jacket over it.

"Rainey Sidorova?" Hana's brow furrows, and she waddles around the bar to where we stand, glancing from her to me. "What are you doing in Hamiltown? With Dirk?"

"I don't have time to explain everything. She can fill in the gaps while I'm gone, but she's here to help us."

Blake snaps to attention, coming to where I stand and grasping my arm. "What's wrong? Where is Hutch?"

Using all my control, I keep my expression neutral. "Hutch and Scar need backup. I've been watching, and I know where they are. It's all going to be okay, but I've got to get to them tonight."

Blake studies me, her gray eyes moving around my face

and then to Rainey at my side. She's smart as a whip and fiercely protective of her family.

She turns a glare on Rainey. "Last time I saw you, you were Natasha's loyal minion. Now I'm supposed to believe you're here to help us?"

Rainey's eyes drop, and she nods. "It's true. We haven't seen each other in a long time, but a lot has changed in four years."

"I'll say," Hana interjects. "Your hair isn't blonde, and I had no idea your eyes were such a pretty blue. Why would you hide that?"

"I hid a lot of things in those days." Rainey's voice is quiet.

"I can't stay." I take Blake's hand off my sleeve. "You can trust her, and I'll be back with the guys. Don't worry if we lose contact for a few hours. Louie is helping me."

"Dirk..." Panic lines Blake's face, and I catch her hand.

"I won't let anything happen to my brother. You have my word."

"Don't let anything happen to you." Rainey steps forward, and I hesitate.

The roller coaster of obsession, to hate, to needing her has my insides in knots. I want to pull her to me and hold her until I understand my feelings, but we don't have time.

"Or Scar!" Hana calls from behind her. "Although, after everything we've been through, I'm pretty sure he's immortal."

"Nobody's immortal." Rainey's tone is a warning, and I nod, giving her hand a squeeze.

"I'll bring all of us back. You be here when I return."

The flight to New York is excruciatingly long. Neither Scar nor Hutch have their phones, but I'm communicating with

Louie the entire way. He's working on the search warrant, the fire department is on alert, and police officers are in the area around the building, waiting for the signal to act.

When we finally touch down at LaGuardia, I've got a taxi lined up, and I'm ready to get to the bar in the Financial District. I shoot Louie a text letting him know I'm on the street, and he tells me other than the usual crowd, everything is quiet.

My head aches from trying to cover the miles faster, and when we finally arrive at the block, I shove a handful of cash at the driver and hop out at the first stoplight. I'm walking fast, doing my best not to break into a run.

It's after midnight, and Natasha's words are on repeat in my head. I can't stop seeing my brother and Scar locked in that room as the entire club goes up in flames. The one thing giving me hope is the clientele. Louie said the club was open for business, and they wouldn't torch it while it was filled with people.

At least I hope they wouldn't.

When I finally reach the block where it's located, I cut down the alley to the side entrance I've watched for years. It's the first time I've seen this place in person, but I know it inside and out from all my surveillance.

Leaning against the wall, I hit the call button. Louie answers on the first ring. "Where are you?"

"I'm in the alley behind the bar. I'll drop a pin, so you can send backup. I don't think it's safe to go in there alone. They might be waiting for me." Rainey's guess that Natasha knew I was watching is also on my mind.

It takes two seconds to send him my location.

"Got it," he verifies. "I'll get a plainclothes officer out there. The two of you can enter together in case anything goes down."

"Hurry."

We disconnect, and I shoot a quick text to Rainey, filling her in on where I am and my next moves.

Her reply is equally quick. ***Be on guard. Natasha has hired muscle since I was there.***

I let her know I'm waiting on a plainclothes officer and ask her to let Hana and Blake know. The moment I hit send, the noise of footsteps in the alley snaps me to attention. Falling back, I turn so it appears I'm taking a leak behind a dumpster.

The benefit of it being my first time here is none of the regulars would recognize me. The man approaching now is short and round with dark hair and heavy features. He reminds me of one of the cast members from that old TV show *The Sopranos*.

"Ay," he snaps at me. "This ain't no toilet."

"Ah, no. That's not what's happening." I look down, slurring my words and not making eye contact.

If he's the undercover cop, he'll threaten to arrest me. If not, I've got a gun in the back of my jeans.

"You're not supposed to be here. This is a private entrance, now beat it!" The guy growls, waving his hand like he's shooing a dog, and I take a few steps towards the street, making a mental note of his face.

He yells louder, "Quit looking at me like that!"

I hold up both hands like he has a gun on me. "Be cool, man. I'm just waiting for a friend."

"Wait on the street."

Nodding, I lower my hands and act like I'm headed to the top of the alley. As soon as he turns his back, however, I'm on him. Jumping on his back, I secure his thick neck in the bend of my elbow. It's a classic sleeper hold, but he's a fighter.

"Fuck you," he grunts, ramming his elbow hard into my solar plexus.

"Oof," I grunt, but I tighten my grip.

He twists his body as if he'll throw me off him, but I've

got probably fifteen years and more cardio on him. I'm not going anywhere.

"Get off…" He growls, turning to slam my back against the brick wall, but his energy is failing.

"Don't fight," I snap through gritted teeth as we go down to one knee.

His hands fumble in his jacket, and I turn him fast, pinning his arm to the ground with our bodies. "Oh, no you don't."

He's taking longer than I expect, and I've got to keep his hand away from the gun I'm sure is under his arm.

We're far enough down the alley that we shouldn't attract attention. Still, the sound of footsteps running up behind me makes my heart beat faster. If it's muscle from Gibson's, I'm screwed.

"Dirk Winston?" A sharp male voice calls to me.

"Yeah." Lucky for me, it's my backup. "Get his gun."

I fall back against the wall, still holding the big guy around the neck, and a slim man with light brown hair in a khaki suit reaches in and removes a beretta.

"Got it."

"That might not be all he's carrying."

"Yeah, but I don't think he's reaching for anything now."

The big body collapses, and I release him with a groan, rubbing my shoulder as I stretch out my side. He got a good hit in when I first grabbed him. "That's going to leave a bruise."

"I'm Jack Price. Louie said I should meet you here." He holds out a hand, and I shake it briefly. "I have to say, I thought we were going inside the club. I'm not sure what's happening right now."

"If you think we're going to walk into Gibson's and go straight to the room where they're holding my brother, you've got another thing coming." Kneeling beside the guy on the ground, I search his pockets.

"But why him?"

Finding what I'm looking for, I hold up a set of silver keys. "We'll wait until everyone leaves, then we'll let ourselves in."

"I'm not authorized to—"

"I know, Jack. You've got to color inside the lines, but I don't. I need you to take this guy downtown and detain him. Say you found him passed out in the alley, public intoxication, whatever it takes to hold him until tomorrow."

He hesitates a minute. "Louie said you guys have your own methods."

"I'm getting my brother out of this hell hole before it goes up in flames. I could use the backup, but even more, I don't need him waking up and causing problems."

"Understood."

"Now help me get him out of here."

Jack and I carry the big guy to the street, where he calls for a patrol car to take him to the station. "Put him in a cell 'til he sobers up," Jack tells the guy in the car, passing over his gun. "I recovered this from his pocket."

One obstacle down, I camp out in the alley to wait until everything's quiet and hope for the best. Hurry up and wait is the mantra of this business. I thought I'd gotten out of it, but here I am, on pins and needles, pacing a dirty alley, counting down the minutes.

When it's finally after 3:00 a.m., I signal Jack, who leaves his post on the street to follow me down a short flight of stairs to the back entrance. It takes a few minutes to find the right key, but at last it turns, and the door loosens.

I reach behind me to retrieve my 9mm, and Jack's eyes widen. I hold my hand up to signal silence, and I wait at the cracked door, listening. The bar's been closed long enough for the staff to be gone, but I'm on alert for Natasha and any of her goons. Rainey's warning is in my head—she hired help, and there's no telling what she has planned.

She told Scar she was cleaning out the office before she torched the place, and the pressure is on me to get us all out of here before that happens.

After several minutes of silence, I slip into the anteroom at the back door, Jack close behind me. The main area is dark except for track lighting around the walls and bar. Thick velvet curtains surround smaller sections in the room. They'll absorb any sound we make, but they also provide a hiding place for anyone.

Straining my eyes, I check the direction of the office, but no other lights are on. Is it possible they've already deserted the place? And if they have, does that mean the fuse has already been lit? My chest seizes at the thought. A gas leak would be the easiest way to do it.

"Let's move!" I hiss, dashing across the empty bar, going straight to the back room where Scar hid the small camera years ago.

Feeling all over the dark wall, there's no latch, only a deadbolt. *Fuck.* Hoping against hope, I take out the set of keys again, trying each one with shaking hands until...

"Yes!" I yell, turning the bolt and ripping the door open.

"Duck!" Jack grabs me by the shoulder, ripping me down to the floor seconds before Scar's fist slams into the wood.

"Fuck!" he yells, shaking his hand. "Dirk? Dammit, I almost knocked your head off."

"Punch first, questions later?" I chuckle, pulling him into a bro-hug. "Hutch?"

"Hey, little brother." He's hanging back, sitting on the edge of the booth, and my stomach pitches. My oversized brother struggling to stand is something I've never seen.

"You okay?"

"Yeah," he shakes his dark head. "They must've given me a fucking horse tranquilizer."

"You're big enough to warrant it." I grab his arm. "We

don't have time to waste. If they're planning to torch this place, it could go up any second."

The four of us head into the dark bar, ready to race out the side door when Scar pulls up short. "Wait. I have to check—"

"There's no time! This whole place could blow at any second."

He's already gone, and I groan. "Help him out." I pass Hutch to Jack and race after Scar, who's in the small office.

He's leaning over an open, empty safe behind the desk. "Fuck. She did it. It's all gone. All the papers, all the records, our phones…"

"We'll worry about it later." Grabbing his arm, we're out the door, racing across the empty bar to the alley door where I entered.

Slamming through it, we collapse against the brick wall to catch our breaths. Jack is across from us with Hutch's arm over his shoulder.

"We need to keep moving." I nudge Scar before stepping over to take my brother from our backup. "If they light the gas line, it'll blow up the whole block."

Quickly, we make our way to the street, across it, and down another block, where we wait against the wall. I'm the only one with a phone, and I send a series of texts—first to Louie letting him know we've got the guys out, then to all three of the girls, letting them know the men are safe.

"What now?" Jack asks, and I look at my partners.

"What do you think?" I ask. Hutch's brow is furrowed, and I know that look. "What?"

"It was a setup."

"Yeah, it was. She confessed as much—"

"No, I mean, all of this. They're not going to torch Gibson's. They weren't even guarding us. They aren't here."

A pinch in my stomach tells me he's right. "If they aren't here, where are they?"

Scar's voice takes an ominous tone. "Natasha said she wouldn't let any of Zander's heirs live."

Our eyes meet, and I straighten. "She wanted us to dispose of Rainey…"

"But we're all here. She made sure all of us came to this location."

A fist tightens over my throat as I realize the meaning of his words. She knew I was watching when she made her threat, when she showed me exactly where my brother and Scar were being held. She made the phony threat about cleaning out the office and burning it to the ground. It was all bullshit, but she knew I'd come running.

"They're headed to Hamiltown." I'm in motion, ordering the plane as the words leave my lips, adrenaline surging in my veins. "They're going back for Rainey."

Scar's voice is deadly. "And my son."

CHAPTER 28

Rainey

WE'RE SITTING AT A SMALL, ROUND TABLE IN THE KITCHEN LADEN with slices of baked ham and pineapples on a platter, a plate of long-cut green beans, and a bowl of small, golden potatoes, and my stomach is too tight to eat.

Hugh van Hamilton is out of town, but Norris has prepared the sisters' favorite dishes for our dinner. I spear a small potato and put it in my mouth. It's buttery and delicious, but my head is still spinning from everything we learned. I was always pretty sure Simon had a hand in my father's death, but learning why... He killed his own brother to steal his inheritance. Not only that, is it possible Scar could be my brother?

Add to all of it my fears about what Dirk could be walking into. I should've gone with him. He has no idea how sneaky Natasha can be—and how driven she is to get what she wants.

"You're so different now." Hana smiles at me from across the table, where she's working on large plate of everything.

"You were so... I don't know," she waves her hand, "before, but now you're like, umm... Oh, I know! Lara Croft!"

That almost makes me laugh. "I'm not the tomb raider."

"What *are* you doing now, Rainey?" Blake's low voice is smooth, and she's as polished as she ever was.

She eats with her knife and fork, and her dark brown hair is parted in the middle and hangs in waves behind her shoulders. She's dressed in a tan, curve-hugging dress, and her gray eyes study me seriously. No Lara Croft references from Blake.

She's always been the exact opposite of her sister, whose spiral, light-blonde hair is piled on her head. Hana is playful and impulsive, and she looks like something between a waif and a fairy.

"Up until last week, I was a student." I say with a bitter laugh, but Hana gasps.

"*You're* the student Dirk's seeing?" Her eyes are wide and sparkling with excitement, and heat rises in my cheeks.

"You knew about that?"

"I knew he was interested in one of his students, but I didn't know who she was. Only..." Her brow furrows, and she seems to be connecting the dots. "But wait... Didn't you already graduate from Columbia?"

"Yeah." My eyes drop to my plate, and I push another potato around with my fork.

I wish Dirk had stuck around a little longer. These sisters are not going to be happy when they find out what I've been doing for the last several weeks.

"Were you going back for a post-baccalaureate degree?" Only Blake would ask something like that.

"Not exactly." I lift my eyes to see both of theirs fixed on me, eagerly waiting for me to explain myself. "I, uh...well, Natasha sent me to get the book Andre Bertonelli stole from Simon."

Both sisters recoil and glance at each other. Blake places her knife and fork carefully beside her plate, but Hana asks the million-dollar question. "Are you saying *you're* the person who broke into Hugh's study?"

"Guilty." I try to say it in a joking way, but it falls flat.

Blake is not amused. Her accusation is sharp. "So you're still Natasha's little minion."

"No, I'm really not." Shaking my head, I lose the casual approach. It's not working. "I only did it because I didn't have a choice."

Blake crosses her arms. "In my experience, you always have a choice."

"Your experience is nothing like mine." It sounds like a challenge, so I quickly add, "I literally didn't have a choice, but I had a plan."

"Which was?"

"I planned to come here and get the book, but I wanted to use it against them. I had hoped Dirk could help me, because he's so good at finding things on the Internet and tracking down information."

"He really is." Hana's tone gives me courage.

I can tell she wants to believe me, which twists the knife in my stomach. Dirk said she's the sweetest person he knows, and I'm realizing I never knew her at all.

"Scar caught me with the book, and he didn't believe me at first…"

"But he believes you now?" Blake still has her side-eye on me.

"I don't know about Scar, but as Dirk and I were listening, he realized I was telling the truth. Natasha has a much darker plan than getting that book. She wants to finish what Simon and Victor started. Then she wants to take over everything they left behind."

"What did they start?" A note of fear enters Hana's voice, and knowing about her past, I don't blame her for being afraid.

I'm afraid, and I was never abused—physically.

"The heir to the Petrovich fortune, all the land, the money, the power, was their oldest brother Zander. He was my father, and they murdered him for it."

"Does she wants to murder you?" Hana's eyes are wide.

"Definitely." I nod, not even surprised. "I don't know why she waited so long. I guess she thought I was too weak or too stupid to figure it out, but now I know." The tension at the table is at an all time high, and they watch me silently. "That's not all, though. I have an older brother, who she confirmed is still alive."

"They want to kill him, too?" Hana whispers.

"It's why Dirk went to Gibson's. To stop it from happening."

Hana's slim hands fly to cover her mouth, and Blake stands from her chair, going around behind her. "Who is your brother?"

"I don't know for certain, but I'm pretty sure it's Scar."

The back door bursts open, and we all jump out of our seats. Hana lets out a little yelp, and Blake's arms go around her protectively.

"Somebody get me a drink!" A woman with bright-red hair storms into the room followed by a sulky teenager.

"Carmen!" Hana sighs, covering her face and starting to laugh. "Oh, my God, you scared the pee out of me."

"From what I understand, that's one of the hazards of getting pregnant." Carmen's at the cabinet, taking down a glass.

Hana waddles over to greet the frowning teen, who I sort-of recognize. "Hey, Pepper. Why the long face?"

"Vodka," Carmen demands, and Blake shakes her head as she turns to open a cabinet near the pantry, muttering under her breath about heart palpitations.

"Dad decided I have to learn how to drive," Pepper starts, and Carmen makes a loud noise as she pours a healthy glass of liquor. The girl rolls her eyes and continues. "He wanted to hire a driving instructor, but Carmen said that's not how we do it here in Hamiltown. She said she would teach me, and she's the *worst!*"

Pepper's voice grows louder by the end of her sentence, and Carmen lowers the glass pointing her finger. "*You* are the worst. I've never seen such a shit driver in all my life! You have no intuition, you make the most bizarre choices…"

Hana cuts her eyes, stage-whispering to Carmen. "Harsh words, my friend. Aren't we supposed to encourage our students?"

"I should've known this was doomed from the start. You want to know what she said to me?" Carmen's country accent injects a sense of humor, but I don't dare laugh. "I told her to put her foot on the brake to start the car. She asked me which one is the brake!"

"Why is that bad?" Pepper yells.

"You don't even know the difference between the pedals! You probably used both feet to work them."

"Why can't I use both feet?"

"Okay, time out, time out." Blake steps between the two. "So she didn't know the brake from the accelerator. That's an easy fix."

"Uh… yeah." Carmen takes another slug of vodka. "She drives slow as molasses in January, until it's time to actually slow down, at which point, she speeds up!"

"I confused the pedals!"

"She nearly had a head-on collision with a tree!"

Hana gasps, putting a hand over her mouth. "Oh, no, Pep!"

"This is so dumb. I can ride a horse if I need to go any-where." Pepper stomps around the kitchen. "Do you know how many people are killed in car accidents every year?"

"And I was almost one of them," Carmen quips, the alcohol seeming to take the edge off her fury.

Blake puts her hand on Carmen's shoulder, her voice gentle. "Maybe you should hire a professional. At least it would save your relationship."

"Hana can teach me to drive." Pepper crosses her arms hard. "She's the only one who listens to me around here."

"Oh, I don't know, Pep." Hana puts a hand on her massive baby bump. "I might go into labor, and then we'd really be in trouble."

Chewing my lip, I scan the group of friends before suggesting quietly, "I could try to teach you to drive. It hasn't been that long since I learned, and I was confused by the pedals at first, too."

Pepper's brown eyes land on mine, and she hops over to where I'm sitting. "Who are you?"

"Pepper!" Carmen scolds. "Don't be rude."

Pepper turns to me and mutters, "She's always riding me."

"We're actually the rude ones," Hana jumps in. "Carmen, Pepper, this is our friend from New York, Rainey Sidorova... or actually, Petrovich?"

"Petrovna." I note, and she frowns. "Russian surnames are gendered. It's confusing until you're used to it."

"Rainey Petrovna," Hana continues, "This is Carmen, who runs the most adorable boutique shop in town, and Pepper is Dirk and Hutch's niece."

"I've heard about you." I smile at the girl. "I saw your picture in the softball uniform with the donuts."

"Oh, that was a million years ago." Pepper sits in the chair beside me, the quarrel seemingly forgotten. "You're from Russia? Is it really super-freezing there all the time?"

"I only lived there as a little girl. I grew up in Manhattan." Her face falls, so I quickly add, "Russia's a really big country, but where I lived was kind of like here."

"I'd like to visit sometime. My uncle Hutch was in the Marines there."

"I bet he might take you if you asked him."

"Maybe." She scrunches her nose like she doesn't believe he will.

Carmen walks over to pat her side. "Come on, it's late. Your dad's going to think we had an accident."

"Stop by tomorrow, and we can practice driving," I tell her. "If you want, I mean."

"Carmen! You just had a vodka," Blake scolds. "I'll drive you back."

Hugs are shared, and Pepper shakes my hand. They head out the door, and the room feels quieter with them gone. I start collecting plates, and Hana takes out plastic storage containers for the leftovers.

"They're always such a whirlwind," she laughs. "Carmen's dating Pepper's dad, but she's known Pepper her whole life. It's okay if you decide to change your mind about the driving thing."

"No, I want to. It'll give me something to do."

Otherwise, I'll be going crazy worrying about Dirk the whole day.

Norris appears and takes the plates from me, claiming it's his job to clean up. Hana puts the leftovers in the refrigerator, and we walk into the living room. It's so different being here legitimately and not sneaking around in the dark.

"I'll be glad when the guys are back," I say quietly.

"Shew, me too. I'd like to sleep in my own bed again, but Blake said we have to stay here together. My overprotective big sister."

Looking down, I pick at my cuticle. "Dirk told me what they did to you. When you were younger, I mean. I'm so sorry."

Her lips tighten, and she touches my hand. "You couldn't have done anything to stop them. You're younger than I am. We were both their victims."

I walk to the window, looking out at the barn. "I wasn't born in that cage, but I couldn't get out of it. Then when Simon died, and only Natasha was left, it was my chance to try."

"So you took it. I understand that." She walks up beside me. "And if Scar is your brother, that means we'll be sisters. We'll be family!"

If we're lucky. The unwelcome thought drifts through my

head, so I push it away for something brighter, forcing a smile. "Are you ready to be a mom?"

"I certainly hope so." She exhales a soft laugh. "I'm pretty close, so I'd better be. Scar wants a family so much."

"I never wanted a man or a relationship. Every relationship in my life has been transactional, except for my dad. And Dirk."

"You love him?" Her lips press into a smile, and I blink down, unable to stop the smile curling my lips, the warmth squeezing my chest and stomach. "You do! I knew it!"

"I've got a lot of making up to do."

"That's the best part." She puts an arm around my shoulders, giving me a side-hug. "I've got to take a bath, then I'm headed to bed. This baby is wearing me out, and he's not even here yet. Did Norris show you your room?"

"Yeah, I'm on the same side as you guys."

"In that case, I'll see you in the morning."

In the middle of the night, I sit straight up in bed with a start. It wasn't a nightmare, but something is definitely wrong. It was a noise, something horrible I've never heard before, yet it's a sound I recognize nonetheless.

My heart beats too fast, and an orange glow emanates from outside my window.

"Oh, God!" I throw back the covers, stumbling in the darkness as I search frantically for my jeans.

Jamming my feet in the pants legs, I grab the sweater off my chair and pull it over my head, over the T-shirt I was sleeping in. Running as fast as I can for the back door, I'm grateful I've been in this house in the darkness. I don't fall as I tear through the kitchen, jogging down the back steps and skidding to a stop as my eyes widen in horror.

The barn is on fire, and the horses are squealing in the most blood-chilling way. They're trapped in the inferno.

"We've got to get them out!" Hana screams, and I look back to see her running from the house as well in her nightgown and cowboy boots with a long coat pulled over her shoulders.

She holds the bottom of her belly as she passes me in a waddle-jog, and it only takes a moment for me to spring into action.

"Stop, Hana!" I catch up to her, grabbing her arm. "You can't go in there! It's too dangerous."

We're yelling, but there's no time. Behind me, I hear the door open and close and Blake is running to join us. Hana takes off again, running straight into the burning structure.

"Hana!" I scream.

"I'll call the fire department!" Blake yells, and I nod.

"I'll get her out!" Charging into the barn, I'm hit with the full force of the blaze.

Holding up my hand, I squint through the heat and the smoke until I see her already at Training Day's stall, opening the door and trying to get the frightened horse to run out.

"He won't budge!" she yells as I run down the row, opening all the stall doors.

None of the horses will leave their safe spaces. They're too afraid.

"We have to cover their heads!" I yell back to her. "I saw it in a movie once. They won't run if they see the fire."

Blake runs into the barn and goes straight for the tack room. When she emerges, she has bridles and lead ropes.

"Fire department is coming, but they're a half-hour away. Use these!" She tosses each of us a bridle. "Take them to the paddock so they can't run back into the barn. Hurry!"

She goes to Regency's Honor and quickly slides the bridle over the horse's head, staying close as she guides the large horse out of the small enclosure, trotting with him to the outdoor paddock. I go for Dancer, but a scream from Training Day's stall makes me double back.

"Hana?" As soon as I enter, everything goes black.

A dark hood is pulled over my head, and my arms are pinned behind my back. I'm lifted off the ground in a strong grip, and whoever has me drags me down what feels like a long passage. My mind is spinning, but trying to remember, it has to be in the direction of the large arena in the center of the building.

Kicking my legs, I struggle to get free, when all at once, I'm thrown to the floor. I fall all the way to my face, but I manage to catch the edge of the hood and rip it over my head. Scrambling quickly to my feet, I'm confused to see Hana standing to the side of a small room filled with hay, and Natasha holding us at gunpoint—with my pearl-handled 9mm Ruger.

"What the hell?" I gasp. "What are you doing here? You're supposed to be at Gibson's! How did you get my gun?"

"Put it in her hand!" Natasha yells, and Rick steps forward.

Gloves are on his hands as he shoves the weapon in my grip, lifting my arm and holding it over my head as he pulls the trigger. Hana screams again, and he snatches the gun away, carrying it to Natasha.

Flames are just reaching this area of the barn, and thick smoke is drifting in above our heads. The noise of horses squealing, the roar of the fire, and the creak of wooden beams splintering in the heat surrounds us.

"What do you think you're doing?" I yell, watching as Rick hands the gun to Natasha, who is also wearing gloves.

"Gunpowder residue is now on your hands. You used this gun to put a bullet in your pregnant friend before taking your own life." Natasha tilts the gun to the side, waving it between Hana and me. "It's so sad how they trusted you. They left you here to protect the girls, not burn down the barn and kill Scar's wife and son."

"You won't get away with this!" Hana yells savagely. "Blake is here. She already called the fire department, and she knows what's happening. Blake will stop you."

"It's true, she would've stopped us. If only she hadn't fallen while trying to save the horses and hit her head. It was a pretty bad lick. She might have a concussion."

"Noo…" Hana's voice is a wail.

My chest tightens, and I can't breathe. They've taken out Blake. If the fire department doesn't get here soon, she could die along with all the horses. Now they're planning to kill Hana and frame me for it—before they kill me as well.

Adrenaline vibrates in my muscles. I can't let this happen. Natasha is a power-hungry, heartless villain who's gotten away with murder three times by my count, but I won't let her get away with it again.

Keeping my eyes on them, I take a step back and hold out my hand. "Wait a minute. Let's talk about this. Maybe we can make a deal."

"I'm not making any deals with you, cousin. I'm ending Zander's legacy right here and now."

I take another step back. "But you don't have Scar, and when he finds out, he'll murder you, after he tortures you in ways I don't even want to imagine."

I'm stalling for time, taking another step back so Hana is just in front of me to the left. Her head is bowed, and her blonde spirals hang in a curtain, hiding her face. Her shoulders shudder, and I'm afraid she's crying.

One more step, and I'm at the back wall. I slowly move my hand around behind me, and my fingers land on the slim handle of a shovel. Closing my eyes, I say the shortest prayer I know, *Guide my hands.*

My fist closes over the wooden pole, and I scream at the top of my lungs as I rip it from the hay and swing it with all my might. A gunshot rings out, but I don't register being hit. I only register the vibration of the shovel through my arms and elbows as it makes contact with Rick's skull.

Blood spatters against the white wall, and he drops like a tree. *I hope I killed him,* is my last thought before I fall to my knees. My head spins, and a heartbeat is in my side. The sounds of struggle draw my attention, and I look up to see Hana and Natasha fighting for the gun.

"God, no!" I gasp.

Hana apparently lunged at Natasha after the shot was fired, and my stomach knots as I watch the barrel of the gun swing wildly. Another beat in my side, and I look down to see an ugly crimson circle growing larger on my side. It's sticky. I've been shot, but it's so strange... I don't feel pain.

I try to stand, but my legs won't cooperate. Hana screams as Natasha tries to throw her down. I can't seem to get my footing, so I decide to crawl, lifting the shovel and swinging it like a scythe at Natasha's legs. It works. The metal makes contact with her knees, and a horrible yell rings out.

Natasha falls, leaving Hana holding the gun. My old nemesis is on the ground, her leg bent at a sickening angle. I'm not sorry I broke her leg. In fact, I'm a bit pleased until I realize she's digging in her coat.

"She's got another gun!" I yell, looking up to see Hana's hands gripping my Ruger.

Her blue eyes close briefly, and she exhales slowly as if she's been trained to shoot.

"You won't shoot me, Hana van Hamilton." Natasha's voice is a hoarse snarl. "You're nothing but a spoiled, Upper East Side socialite who's been coddled her whole life."

"I'm a mamma bear, and I will protect my family." Hana's eyes open, and she pulls the trigger slowly.

I fall onto my forearms and army-crawl away from her line of sight just in case. One staccato pop echoes in the small space, and I look over my shoulder to see Natasha lying on her back in the hay, eyes open, staring blankly at the ceiling overhead.

My head drops, and I begin to sob.

It's over.

The murders, the cruelty, the revenge...

"Rainey, can you get up?" Hana kneels beside me, touching my shoulder. "You've got to get up, Rainey. We've got to get out of here. I've got to find Blake. The barn is still burning, and the horses… We've got to save the horses."

She's talking so fast, I think she might be in shock, and I want to tell her it's all going to be okay. It's over. Doesn't she understand? She ended it. She ended all of it—her pain, my pain, the years of lies and torture. Tears blur my vision, and I can't make my mouth speak. I'm so cold, and my legs are completely useless.

"Rainey, please get up!" Hana's voice shakes, and I see tears on her face now. "You've got to hang on a little longer. Help is coming. Help is coming, Rainey, please…"

Help is coming…

This makes me smile. Help has never come for me, and now someone wants to save me. Does this mean I've made it to redemption? I must have, because as I close my eyes, I see the most brilliant white light, and the purest joy warms my chest.

CHAPTER 29

Dirk

AFTER HOURS OF NO ONE ANSWERING MY TEXTS, WE MADE IT BACK to the airport in Charleston just before dawn. All three of us were on edge as we flew to my Jeep. I burned rubber out of the parking lot, holding the pedal to the floor as we broke every speeding law to cover the short distance to Hamiltown.

When we arrived at Hugh's, the place was in chaos. Fire trucks were on the scene, and while the barn fire was under control, it was still burning.

Hutch ran immediately to Blake, who was sitting on the edge of an ambulance with an oxygen mask on her face and a bandage on her head.

"I had just left Reeg at the paddock," her voice shook as she explained, "and I was racing into Dancer's stall when someone or something hit me in the head."

Hutch's jaw clenched, and he held her in his arms as the emergency workers filled in the rest of the details.

"We sent Mrs. Lourde and her friend on to the hospital

in Miranda Bay." Scar was moving before the worker finished speaking.

"Hana and Rainey were helping me evacuate the horses when we all got separated." I waved to Blake as I turned and jogged to catch up with my partner.

Now we're both at the hospital. Hana is in a room under observation. Scar is with her, and I've checked in a few times. She didn't suffer smoke inhalation or any other potentially dangerous effects of being in a burning barn while nine months pregnant.

I'm just praying we didn't use up all our miracles on that alone.

I'm pacing the small waiting room at Miranda General, hands clasped under my arms as I wait for another report from the nurse when Hana walks slowly to where I'm pacing.

"I hate to think of you out here all alone." She puts her hand on my shoulder.

Scar has his hand on her arm, but she waves him away. "I'm fine. The doctor said the baby is fine, and I can't just lie in that bed. It's uncomfortable."

"You're lucky you didn't go into labor." Scar's deep voice is slightly less stressed.

"How are you doing?" Hana rubs my shoulder, and I lower my arms to give her a hug.

"I've been better."

"How's Rainey?"

"Haven't heard. She lost a lot of blood. The nurse said by the time they got her here, she was in danger of hypovolemic shock."

"What does that mean?" Hana's wide eyes go from me to Scar.

"It's not good," is all he says.

"They were able to give her a transfusion, but she's still unconscious. She needs to wake up so they can check for more severe damage."

"She was amazing, a real hero."

Hana fills me in quickly on the scene that played out while we were racing across the country to help them. She told me how they were rescuing the horses when Natasha dragged her by the neck at gunpoint. Rick muscled Rainey into the hay storage shed off the inside arena, and there they planned to stage a murder-suicide.

Scar bends forward to wrap his petite wife in his large arms. His eyes close, and he smooths his hands over her belly.

"When Rick shot the gun in the air, I was freaking out." Hana's voice grows animated. "I didn't know how we were going to escape them, when all of a sudden, Rainey swung that shovel like she was hitting a line drive in Yankee Stadium."

My lips press together, and my eyes heat. "She's a pistol."

My voice is thick, and I do my best to clear it. I want to tell her I'm sorry for being so quick to judge her. I want her to know I'm proud of her. I want to tell her I'll help her, and she'll never fight alone again.

I just need her to wake up.

"The doctor said you took down Natasha."

Hana's lips press together, and her chin drops. "I didn't have a choice. I didn't want to do it, but... I didn't have a choice."

She speaks the last part just above a whisper, and I step forward, completing the group hug around her.

"It was you or her, Hana." I step back, meeting her sad eyes. "She drew the line and made the threats. You did what you had to do to protect your baby, Rainey, yourself..."

"I know." Her voice is quiet. "I just wish it didn't have to be this way."

"I wish Rainey would wake up." I turn, crossing my arms over my chest again in what I realize is a defensive move.

I'm holding onto my insides so they don't spill out on the hospital floor. All the things I said to her. I said I wanted to hurt her. I made her sleep on the fucking floor.

A strong hand grips my shoulder, and I glance up at my

partner. "She's going to be okay. It takes a lot more than a bullet to stop my family."

I put my hand on his wrist, on the place where his scarred flesh meets his hand. "A lot more than a fire?"

We're in the group together when the nurse comes out to the waiting room. "Are you the family of Miss Sidorova?"

"Yes," Scar answers. "I'm her brother. This is my wife and her…" he hesitates, giving me a glance, "her loved one."

The woman nods, glancing at her iPad. "She's awake and stable."

My arms drop, and the breath I've been holding rushes from my lungs.

"Oh, thank God!" Hana whispers, and Scar grips my shoulder again.

"Can we see her?" he asks.

"The doctor said short visits, one or two at a time." She scans her eyes over us and smiles warmly. "Since there's only three of you, I think it will be okay."

Rainey's face is pale, and a series of monitors and tubes are connected to her when we enter. The noise of beeping machines surrounds us, and her head is turned to the side, her eyes closed.

"Rainey?" Hana says softly. "Are you asleep?"

Her dark hair is smoothed over her shoulders, and when her blue eyes blink open, she smiles weakly at us. She's the most beautiful thing I've ever seen.

I cover the space between the door and her bed, bending so I can hold her hand and be near her. "How are you feeling?"

Her slim brows lift, and she raises her hand to touch my face. "You were worried about me?"

So much wonder is in her tone, and I want to gather her in my arms and hold her until she never has to ask that type of question again.

"We were so worried about you." Hana slides her hand over Rainey's hair. "You're my badass Lara Croft bestie."

A weak smile curls her lips, and she shakes her head. "We're more like Natasha and Yelena."

Scar exhales a soft laugh, and Hana looks up at him confused. *"Black Widow."*

That makes his wife smile. "I can live with that."

"Come on." Scar takes Hana's arm. "We're going back to your room, and you're going to rest."

Hana glances from me to Rainey before surrendering, pointing at both of us as she leaves. "To be continued."

Rainey blinks after them, pulling her bottom lip under her teeth before turning to me. "She's not an easy one to keep safe."

"Are you kidding? No one's been able to make Hana cooperate as long as I've known her. Now you've got her on your superhero team. I'm impressed."

A real smile curls her lips, and my chest warms. "She's pretty badass. You should've seen her shoot that gun. I was trying to get out of the way in case she missed, but she didn't."

"I think Scar taught her to shoot because it was the only way he could have peace of mind letting her out of his sight." My voice cracks. "I'm never letting you out of my sight again."

"But you can! Hana and I saved the day."

"You and Hana… the smallest of us."

"What's the saying? Small but mighty?"

"I wish I'd been there. I'd have beaten the shit out of all of them."

"My fighter." Her eyes drop, and she glances up at me. "I love your strength."

I meet her gaze. "I love you."

"You do?" Her voice cracks, mist glistening in her eyes. "After everything I've done?"

Warmth burns in my chest, and I slide my hands up her arms, avoiding the wires. "Of course I do."

"I love you." Her hands cover my forearms. "I still want you on my team."

"You've got me." I kiss her hand. "You'll never fight alone again."

"Just like my dream."

"No more dreams, no more nightmares. I've got you. Understand?"

She nods quickly. "And I've got you, professor."

Lifting my hand, I cup her cheek, sealing my lips to hers as our mouths part. Our tongues slide together, and the lash across my heart is healed.

CHAPTER 30

Rainey

"**B**UT WHAT ABOUT YOUR FINAL GRADES?" ALI STANDS AT THE edge of my bed, sad-faced as she watches me pack my final belongings into my large suitcase.

"They're giving me an incomplete. I can't attend classes like this." I hold up the polished wooden cane I've been using since I left the hospital.

The bullet caused nerve damage in my left hip, and while the physical therapist says I'll make a full recovery, for now I have to do biweekly exercises using parallel bars, I have to tread water in the pool, and I have to walk with this stick.

Hugh van Hamilton was kind enough to loan me one of his. "If you have to use a cane, you might as well do it in style," he'd said. It was after he'd visited to thank me for saving his grand-nieces and his horses, although Blake and Hana helped with the horses.

"Are you in terrible pain?" Ali strokes the side of my hair. "I can't believe your friend shot you while cleaning his gun. With friends like that... you just need to stay here."

"I'm not in pain. It's just weakness and numbness in my leg. And that's the importance of gun safety—always make sure your gun is completely unloaded."

It was the only lie I could come up with—a horrible accident, and I'm lucky it wasn't worse.

"Does this mean you'll have to come back next semester to finish?" She's so excited by the prospect, I don't have the heart to tell her I'm already finished. I already have a degree.

"Maybe..." I close my suitcase, sliding the zipper around the edge. "My family wants me to come home and recover, where they can help me."

A bubble of warmth grows in my chest at the word *family*, at knowing what it means now. Scar doesn't say much, but before I was released, he visited me in the hospital alone.

"I never knew I had a sister," he'd said, standing tall at my bedside. "But the way you rushed into a burning barn to save Hana, to save the horses, it's clear we're related. It's what I would've done."

His long hair was pulled back in a bun, and the imposing tattoos covering the scars on his arms were visible beneath the short-sleeved shirt he wore.

"I think our hair and our eyes make it pretty clear we're related as well," I'd teased, strangely comfortable with his demeanor.

He cut his wolf gaze at me, the same color as my own, then a rare smile curled his lips. He stepped forward to kiss the top of my head, and so much happiness rose in my chest it hurt. My father's spirit was with us. I had them both again.

"And your sister-in-law is having a baby..." Ali's pout pulls me back to the present. She crosses her arms. "You're going to forget all about us."

Exhaling a laugh, I put my arm around her shoulders. "I'll never forget about you." It wasn't so long ago I was pissed to see her walk through that door. I thought of her as a complication to my plans. Who knew we'd get so close? "I'll come back for a visit, and I'll actually be in the same town as Professor Winston."

Dirk and I decided to say we're from the same hometown on campus, considering he'd still like to continue his teaching job at Thornton.

Ali's eyes go wide. "You are *not!*" she cries. "You'll be in Hamiltown with Professor Panty-dropper for the holidays?"

"I don't know that I'll be *with* him…" *Yes, I'll be with him.*

"You are definitely coming back for a visit, then. I want to know everything."

"Okay." I exhale a laugh as she pulls my suitcase out the door and to the elevator for me.

Scar and Hana are waiting in the parking lot when we exit the dorm. I introduce them to my roomie, who clutches my arm at the sight of my oversized brother.

"Your brother is scary," she whispers in my ear. "Scary hot!"

A laugh huffs through my lips. Scar and I are still getting used to this sibling thing, although I might be more excited about it than he is. I dreamed so many years of finding him, and like Hana said, overnight, I'm surrounded by family.

Giving Ali another hug, I take the suitcase. "I'll text you all the time, and I'll be back for a visit as soon as I'm off this silly cane."

Perhaps I can even come clean as Professor Winston's significant other…

"I'm holding you to it." She gives me another tight squeeze, and Scar takes my things, putting them in the back of his big black truck.

Hana's up front, and he helps me climb into the small backseat. With that, we're headed out of Thornton, and my second round as a college student ends. Dirk and I agreed it would be better if I didn't visit him on campus, but he's coming back to his place tonight, and I'll be waiting for him.

"Thornton is adorable!" Hana coos as we drive off the campus, approaching the interstate highway. "I'd like to attend as a student, too!"

"Dirk really likes it." I glance back at the large academic buildings with their ivy-covered façades. "He's a really good professor."

"Who knows? Maybe in eighteen years, we'll be dropping off a little Lourde at the university," Hana adds.

"Let's not get ahead of ourselves," Scar growls, and Hana and I both snicker.

After helping me transport my things into Dirk's massive loft, Hana tells me she brought the golf cart for me to use.

"My pregnancy brain is so bad, I completely forgot I'd left it here last time." Her voice catches, and worried eyes meet mine. "I guess you already knew that."

"Yeah..." My past indiscretions pop up at the most awkward times.

Luckily Hana is a master at forgiveness. "So you know the way to Hugh's, and we'll see you around suppertime?"

Chewing my lip, I look around the place, thinking of Dirk coming home later. "Maybe I can get ours to go?"

"You definitely can." She gives me a wink and a hug, and I'm alone in the space Dirk says we're making ours.

Opening my suitcase, I slowly remove my clothes and set them on the bed, carefully carrying them to the new dresser he put in the bedroom for me.

Dirk wouldn't hear of me returning to New York, so I let my old apartment in Hell's Kitchen go, not that I was overly attached to it anyway. He hired a service to box up all my belongings and ship them to us here.

I suggested I find my own apartment in Hamiltown, and Carmen offered to help me. Dirk's *no* was so fiercely emphatic, I was turned on and a little defiant. I do love wrestling with him, after all.

Having to get around with a cane means it takes several

hours to get all my clothes and books and accessories arranged to my liking. I've never been more annoyed and frustrated with my body, but I'm doing my best to stay positive. The nice physical therapist said because of my age and athleticism, my body should recover more quickly. I'm a week in, and it's already taking too long.

By seven, I'm standing at the top of the stairs wondering how I'm going to get down them and over to Hugh's to collect our dinner when I hear a vehicle pull up in the driveway. My chest sinks, because I wanted to have yummy food smells in the house when Dirk got home.

Yes, it's old-school housewife vibes, but I love it. I'm leaning into this new relationship. I want to give him all the care he deserves.

"Miss Hana apologizes for not bringing this to you herself." My eyebrows shoot up when I see Norris standing at the bottom of the stairs. "She helped me prepare everything, and she selected the wine…"

"Please don't apologize! This is so nice."

I carefully take one step down, and the older gentleman jogs up to me. "Stop right there. I was told you weren't to do anything."

He takes my arm, leading me back into the loft. I watch as he quickly empties the large basket containing a small rotisserie chicken, steaming hot and smelling delicious. Up next are containers of scalloped potatoes and roasted butternut squash.

"I'm going to have a hard time waiting for Dirk." I rub a hand over my growling stomach, and he uncorks a bottle of sauvignon blanc.

He pauses, taking out one last bundle. "Miss Hana sent you these butter cookies."

A sad smile curls my lips. "I remember having these in New York a long time ago."

"If that's everything, I'll be getting back to Mr. Hugh's."

Leaning forward on my cane, I give the man a tight hug.

"Thank you so much. No one's ever taken care of me like this before."

He seems startled, straightening his coat when I release him, but I notice a hint of a smile on his formal lips as he nods and quickly leaves me alone. I carefully walk over and light a few candles, turn on the gas log in the fireplace, then I take a minute to change into a silky black dress with spaghetti straps. It ends at the top of my thighs, and of course, no underwear.

At least my injury doesn't cause pain. It causes my leg not to respond properly, but when I painted my toenails red this afternoon, I was able to wiggle all of them, which made me as happy as when I got my black belt.

I'm just pulling a chunky cardigan over my shoulders when the door opens, and the heavy thud of boots running up the stairs sends my heart flying. Until he appears, and I lose my breath all over again, just like that first day in class.

He doesn't stop until he's with me, pulling me into his arms and kissing the side of my neck. "I'm pretty sure this day couldn't have been any longer."

My eyes slide closed as my fingers curl in his shirt, and I inhale deeply his clean citrus scent. Turning my face, I kiss his lips. "I had the opposite experience. This silly cane makes everything take twice as long."

He steps back, holding out my arms and running his eyes from my lips, slowly over my breasts and down to my bare feet in a hot caress. "You look great, although I can't get over you with this thing."

"Check it out." I hold it up, lifting the brass cover off the top of the polished cherry wood. "It has a watch on the end. Although if I had to use one on a permanent basis, I'd want something more elaborate. A bear claw... or a hand holding my hand."

"I'm the only one who holds your hand." He steps closer, wrapping his arm around my waist again.

"So possessive, professor," I tease. "Come look at this."

Holding his arm and the cane, I do my best to lead him to the kitchen table. "Hana and Norris packed dinner for us!"

"Are you hungry?" Wrinkling my nose, I nod, and he laughs. "Then I'd better feed you."

Plates are served, wine poured, and we're sitting across from each other like an actual couple on a date—something we've never done.

"I'm glad you stopped fighting me about living here." Dirk takes a sip of wine, watching me over the candles.

Sliding my right foot under the table, I tickle my toes under his pants leg. "I'll fight you. Just give me three to six more weeks."

Heat fills his gaze, and he nods. "I'm looking forward to it. In the meantime, I'm taking care of you."

"I've never been taken care of before, professor."

He places his fork beside his plate, leaning back to take a long sip of wine. "You are now."

"Tell me about class." I take another bite of the buttery potatoes.

"Class was pretty quiet. I covered a surprising amount of material, almost like I wasn't distracted by anything... or anyone."

"Are you saying there were no flirtatious female students?"

"Maybe a few, but I wasn't interested."

"What about your friend Sharon?"

"Sharon got a boyfriend over fall break. Some guy from her hometown, which leads me to believe he was always waiting in the wings."

"I'm very happy for her."

Dirk grins at me as he shoves a slice of chicken into his mouth. "Either way, she's almost finished with her dissertation, so she'll be graduating in May."

"I wish her well. She should move far, far away." I take a long sip of wine, feeling happily full of a delicious dinner.

"And Evan?" Dirk's tone turns dark, and a thrill races to my core.

Grasping the cane, I carefully rise from my chair and make my way around to straddle his lap. "Evan meant nothing. He was only a tool."

"You bet he was."

I exhale a laugh, lifting his glasses off his eyes and placing them on the table.

"Hana sent these for dessert." I show him the small bundle of cookies.

He takes them out of my hand, setting them behind me before grasping my thighs and standing, taking me with him. "I want something else for dessert."

A thrill races to my core, and I wrap my arms around his neck, kissing his jaw as he walks to the bedroom.

My lips pull the shell of his ear between my teeth. "What might that be, professor."

He lays me back on the bed, sliding his hands up the sides of my smooth thighs. "I've been wondering what was under this dress since I got home."

The silky fabric rises higher, and a cool breeze sweeps over my skin as he gets closer to…

"Nothing," I hum, heat flooding my core as his hot breath whispers over my skin. "Just how you like it, professor."

"It's exactly how I like it." He gives me a naughty grin before putting his mouth directly on my pussy.

"Oh, fuck." My knee rises as a moan slips from my mouth.

His tongue moves quickly, sliding around and over my clit as the scruff of his beard brushes my inner thighs. Surges of pleasure race to my core, and my fingers thread in his soft hair.

I gasp, my jaw dropping, and he groans against my clit. The building pressure makes me squirm, but he jerks me closer. His warm tongue is joined by teeth and intense suction, and I writhe, chanting, my eyes squeezed shut.

He drags me closer to the edge of the bed, inserting two

fingers and curling them against that place deep inside me. The moment he touches it, I stiffen as if electrified, and the orgasm fires through my lower belly.

"Oh!" I scream, and he stands, unfastening his jeans and shoving them down roughly.

His hard cock bobs out, pointing directly at me, and he slides it in with a low moan. My orgasm still spasms, and he reaches forward to grip the back of my neck as he slams into me hard and fast. He's moving so vigorously, his tip ignites my G-spot, and I grip his arms, moaning as my second orgasm flares to life.

My breasts bounce fast with every rapid thrust, and he groans deeply. His eyes squeeze shut, and his grip on my neck moves to my shoulders as his lips part.

"I want to see it," I gasp, and he quickly pulls out, grasping his cock and jerking it fast as his orgasm sprays onto my belly, up to my breasts in white streams.

"Oh my God, that's so hot," I moan.

His ejaculation slows, and he shoves into me again, holding my arms and slamming faster, moaning deeper as he continues thrusting. My core bursts into violent flutters as another orgasm blazes through me, and my back arches off the bed.

Releasing my arms, he leans back, using two fingers to slap my clit repeatedly until it happens again, wetness leaks from my body, and I scream, squirming to get away from the intense pleasure blanking my mind.

"Come here," he growls, pulling me under him and covering my shaking body with his big, warm, muscular one.

My pussy clenches wildly around his cock, and my thighs tremble with aftershocks.

"Fuck you feel amazing," he groans.

"I can't take anymore," I gasp. "I'm going crazy."

Warm lips cover mine, and I open my mouth for him, hungrily finding his tongue, curling it with mine and sucking, pulling his lips. I'm desperate for more of his kisses, and I drive my fingers into his hair as he moves his lips lower, pulling the soft skin of my jaw between his teeth.

His mouth moves to my ear, and he whispers, "One more."

His hips move, and he's thrusting into me again, hitting that spot and making me scream as our skin slaps together. He slides his warm hand over my breasts, squeezing my hardened nipples and closing his eyes as he groans raggedly. His hips shudder and hold as his cock jerks inside me, filling me.

I'm breathing fast, the intense sensations in my body unlike anything I've ever felt. He slides his warm body over mine, holding me tightly, smoothing his hands down my back and whispering in my ear.

"That was amazing." Soft lips touch my temple, my cheek. "You are so beautiful."

I stretch higher to find his mouth again. Our lips seal, and as I taste him, soothing waves of comfort flood my body. My arms are around him, and our breath slowly returns to normal. I'm slowly aware of my surroundings again.

Lifting his head, warm hazel meets ice blue. "How are you feeling?"

Blinking slowly, I smile, tracing my finger over his square jaw and that dimple in his cheek. "I've never fucked like that before."

"Was it too much? You are still recovering." He leans down to kiss me again.

I start to laugh, and our teeth clink together. "I think you healed me."

Standing, he goes to the bathroom, returning with a warm cloth he uses to clean me gently, then himself. I'm loose and sleepy, and when he returns, he smiles, tracing his eyes over my body.

"Come here." He pulls my back to his chest, and I slide my hands over his strong arms holding me so close.

I drift to sleep for a little while, and when I open my eyes again, he's still holding me in the same position, only now he's also holding *The Goblet of Fire*.

"When I would read this after mom died, I wished we had a Molly Weasley, even if she was a bit much." His voice is quiet, and I thread my fingers with his, a pinch of sadness in my chest. "Hutch did his best, but it was never the same."

Turning in his arms, I place my hand gently on his cheek. "I'll take care of you."

He lowers the book, sliding his finger along my hairline, seeming like he wants to say something, but instead, he changes course. "You never told me what you got your degree in."

Lifting my chin, I give him a little smile. "Education. I wanted to be a teacher. I thought the kids could be like my family, and that way, I could get a little of what I'd lost."

His eyes warm, and he kisses me gently. "And now you have a family of your own."

"I do." My eyes shine, and I snuggle close in his arms.

"And you're going to be my assistant at Thornton starting next semester."

"What?" Pulling back, I study his face. "Can you do that?"

"Of course." His tone is so sure, so final. "We have field experience together. You're just as qualified as I am, perhaps more, since you have educational training. You can help me with my research."

"Okay," I laugh. "What are we researching?"

Hesitating, he looks around the room as if he's deciding. "The effects of... Ah, I know, the effects of explosive chemistry on the marital habits of college professors."

"Marital habits?" My chin pulls back. "You don't think it might be a bit sudden?"

"They say when you know, you know." Bending his elbow, he leans his head against his hand... so sexy. "Do you know?"

"I knew the first day I saw you I'd do anything to have you. Now I'm in love with you." His hand smooths the hair off my cheek, and his expression turns serious. "It hit me like a ton of bricks when we were stuck in Scar's house. I realized even with all that had happened, even before I knew the truth, I was still in love with you. I wanted to get you away from that life. I wanted to take care of you and keep you safe."

Heat floods my eyes, and my breath hiccups in my chest. "I would've done anything to know that. I was so miserable that I hurt you when all I wanted was to love you."

His mouth covers mine, and my hands are on his cheeks. Our tongues curl, and I roll us so he's on his back, and my body is over his, ready to be joined once more. With a sigh, I lift my chin, rising to a sitting position with my legs straddling his waist.

Looking down at his muscled torso and his hungry grin, I arch an eyebrow. "Will you still want me if I'm no longer your naughty student?"

His eyes darken, and his hands slide up my thighs, squeezing my ass and flooding my core with heat. "You'll be my naughty assistant."

I lean forward, peppering his lips with kisses. "We'll never get any work done."

Reaching up he catches my cheeks, moving my hair back and looking into my eyes. "Just wait 'til you're my wife."

Leaning down, I press my lips to his. "We should give it a year."

"You think you'll be sure then?"

"I'm sure now, but let's go through all the seasons, and then you can be sure you're sure."

"I'm sure." His hands slide down my back, cupping my ass, and I slide my lips lower, kissing his neck, his collarbone, the top of his chest. It's not long before we're coming together, our bodies uniting the way our hearts are.

Our love might have started as a scheme, a plot by evil people to do bad things, but the strength of what we have, the undeniable force of our attraction, broke through their plans. What started out as forbidden, dissolved under the strength of two lonely souls searching for family, for belonging, for the missing piece.

We found it in each other. We're silent yet strong, wounded, but still fighting, and we earned our happily ever after. I didn't believe I deserved it. I thought it wasn't mine to have, but he changed my destiny. We're magical yet real, healing and transformative. From the ugly and the cruel grew beauty and life, and we made it ours.

EPILOGUE

Derk

Nine Months Later

A COOL SUMMER BREEZE SURROUNDS US AS WE DESCEND FROM THE private jet onto the tarmac of the small airport in Minsk.

"It's colder than Hamiltown in the summer." Pepper leans into Rainey's side.

"It's probably the same as Minnesota," Rainey whispers back.

The two of them have been tight since Rainey taught Pepper to drive last fall. It was when she was still recovering from the gunshot wound, and they started on the golf cart, ostensibly so Rainey could jump out if Pepper tried to wreck it.

The only problem with that plan was Rainey couldn't have hopped out to save her life. Fortunately, Pepper caught on quicker than Carmen's predictions, and by the end of the week, she was driving Rainey to all her physical therapy appointments.

They became such good friends that Rainey insisted Pepper come with us on our trip to meet with the man from Minsk, who we now know as Dmitri Usmanov, who has been helping piece together what happened to their father and track down Scar and Rainey's official records.

"Oskar, my friend." The older gentleman shakes Scar's hand with both of his. "Is this your beautiful wife and son?"

Hana is beside him holding eight-month-old Lourde, who is wearing a little blue beanie over his jet-black hair. His pale blue eyes are alert, and he smiles at Dmitri. "It's wonderful to meet you, Mr. Usmanov."

"The pleasure is all mine." He turns to look up as we reach the bottom of the steps. "And you are Reanna?"

"I am." Rainey takes the hand he offers, and I hang back with Pepper. "Of course you are. The resemblance is remarkable."

"Funny how we never saw it," Scar notes.

"To be fair, I wore a disguise most of my life," Rainey replies.

Dimitri frowns. "Why would you do that?"

She glances down and shrugs. "I was alone. It felt safer."

Stepping up behind her, I take her hand in mine. "She's not alone anymore."

The six of us climb into a waiting limousine, and Dimitri fills in the blanks. "With the help of local investigators, we located your father's body, and using the DNA sample you sent, we were able to establish a clear identification. It was as you said, Reanna. Your father was murdered near his home. However, as you know, the killers took a page from the Bolshevik handbook, which is why we needed the DNA sample."

Rainey's eyes move from mine to Scar's, and her brother answers in a low voice. "They destroyed his body, covered it in acid, and burned his clothes to prevent a positive ID. Without our DNA, it would've been impossible."

Her lips tighten. I cover her hand with mine, but she keeps it together. "I saw them shoot him. I knew what they did."

"Yes, and it's interesting they allowed you to live. In your brother's case, they gave him a new name and a new birth certificate. He could have lived his whole life never knowing the truth. Perhaps because you were a little girl, they didn't see you as a threat."

"I'm sure that's what it was." An edge is in her voice, and I give her hand a squeeze.

"They didn't know you very well."

Dmitri takes a large brown envelope from his case and hands it to Scar. "In any event, here are your official documents, your passports, and the deed to the house. All of the bank accounts are now in your name, and you are the legal owner of all your father's properties as well as *Aurora*."

"*Aurora*?" Scar opens the envelope and two small, crimson booklets slide out. They're printed with gold lettering, and I recognize them as Russian passports.

Scar hands one to Rainey.

"*Aurora* is the super yacht that belonged to your family. It's a two hundred and fifty foot luxury liner currently off the coast of Spain."

"I thought that was an exaggeration." Scar's voice is quiet, and he opens the passport studying the name. Hana slides her hand in the crook of his arm, and his brow furrows. "I still feel more like a Lourdnikov than a Petrovich."

"Yet that is who you are." Dmitri claps his knee. "You're a very powerful man, and as such, you can tell everyone to leave you alone."

Hana's nose wrinkles, and she laughs. "Perfect."

We spend the night at Dmitri's estate, which is the size of a palace. We dine on borscht, which is a sour red soup made with beetroots, and beef stroganoff. We drink expensive vodka and look at pictures of his granddaughter, who's a grown woman now. He takes time to walk Scar and Rainey through the details of their properties and holdings here and in the United States.

Most everything goes to Scar as the eldest son, but Rainey inherited a good bit of money stored in Swiss bank accounts. The investment group belongs to them along with interests in a few thoroughbreds and a certain club we're all very familiar with.

"I'm not interested in keeping Gibson's," Scar says under his breath. "Hana has too many bad memories associated with that place."

Rainey looks at me, and I shrug. "I don't think I'll ever go back there."

"I have no interest in the place," she agrees.

We decide to cross that bridge when we return home, and the next day, we take another small plane from Minsk to Odesa, where a car is waiting to drive us to the house on the coast of the Black Sea.

It's actually more of a small villa with a domed roof and a wrap-around porch. Dmitri says a caretaker has been managing the property, and it has remained virtually untouched following Zander's death.

Entering the arched doorway, the interior is dark, lit only by sunlight shining through oversized windows. A large, rough-hewn table is in the kitchen with bench seats, and Rainey reaches for my hand as she takes her first steps into a painful past.

"I want to see my room." Her voice is quiet, and I stay with her, following her through the silent halls to a small, pink bedroom.

Stepping inside, her breath catches. She walks around the space with her hands clasped at her chest, looking up at the wallpaper, the pictures, the bed. When she reaches a small, wooden dollhouse, she stops, dropping to her knees in front of it and opening the doors.

"It's here," she whispers, and her head bows. Her shoulders shake, and I rush to kneel beside her.

Hesitating a moment, I put my hand gently on her shoulder. "Are you okay?"

Turning to me, she takes my hand, opening my palm. In it she places a tiny painted object. It takes me a moment to realize it's the smallest piece from one of those Russian nesting dolls.

"I thought Natasha threw it in the fire?"

"I had another one, left behind here in Papa's house." Our eyes meet, and hers are shining with tears and happiness. "I never thought I'd see it again."

Pulling her into my arms, I hold her as she rests her face on my shoulder. Her hand clutches my shirt, and if only to retrieve this one, tiny object from her past, this fixture of her nightmares, I'm glad we came.

We stay at the house most of the day, collecting photographs and letters to take back with us. Scar holds his tiny son in his arms as he inspects his father's tools and the furniture Rainey explains their father made.

Hana and I hang back, and she's alternately smiling and wiping her eyes as she watches the two of them discover and rediscover their history.

"Isn't it wonderful?" Hana whispers, and I put my hand on her back.

"It's pretty amazing."

Our trip lasts five days, during which time we explore Odesa. Rainey takes us to all the local sights. She takes us to see the places she would play as a child and the places her father worked. We visit an outdoor market where stooped little ladies sell more of the beautifully painted nesting dolls along with other tapestries, blankets, and pottery. One shop in particular catches my eye, and I slip away while Rainey helps Pepper choose her favorite of the matryoshkas.

A special gift is hidden in my pocket when I return, and I find Pepper on the edge of her seat, listening as Rainey describes the underwater museum at the bottom of the Black Sea, the more than fifty exhibits, including statues of Lenin and Stalin and a replica of the Eiffel Tower. We make a note to include time for scuba diving on our next trip, and when we're finally on the plane back to America, she seems content.

In our private sleeping quarters, her cheek rests on my chest, and I thread my fingers in her hair as we listen to the noise of the jet engines. "Did you get what you needed on this trip?"

She slides her arm around my waist. "I had what I needed before this trip, but coming here and seeing it all again, seeing his grave, gave me closure."

Eleven hours later, we're touching down in South Carolina. The drive to Hamiltown is quiet but content. It seems everyone got what they needed from the trip, except for Lourde, who's fussy.

"He's ready to be back with his things," Pepper notes. "I know the feeling, little buddy!"

She takes him from Hana and bounces him on her hip as we stop by Hugh's place, following a text from Blake asking us to meet them there.

"We'll keep it short." I kiss the top of Rainey's head, ready for my own things as well.

One thing in particular.

We enter the small kitchen last, and at Hana's squeal, Rainey and I exchange a look before hustling up the steps to see what's happening.

"When did you get in town?" Hana cries.

"Gia has a meeting with designers in New York all week, so I decided to take a little field trip down south to see my favorite neighbors."

The casual male voice is familiar to me, something out of the not-so-distant past.

Rainey hesitates inside the door, her voice cautious. "Trip?"

"Well, I'll be damned." A slim man with longish hair and an expensive suit steps over to where we're standing.

They both start and stop as if they'll hug then change their minds.

Finally, Rainey laughs and steps forward, wrapping her arms around him briefly. "You look good."

"You've changed." He sizes her up in a way I don't care for. "In a good way. And Dirk. It's been a while."

Trip Alexander turns to me, extending a hand. I carefully shake it. Hana slips her hand in the crook of his arm. "It's okay, Trip's a friend."

I narrow my eyes. "Is he?"

"It's been a long, *long* time since I've seen you." Rainey jumps in, and I guess they were on the same team for a while. "Where have you been?"

"Milan."

"He has a gorgeous Italian wife, and he's turned over a whole new leaf." Hana lifts her chin like she had something to do with it.

He pats her hand. "Who would've thought when all the dust settled, we'd be the ones left standing?"

"I knew." Hana, the eternal believer, smiles at the group.

Blake enters the room holding Lourde on her hip, followed by Pepper holding his chubby fist. Hutch is behind them, speaking in low tones with Scar, who appears to be filling him in on all we've learned.

I think about this crew—brought together by a death now formed into a family, a team ready to fight for each other—and able to do what it takes to keep each other safe.

"I have an idea." Hana puts her hand on Trip's shoulder. "How would you feel about buying Gibson's?"

His eyebrows rise, and he studies her expression. "I might be interested. Perhaps I could come home more often, if only to visit."

"I knew it!" She claps. "And I'll get to meet Gia!"

"Then you'll see what I've been saying," Trip winks. "She's too good for me."

"I have no problem believing that." Blake quips, and he laughs.

"Always my biggest fan."

Hana circles the small table, reaching for her husband. He immediately slides his arms around her waist. "Scar, we should sell Gibson's to Trip. He's probably the only person who would appreciate it."

Scar lifts his chin, sizing up her friend. "Let's talk."

Hutch walks up to grip my shoulder and pull me in for a hug. "Glad you made it back."

"It was an amazing trip."

"I bet." He touches Rainey's arm lightly. "You good?"

She smiles up at my brother, nodding her head. "Really good."

He pulls her in for a hug, and I'm gratified that my protective big brother has accepted her completely into the family.

Later that night, when we're lying in our bed, sweaty and breathing hard from catching up on lost sexy times, I pull her into my arms. She lifts her chin to look up at me, and I slide my palm over her pretty face.

"Watching you holding Lourde had me thinking down the road a ways."

Her nose wrinkles and warmth fills her eyes. "You want a little boy with dark hair and blue eyes?"

"I want all our babies to look like you." Leaning down, I cover her lips with mine.

Our tongues touch lightly, and I don't want to wait anymore. Hopping out of the bed, I walk over to the desk where I stowed the parcel I picked up in Odesa. Carrying it back to the bed, I fluff the pillows so we can lean against the headboard.

She pushes against the blankets to sit up. "What do you have?"

"I picked this up in Odesa."

Her eyes widen, and her lips part. "What…"

I unwrap the tissue, placing a small blue matryoshka in her hands. "You got me a nesting doll? That's so sweet. She's beautiful."

"Let's see the littlest one." I guide her hands to open it.

It's a small doll, only five sizes in all, and at the very bottom, wrapped around the baby sits a pear-shaped Alexandrite stone with sapphires on each side surrounded by diamond baguettes.

"Dirk!" she gasps, blinking her eyes up to mine. "It's so beautiful. What does it mean?"

"Rainey… Reanna Petrovna, you're the strongest, kindest, sexiest woman I've ever known. You're the air I breathe, the piece I've been missing, and I can't imagine my life without you."

"Are you saying…"

"At first, I thought I'd hold it for three more months, but I want to give it to you now. I want you to know my intentions are real and forever."

She blinks quickly, mist filling her eyes. "I don't know if I should be rewarded for all the scheming I did to have you."

"I'm willing to be your target any time, if means you'll be my wife."

Her nose wrinkles, and a tear falls on her pretty face. She's shaking her head, and I start to laugh, cupping her cheeks and wiping her tears with my thumbs.

"Is that a yes?"

Nodding quickly, she chokes out a "Yes!" then adds quickly, "Yes, yes, yes!"

I slide the ring on her finger just before she wraps her arms around my neck, covering my mouth with hers. Our lips part, and our tongues slide together, and we move lower in the bed. Her naked body is pressed against mine, and I'm in fucking heaven.

It was only a year ago I didn't know where I was going or how I'd gotten so off course. I didn't think I'd have the things my brother had or my partner had, then this little vixen appeared like a tornado in my house of cards. She threw all my chess pieces in the air, and I've never been happier.

Calm fills my chest. I don't question anymore, my restlessness is gone, her nightmares are gone, and they're replaced with new dreams.

I've found my course, and she's right here in front of me. Holding her in my arms, she saved me as surely as I saved her. We've both found a home, and we'll build it strong together.

Thank you for reading *Forbidden!*

Need more fiery-hot, small-town military romance with a touch of suspense?
Read *One to Hold* Now!

Keep clicking for a short sneak peek...

It's also available as an Audiobook.

Learn about all of my books on TiaLouise.com/Books, including a downloadable Reading Guide.

ONE TO Hold

Special Sneak Peek

Derek Alexander is a retired Marine, ex-cop, and the top investigator in his field. Melissa Jones is a small-town girl trying to escape her troubled past.

When the two intersect in a bar in Arizona, their sexual chemistry is off the charts. But what is revealed during their "one-week stand" only complicates matters.

Because she'll do everything in her power to get away from the past, but he'll do everything he can to hold her.

(A stand-alone adult contemporary military romance with a touch of suspense. No cheating. No cliffhanger.)

One

A ONE-WEEK STAND

IN THE COOL DARKNESS OF THE SEMI-CROWDED BAR, I COULD ALLOW the last year to dissolve into a hazy fog, a far-off memory. Each low thump of bass that disappeared into the dull roar of voices beat it further down. With a little more alcohol, it could even become a dream—something that never occurred in real life. Something that could be brushed aside like a phantom, not a true form. Not a reality that burned shame, low and deep in my stomach.

Bars had become a thing of my past, along with flirtatious passes from unfamiliar men, but sitting alone in this hotel club, hundreds of miles from home, I felt wonderfully liberated. I could be anyone. Any anonymous woman having a drink before bed. I could pretend to be free.

My eyes traveled to the dance-floor where younger women in shiny slip dresses and chunky stilettos twisted and swayed, their smooth blonde or red hair matching their movements. They squeal-laughed when songs they liked came on, and the lines around their eyes disappeared as soon as their cheeks relaxed. They could dance all night and still make it to work tomorrow, eyes sparkling.

A bitter laugh slid from my throat as I stared back into the amber drink I'd ordered. The thought of dancing all night made me tired.

The bartender didn't notice me. I'd stood for almost five minutes trying to get his attention to order this drink, and it was gross. "Seven and seven" was all I could remember from the days when I used to order drinks for myself. It was a popular combination then, but I never liked the flavor. Refreshing citrus dragged down by a heavy undertone of bitter syrup. I took a long pull from the tiny red straw and winced.

I should've gone back to the room with Elaine. My best friend since childhood said what I needed was a trip to the desert. She'd booked us a week at the Cactus Flower Spa in Scottsdale, where we could get massages, sit in steam rooms, soak in mud, and let our tensions melt away with hot-wax pedicures. She said it would break me out of my "funk," as she called it.

I didn't have anything else to do this week.

It was with those sunny thoughts in my head that I saw him. At first I thought it was an accident, my eyes flickering across the square-shaped bar at the same time as his. Blue eyes, strikingly blue because of the way they stood out beneath his dark brow, coupled with collar-length, thick dark hair. He had a beard. I didn't like beards—not even close-trimmed ones like his. He was huge. I could see his muscles from where I sat. His chest strained against the tight, black shirt he wore, and his biceps stretched the sleeves. I preferred smaller men, long and lean model-types.

But he didn't look away. And like a deer caught in headlights, I couldn't either. My breath stilled as my eyes stayed on his, as I waited for him to release me. He would release me. I knew he would. I simply had to wait.

Men in bars were after those baby-faced innocents on the dance floor, not me. They wanted energetic young ones with their tight bodies, high-pitched breasts, and even tighter vaginas. Those were the girls men wanted to fuck. They would scream and moan all night and tell them they were the best ever, the king. I wasn't looking for a king. Still, in the next moment, when the mountain of sex holding my gaze stood and began his slow glide in my direction, all I could think was *maybe...*

I watched as he passed the patrons facing each other,

talking and laughing. Some were more animated than others, waving their arms and putting their drinks in peril. They all shone in the yellow lights hidden above, in the recesses of the wooden shelves that held dozens of upside-down glasses in all shapes and sizes. Liquor bottles were arranged on the top shelf. For some reason, though, the lights didn't seem to reach him. Or me. We were in our own secret, shadowy place.

When he rounded the final corner and I could see him in full, my breath caught. My eyes traveled quickly from his broad shoulders to his narrow waist, down his grey pants ending in sleek, black loafers. Just as fast, they were back to his face, and he was in front of me. I'd never been confronted with so much male presence focused on me in my life. He had to be six-two and twice my size.

"Can I buy you a drink?" The low vibration of his voice shot a pleasing charge right between my legs, and my cheeks warmed.

Blinking back to my glass, I poked the half-empty contents with the straw. "I have this," I said, my voice softer and higher in contrast to his.

"But you don't like it." A small smile was on his lips. It made him the slightest bit less intimidating.

"How do you know?"

He leaned against the bar in front of me, bringing his face closer to my level, his body almost touching mine. A faint scent of warm cologne swirled around me, tightening my chest.

"You make a face every time you sip it," he said. "I've been watching you since you walked in with your friend earlier."

My brows drew together. "Why?"

His tongue touched his bottom lip, and my jaw dropped. I quickly closed it, thinking how insane it was the way my body responded to him.

This was not me. I did not fantasize about hooking up with strange men in bars. And a cocky alpha who studied me like I was a frontier landscape he was ready to conquer had never been my type. He probably wanted to tie me up or handcuff me to something. A delicious shiver passed through me at the thought. I put my eyes on my drink.

"Maybe I should introduce myself," he said, holding out a large palm. I stared at it a moment. "Derek."

My eyes lifted to his blue ones, which were still holding me in that intense gaze. He had a small nose and a full mouth. A million pornographic images flooded my brain of that nose nudging into my dark spaces, of that mouth kissing areas long-neglected. That beard scratching the insides of my thighs as I moaned and twisted in white sheets, threading my fingers in his silky hair. I cleared the thickness in my throat, feeling heat everywhere in my body.

"Melissa," I said, placing my noticeably smaller hand in his. His fingers closed over mine, and instead of overwhelming, it felt… right.

"Sweet Melissa," he said with a little grin. The side of his mouth lifting the way it did made me want to kiss him.

"I'm not so sweet," I said, taking my hand back.

"Aren't others supposed to make that judgment?" His eyes never left me as he motioned to the bartender, who immediately came to us. Apparently it wasn't only the perky blondes who got instant service.

"Two glasses of your best cava," Derek said, giving the boy a quick glance before turning back to me.

"Cava?" I did love the crisp, Spanish sparkling wine. Why I hadn't thought to order that instead of my tan cocktail-disaster? "That's sort of a celebratory drink, isn't it?"

"So let's celebrate."

"Did you get a promotion or something?"

He leaned closer, bringing his eyes to my level. My throat tightened, but I didn't move away. "I met you," he said in that low tone I felt in all the right places.

Two slim glasses were placed in front of us, but I wasn't sure I could lift mine without my hand trembling. Derek picked up both and handed one to me. I took it and carefully sipped, watching as he did the same.

"Are you here on business?" I asked, trying to diffuse the ridiculous amount of sexual tension between us. I considered the possibility I was the only one feeling it.

"Banker's conference this week," he said, taking another, longer drink and then setting the glass back on the bar. His muscles fought against the thin fabric restraining them with every movement.

"You're in banking?" I hated the tremor in my voice. It made me sound like a little girl, when I was striving to be an independent woman. A strong woman who was bigger than her past.

For once, I wanted to forget what happened last year. Let it go and be somebody else. I was out of town, in the desert, in a bar being hit on by a gorgeous stranger. Fate was giving me my chance.

"More like upper management," he said, not seeming to notice my distraction. "I'm doing a workshop on international trade and finance tomorrow. You?"

"Spa vacation," I said. "My friend Elaine said it would be a week to change my life. Or at least my outlook."

A little spark hit his eyes, and I bit my lip. Did I just proposition him? Did I want to? It had been a long time since I'd wanted to be close to anyone in that way. Was I brave enough to let him in?

Internally I shook myself. *Yes.* If that was what I wanted, of course I was. I had always been strong before, and I was still strong. I wouldn't let that be taken from me, too.

"Elaine is who you're here with?" he asked.

I nodded, taking another, longer sip. I allowed my mind to release the past and return to better thoughts, like those of him removing that shirt and setting that massive physique free. My desire to see what was under it grew stronger by the minute.

"Will she worry if you're out late?" he asked looking directly into my eyes.

I barely shook my head No. Elaine wouldn't mind. She might even throw a party if I got laid. My breathing had become shallow, and all rational thought was quickly taking a backseat to desire.

"I have a key to the conference room," he said quietly. "There's a small, outdoor patio just off the side. It's very private."

"Why do you have a key?"

"So I can set up in the morning." With that, he straightened up and placed two bills on the bar beside his drink. "Let me show you the desert sky."

"That sounds like it might be dangerous."

His hand touched my arm. "I'll keep you safe."

Safe. It was a word almost erotic to my ears. My eyes traveled from his waist up his torso to his broad shoulders to his lips, past that perfect nose to his darkening eyes. The temperature in my body rose with my gaze.

"You're not safe," I whispered.

"And you're not sweet." His low voice caused my tongue to press against my teeth. I was dying to kiss him. "I'll only do what you let me."

As he said it, I already believed him. His tone was calm, and his eyes said he wasn't lying. Somewhere in my head, the voice of reason was telling me to slow down, but either the cava or the anticipation of what might happen had me floating up, out of my body as I watched him take the slim glass from my hand and help me off my stool. I followed him from the bar, past the dancing girls, and out the narrow exit. Against everything I knew to be prudent, I was doing this.

Read *One to Hold* today!

Also available on audiobook, ebook, or in paperback.

BOOKS BY TIA LOUISE

ROMANCE IN KINDLE UNLIMITED

THE BRADFORD BOYS
The Way We Touch, 2024★
The Way We Play, 2024★
The Way We Score, 2025★
The Way We Run, 2025★
The Way We Win, 2025★
(★Available on Audiobook.)

THE BE STILL SERIES
A Little Taste, 2023★
A Little Twist, 2023★
A Little Luck, 2023★
A Little Naughty, 2024★
(★Available on Audiobook.)

THE HAMILTOWN HEAT SERIES
Fearless, 2022★
Filthy, 2022★
For Your Eyes Only, 2022
Forbidden, 2023★
(★Available on Audiobook.)

THE TAKING CHANCES SERIES
This Much is True★
Twist of Fate★
Trouble★
(★Available on Audiobook.)

FIGHT FOR LOVE SERIES
Wait for Me★
Boss of Me★
Here with Me★
Reckless Kiss★
(★Available on Audiobook.)

BELIEVE IN LOVE SERIES
Make You Mine
Make Me Yours★
Stay★
(★Available on Audiobook.)

SOUTHERN HEAT SERIES
When We Touch
When We Kiss

THE ONE TO HOLD SERIES
One to Hold (#1—Derek & Melissa)★
One to Keep (#2—Patrick & Elaine)★
One to Protect (#3—Derek & Melissa)★
One to Love (#4—Kenny & Slayde)
One to Leave (#5—Stuart & Mariska)
One to Save (#6—Derek & Melissa)★
One to Chase (#7—Marcus & Amy)★
One to Take (#8—Stuart & Mariska)
(★Available on Audiobook.)

THE DIRTY PLAYERS SERIES
PRINCE (#1)★
PLAYER (#2)★
DEALER (#3)
THIEF (#4)
(★Available on Audiobook.)

THE BRIGHT LIGHTS SERIES
Under the Lights (#1)
Under the Stars (#2)
Hit Girl (#3)

COLLABORATIONS
The Last Guy★
The Right Stud
Tangled Up
Save Me
(★Available on Audiobook.)

PARANORMAL ROMANCES
One Immortal (vampires)
One Insatiable (shifters)

GET THREE FREE STORIES!
Sign up for my New Release newsletter and never miss
a sale or new release by me!
Sign up now!
https://geni.us/TLMnews

ACKNOWLEDGMENTS

Ending a series is such an emotional experience. I've found so many new readers through this Hamiltown world, and *I love you all!*

THANK YOU for loving my books so much. I'm incredibly blessed to have so many amazing, enthusiastic, *supportive* readers and friends cheering me on and anxiously awaiting each new adventure.

Huge thanks and so much love to my husband "Mr. TL" for his encouragement, for helping me brainstorm, and for always wanting to read my books.

Thank you to my beautiful daughters who have left the nest but still believe in me, make me laugh, and support me from afar. I love you ladies!

Thanks so much to my alpha readers Renee McCleary and Maria Black for your immediate love (*lust*?) for Dirk and Reanna's story. Your funny notes and sweaty emojis kept me writing.

Huge thanks to my *incredible* betas, Leticia Teixeira, Corinne Akers (even in the ER!), Ilona Townsel, Amy Reierson, Courtney Anderson, Jennifer Christy, and Jennifer Kreinbring. You guys give the *best* notes!

Thanks to Jaime Ryter for your eagle-eyed edits and to Lori Jackson for the killer cover designs, my dear Wander for the *perfect* Dirk, and the amazing Stacy Blake, who helps me make my gorgeous paperback interiors!

Thanks to my dear Starfish, to my Mermaids, and to my Veeps for keeping me sane and motivated while I'm in the cave.

I can't begin to put into words how much I appreciate the love and support of all the influencers on BookTok, Instagram, Facebook, and to my author-buds! I love you guys so much...

I hope you all adore this new story and get ready for new adventures to come in 2023!

Stay sexy,

<3 Tia

ABOUT THE AUTHOR

Tia Louise is the *USA Today* and #4 Amazon bestselling author of (*primarily*) small-town, single-parent, second-chance, and military romances set at or near the beach.

From Readers' Choice awards, to *USA Today* "Happily Ever After" nods, to winning Favorite Erotica Author and the "Lady Boner Award" (*lol!*), nothing makes her happier than communicating with fellow Mermaids (*fans*) and creating romances that are smart, sassy, and *very sexy*.

A former journalist and displaced beach bum, Louise lives in the Midwest with her trophy husband, two young-adult geniuses, and one clumsy "grand-cat."

Sign up for her newsletter at TiaLouise.com and never miss a new release or sale—and get a free story collection!

Signed Copies of all books online at:
https://geni.us/SignedPBs

Connect with Tia:
Website: TiaLouise.com
Instagram (@AuthorTLouise)
TikTok (@TheTiaLouise)
** On Facebook? **

Be a Mermaid! Join Tia's Reader Group at "Tia's Books, Babes & Mermaids"

www.AuthorTiaLouise.com
allnightreads@gmail.com

Made in the USA
Columbia, SC
23 October 2024

44958089R00183